Dry Bones

DRY
BONES

a novel by
Hope Norman Coulter
author of *The Errand of the Eye*

August House Publishers, Inc.
LITTLE ROCK

© 1990 by Hope Norman Coulter.
All rights reserved. Published 1990 by
August House, Inc., P.O. Box 3223,
Little Rock, Arkansas, 72203,
501–372–5450.
Printed in the United States of America

10 9 8 7 6 5 4 3 2 1

LIBRARY OF CONGRESS CATALOGING-IN-PUBLICATION DATA

Coulter, Hope Norman, 1961-
Dry bones : a novel / Hope Norman Coulter.
—1st ed. p. cm.
ISBN 0-87483-152-0 : $17.95
I. Title
PS3553.O844D7 1990
813'.54—dc20 90-38055

Cover illustration and design: Byron Taylor
Typography: Lettergraphics, Memphis, TN
Book design: Ted Parkhurst
Executive editor: Liz Parkhurst

This book is printed on archival-quality paper which meets the
guidelines for performance and durability of the Committee on
Production Guidelines for Book Longevity of the Council on
Library Resources.

To my parents
with love and admiration

Acknowledgments

Many thanks to John David McFarland of the Arkansas Geological Commission for his time and help on geological matters; to Paul Austin of the Arkansas Indian Center, for insights into Arkansas Indian issues offered in a phone conversation in 1989; and to Sandra Smith, Official Court Reporter of the U.S. District Court, Eastern District of Arkansas, Western Division, who loaned me her transcript of the Arkansas creationism trial.

I would also like to give grateful acknowledgment to the following works: "Who Owns the Past?" by Mara Leveritt (*Arkansas Times,* December 1985); *Creationism on Trial: Evolution and God at Little Rock* by Langdon Gilkey (San Francisco: Harper & Row, 1985); the late Judge William Overton's opinion in *McLean v. Arkansas Board of Education* and Stephen Jay Gould's lectures in his course at Harvard, "History of the Earth and of Life," given in the fall of 1981, the period when he testified in the Arkansas case. Each of these furnished some philosophical background for this book, stimulated my imagination, and was a pleasure to absorb in its own right.

Contents

One

I could be bounded in a nutshell and count myself a king of
infinite space—were it not that I have bad dreams.

Shakespeare, *Hamlet* II.ii

1

"YOU KNOW WHERE WE ARE?" said Jonas Torbett to his father. He didn't wait for an answer. "We're on the crust," he said.

Bryce Torbett grunted and crushed his cigarette out in the ashtray of the pickup truck and passed a navy-blue Lincoln. He glanced up in the rear-view mirror. "That's A.M. Bigley," he said, "going over to the races in Hot Springs, I bet."

"We had it in science last week," Jonas added. There was the core of the earth, a fiery ball, which all the children instantly recognized as Hell. Obviously their science book called it the core only to avoid the bad word Hell. Nevertheless that must be where the Devil lived, and it was satisfying to have a diagram of it, which was never given to them in Sunday school. Surrounding that was the mantle, where you could hang around on your way down to the Hell-core. On top was the crust: the outermost layer of the planet, the floor of the sea and the land alike, where lay the bones of the dead. The crust was where everyone moved and drove and walked around like bugs on the surface of a deep deep lake—where, in fact, their Ford was zipping along right now. And cushioning it all, buoying it all, surrounding it all, was what they called space or the universe, until you died, when it automatically turned into Heaven.

"He'll miss the Daily Double," said Jonas's father, "but he'll get there in time for the Classix."

Except for an occasional exchange of crossing comments, the father and son had been riding in silence: Bryce hunched against his window sunk in thought, driving with a heavy foot as usual and passing slower, older pickups and sedans, and

Jonas gazing out the window and daydreaming. This particular stretch of the earth's crust that they were crossing, this Tuesday afternoon in March of 1981, was very familiar to them, the Crowdersville highway. They lived in a neighboring town, Groverton. In fact, just recently Jonas had decided what his complete and true address must be: Route 1 Box 23-C, Groverton, Wilbur County, Arkansas, the United States of America, Western Hemisphere, Planet Earth, the solar system, the Milky Way galaxy, the Universe. He had scrawled it in the back of his social studies notebook, then sat back and read it with awe.

The highway was an old two-lane, crumbling at the edges and splitting where its cracks had previously been tarred over, but not that much worse off than most roads in the state. It went past cluttered shacks, rolling pastures with Herefords grazing in them, and old white-painted farmhouses with martin houses in the yard. There were lonely-looking brick or frame churches, shuttered-up peach sheds, and every so often a new brick ranch house with a TV satellite dish in front. Between these the road went for miles through nothing but hardwood forests leafed out in a new, sharp green. There were a few rocks cropping up from clay-colored dirt, especially where creek gulches cut through the hills. Sometimes the sun would glint off a dim spread of quartz within the rocks, but more often they just looked dull and rusty.

Then there was a spate of houses occurring more and more frequently, a quick-stop store, and a parts salvage yard, and then they were in Crowdersville. They got caught by the red light on Main Street, and Jonas's heart started hammering high, at the base of his neck. The Big Injun—as people around there called him—was momentarily hidden by the time-and-temperature sign of the Southwest Arkansas Savings and Loan. Then the light changed and they saw him.

He was a huge, faded, weatherbeaten-plywood warrior, with leggings and a feather headdress and a tomahawk and a scalp belt. He towered above the highway, with one hand holding a piece of stretched buckskin—also fashioned of weathered plywood—that said, GIFTS! SOUVENIRS! EDUCATIONAL MUSEUM!

13

BURIAL MOUNDS! and with the other pointing right, to the Mi-Ka-Do turnoff. Mi-Ka-Do was once a fertile hollow in the hills where Caddo tribes had convened for their important meetings and ceremonies. Now it was the private property of Mr. Vaughan Sandifer, who lived there near a little museum of his making, a shop, and a complex of dug-out mounds. He charged admission to the complex. The Caddo people were mostly dead, and nobody much gathered at Mi-Ka-Do anymore except school-children on field trips. Sometimes a lost tourist or two would straggle through.

Bryce Torbett was something of an Indianologist himself, he would say, a collector. A para-archaeologist. Not that Jonas used such terms for him. Filling out forms at school, Jonas printed FARMER in the Father's Occupation blank. And Mother's Occupation? DEAD.

Bryce and Vaughan Sandifer had known each other for years, and Jonas and his older brother, Clint, had more chances than most children to go to Mi-Ka-Do. As small boys they liked walking about the museum store. They would save their quarters up to buy brightly colored tomahawks with dyed feathers on the end, bead belts, or moccasins that turned the skin of their feet a jaundiced yellow. But it was when they were a little older and started to explore the outside exhibits that the real drama of Mi-Ka-Do began for the boys. For Mr. Sandifer had dug right into his mounds—instead of bulldozing them, as their daddy did his—and had uncovered Indian skeletons. Eight in all. Skeletons which you could see, with pots around them, lying at the bottom of the dug-out cylinders of clay. Jonas and Clint would hang over the three-foot chicken-wire fences Mr. Sandifer had put up around the rim of each of the burial shafts, staring down at the bottom of the pits and forgetting to blink for hours, it seemed, or until their father would start calling them from the main museum building. The dug-out chambers were never a place where the boys were inspired to play or rough-house. Instead, in quiet, dramatic voices they would reread the little plaques Mr. Sandifer had put up, and shiver. "... A person of some importance in the tribe, probably a chief." "Eight to nine hundred years ago." "Buried with two young males beneath her." "With other human bones broken and scattered nearby." They knew the skeletons individually and had agreed on affectionate names for them: Ghouly, Needs-a-Pillow, Red Man, Scalp Shark, Look-Ma-No-Cavities, Madam Grunt, Busted-Leg, and Chief of the Pots.

What started Jonas's heart thudding so hard when he saw the Big Injun sign, as much as excitement, was worry. In the last year or so the trips to Mi-Ka-Do had started giving him nightmares. They were always about his mother. Normally, when he was awake, he could never remember exactly what she looked like anymore. The image of her that stayed uppermost in his mind was the photograph on the shelf in his room, of her holding him and Clint each by a hand, smiling into the sunlight with her eyes squinched a little closed and those distinctive bluish shadows in the cracks between her teeth. But during this bad dream he always saw her differently, living, fresh, real, and knew that it was exactly how she had looked most of the time to him. With a sense of boundless relief and joy he would start running to her. Then suddenly she would sink into the bottom of one of these mud cylinders at Mi-Ka-Do, with her head raised uncomfortably, like that of the skeleton he and Clint called Needs-a-Pillow. Her newly recognizable face, with the out-pooching, faintly pink cheeks and the laughing eyes, the bangs that slipped down on her forehead, would fade away and turn to yellowed bone. The eye sockets would stare at him; the teeth would protrude uglily; it seemed the hands reached up to him like claws. He would wake screaming.

After the last episode like that Bryce had forbidden him to go to Mi-Ka-Do anymore. But today he must have forgotten. That was a long time ago, last December. I won't have nightmares, Jonas thought as they bounced down a back street of Crowdersville. Nightmares were just another thing Clint teased him about. He needed to be tougher than that—"with nerves of steel," he told himself, like Kit Carson in the book he had from the library now, "with nerves of steel."

"What'd you say?" said his father.

Jonas jumped. "Nothing." To cover up he asked, "What are you gonna do, sell you a pot?"

"I'm thinking about it," said Bryce. "Want to talk to Vaughan about it at any rate. Plus he's got a quartz arrowhead he wants to show me."

They crunched up Mr. Sandifer's long gravel drive and parked in the turnaround under a pin oak. They walked up to the half-door, where a girl with blond curls on her shoulders and purple all under her eyebrows stood up to greet them. "You're new, aren't you?" said Bryce. "We don't want a tour—I'm a friend of Vaughan's here to see him. He in the office?"

"No sir, he went over to the house," said the girl. "If you wait, though, I'll go get him."

They stood watching her walk on upended cinderblocks that made a little footpath between the museum and the house. A man must have put down the cinderblocks, for they were much farther apart than the girl's natural stride. She had on striped canvas shoes that looked new. Her jeans were very tight and showed how her behind went back and forth as she stepped from block to block, swaying.

"Mmn," said Bryce suddenly, but when Jonas looked up at him he didn't say anything else.

Then Mr. Sandifer came, ignoring the cinderblocks and walking right on the squelchy ground. "Bryce, how are you?" he said. "Came to tell me you need some help digging into your other mound?" He ignored Bryce's scowl and continued blandly, "One of these days you'll see you need a partner to excavate something like that—a professional." He turned to Jonas. "Hey there, Clint. How're y'all today?"

"I'm Jonas," said Jonas.

"Just wanted to visit with you a minute," said Bryce heartily. "We were out this way."

"Come on inside, have some coffee."

"All righty. Thought I'd—what is it, son?" Jonas was tapping his arm.

"I'll be outside, okay?"

"Sure, sure, don't go far." Bryce turned back to Mr. Sandifer.

16

Jonas walked past the signs to the Peepee Teepee toward the first small mound of the complex. He was not too interested in the pots and clay frogs and things. Even arrowheads got dull after a while. "What did they do with these?" he would ask, and when Bryce's answer was too short, he would say, "Well, tell me a story about it. Who made it, Daddy? How come?" But Bryce's voice would get impatient. "I don't *know* who might have made this, son," he said, "but I can tell you this: if I wanted to, I could carry it up to a fellow I know near Muskogee, Oklahoma, and sell it for twelve, thirteen hundred dollars"—he snapped his fingers—"just like that." Talk of dollars, which always came up in connection with the pots, bored Jonas. That was not what he wanted to hear about the Indians. He preferred information like what was in the social studies book, like what Mr. Bledsoe, that substitute teacher, had explained, about *living* Indians: having secret names; setting up their teepees in fifteen minutes; sending smoke signals; diving naked into cold water ...

Instead of going up the plank steps Mr. Sandifer had laid up the slope of the mound, he went to a pine tree a few feet away and sat down under it. He sat Indian-style. Just so might the Caddo chiefs have sat to smoke their peace pipes. Probably in this very place. There were doodlebugs in the soft dust here. Maybe they, too, had been here in the Caddo people's time. Jonas took up a straw to stir up their little holes. His mind began to wander and he forgot to sit Indian-style; he drew up his knees beneath his chin and put his arms around them.

He wished he could build up his nerve to go look at the skeletons. Would he do it if Clint were here? he wondered. Probably so. But would that be because it was easier not to be scared if there was someone with you, or so that Clint wouldn't shame him? He didn't know. Clint said only babies had trouble looking at skeletons. And Jonas agreed. Besides, if he couldn't even look at dead Indians without getting upset, how would he ever behave if a real crisis came along, if he were ever really tested by terrorists or kidnappers or whoever? He needed to not have qualms. What if he were eavesdropping on some thieves who were torturing somebody and he needed to stay

17

strong and brave to jump on the thieves and knock them out and let the tortured person go?

Jonas was always wanting something to happen to him. He liked mystery books—Sherlock Holmes, the Hardy Boys, the Three Investigators, and Brains Benton—and judging from them it seemed inevitable that adventure would come his way. There would be some kidnapping or robbery or even murder that the police could not solve. He, being a boy, would have more time and freedom to investigate the crimes than any adult would. No one would notice him tracking the clues. He would recognize the thugs because he always studied the FBI Most Wanted signs in the post office, which everyone else ignored. He would trap a criminal and become a hero.

Or adventure might come in other forms. He wouldn't have minded finding the body of the canoeist who disappeared during the spring rise of the Cossatot. Or being the first to come upon the eighteen-wheeler that jackknifed on the new bypass, or striking gold or finding a treasure. Sometimes Jonas and Clint would fool around by the mounds at home together, daydreaming about making the really valuable discovery that would shock their dad. "Find of the century," Jonas would muse, scrabbling in the dirt, and Clint would add, "Something that'd sell for a hundred million dollars." But whenever Bryce leveled a mound he worked practically around the clock to sort what he turned up, removing the pots and pipes and arrowheads and necklaces himself, quickly, leaving only chips and trashy stuff behind. The boys often ended up playing trench war or dodge-clod, a game invented by Clint, in the freshly turned dirt of the mounds.

Some people might say things did happen to Jonas. He once broke his arm in a Little League game. Before that his mother had died of breast cancer. But obviously those were not good happenings; those were awful. The kind of excitement he longed for was better than that. Oh, he knew it might not be all fun and games—not at all. Just as long as it was *neat* and didn't cause him, Jonas, pain.

When he was in the third grade, Groverton had had three straight days of tornado warnings and power outages and flash floods, and school had been canceled. In the end the tornadoes had skipped over Groverton, and instead whipped through the little community on the lake road named, ironically, Uncloudy Day. When school took in again the third-graders had had to write a paragraph on how they felt during the bad weather. Jonas wrote, "I loved it. I love when you get your bathtub full of water. You go to the store and get alot of Everready bateries, and food too. You get in the middle of your house. My brother he said Open all the windows! but my Dad says No thats for a Hurricane you do that. I was sad when the tornado went to Uncloudy Day insted of here and we have to come back to school. I ca'nt wait for more tornados to come to Groverton, U.S.A." He had made a C minus on the paragraph. It came back all marked up, and his teacher had written, "That's no way to feel!" His father agreed. "You wouldn't say those things if you'd ever lived through a real tornado," he said. "But I *haven't,*" protested Jonas. His father had whipped him anyway. The boys got whipped any time they made lower than a C, even if it was just a little daily grade.

He heard the side screen door to Mr. Sandifer's house open and shut, and Mr. Sandifer and Daddy came out and stood talking in the sunshine for a minute. Jonas looked up expectantly. But the two men crossed back over to the museum, and that door slammed behind them.

Sometimes it seemed that nothing really panned out. The tornadoes always went elsewhere. A deputy sheriff found the drowned canoeist. And yet—and yet—there was always hope, the hope that something neat would happen next to *you:* and in the meantime you had to make your own adventure out of what really was going on. And that was life; as one of Celie's stories said, that was Days of Our Lives. That was one place where things happened quite regularly—on the stories. When he was out of school and bored Jonas would often lie on the floor in the TV room after lunch, idly pestering Celie, their maid, for another helping of dessert, or waiting for some sort of inspiration for what to do next. Celie would watch the stories and iron at the same time. The room would be fresh with the smells of warm laundry and starch. Every once in a while a tear of Celie's would drip down and sizzle on the iron. She would sigh and say, "Lord Jesus, remember me." Jonas pictured the Lord Jesus, slapping his forehead, struck with a thought: "Why, that's Celie Matthews, down in Groverton!" Sometimes on one of the stories there would be a shooting, to which he attended with longing interest. One day last summer on "As the World Turns" a crazy man had put his hand through the burning candles of his own birthday cake. Celie had noticed that he sat up to watch. "You like the stories?" she asked him.

"I guess," he said. "I like when something *happens.*"

"Makes you forget your own troubles," Celie agreed. "Yes, Lord. Seem like your own troubles ain't so heavy then. Not like theirs." And she had used her elbow to point toward the pained-looking people on the screen, because her hands were occupied with the collar of Bryce's good shirt.

Jonas perked up. Maybe interesting things were happening right under his nose! "What kind of troubles has Celie got?" he asked his father later.

"Celie?" said Bryce. "Lord, I don't know. Why in the world do you ask?"

Jonas said, "She said she has troubles."

"I think A.R. has high blood pressure or something," said Bryce. "In my opinion, Celie ought to be counting her blessings, not talking about her troubles."

Not one doodlebug was coming out. Jonas tossed the straw behind him and squinted up at the tin shed surrounding the dug-out chamber. Just think how close the skeletons were to him right now. The back of his neck crawled. But he had looked at these things lots of times before. There was nothing to it. What would Clint say at supper when his father told him where they'd been and Jonas would have to admit he hadn't looked at the skeletons?

He stood up and started pulling pine bark off the tree. If you were an Indian you would use this for something useful, he thought. You would start fires with it or do an art project, painting on it or something. You might make a boat. Maybe he would take some home to paint on.

A few minutes later he heard his father's voice. "Jonas! Let's go, son!"

"I'm comin'!" he called. He looked around desperately and slowly started for the truck. Just when he was about to break into a trot he paused, turned around, ran up the plank steps two at a time, and ducked into the shadow under the tin roof. He leaned over the fence and stared down into the pit, which stayed glaringly lit by jerry-rigged hanging lights: and there the pale boneheads were, grinning up at him as if to say, "We knew you wouldn't be able to resist us!" As he ran away he imagined they were pointing their long white bony fingers at him. His father was honking the truck horn now.

"I'm—*comin'!*" he hollered, getting a stitch in his side as he ran.

2

IT WAS LATE THE FOLLOWING DAY, and on a remote dirt road in Wilbur County two figures on bikes were stopped. Some thirty yards behind them, a third cyclist was struggling to catch up.

Even at this distance Jonas could tell that the other boys were getting tired of waiting for him. Down the road where they were waiting, their two bikes blazed in the sun, a spiky configuration of silver and gleaming red. Both were ten-speeds acquired the same Christmas Jonas had finally crossed the threshold to a three-speed banana-seat—like the ones the older boys never mounted again from that day forward. *Why didn't somebody tell me?* Jonas remembered thinking that Christmas afternoon. You would have thought even Santa Claus could have brought it up, say when he got Jonas's letter: "Jonas," in a booming voice like God talking to Moses, "look here, you can have 'is banana-seat if you really want it, no problem, but I just thought I'd tell you it's not the toughest thing out there anymore ..." The older boys were straddling the frames as best they could, Jonas's brother Clint with a fist on his hip and Clint's friend Kyle with his arms folded, in exaggerated attitudes of boredom and impatience.

"I'm coming, hang on," yelled Jonas one more time. Finally he tore his pants leg out of the chain. "Daddy's gonna have a cow," he thought. But it couldn't be helped. If he took any longer trying to coax it out intact the guys would leave him. He leaped astride his bike and pedaled furiously, the small front wheel digging into the red clay road, his face sweaty and contorted with effort. Now his chain didn't work so well. It had some threads still stuck in it. Clint and Kyle started riding again before he caught up to them, and by the hardest he managed to stay abreast.

"You'll need to come down to your lowest gear, so he can keep up." Clint spoke sideways, nonchalantly, to his friend.

"It's not that. My pants leg got caught," said Jonas.

Clint glanced across. "Daddy's gonna have a shit fit," he observed.

"I know."

"If you wouldn't wear bell-bottoms—" Clint continued. "They're really out."

"They been out a long time," said Kyle.

"I know, but that's all I get to wear. These are some you used to have."

"Save your Christmas money and get you some straight-legs."

"I can't, I a'r'dy spent it ..."

"Boot-cut," said Kyle. "That's what I get."

"You'd better have something worth seeing," said Clint. "I need to get to bed early. And my bike's getting all muddy."

"Oh, just wait," said Jonas. "This is gonna be so neat. You think the drainage canal is something. Wait till you see this."

"Reason I need to get to bed early," Clint said to Kyle, "is that *he* had nightmares and woke everybody up screaming last night. Never did get back to sleep."

"*My* baby brother used to have nightmares," said Kyle.

Jonas flushed and pedaled harder.

The drainage canal was at the back of the Torbetts' farm. To get there you had to ride down two miles of thick clay road. Two miles was a long way to ride through clay, especially if you didn't have a ten-speed. But on special outings sometimes, to catch crawfish or hunt arrowheads or pick dewberries, the boys would go back there. On this side of the canal were woods, kept fairly clean by foraging cattle, woods with even an old home place in them at one point and a creek for wading. One day Jonas had figured something out. On the other side of the drainage canal there was a long rising slope ending in a ridge that you couldn't see over, which looked so thorny and unpromising that they rarely played there. But what could be on the other side of it but the Red River? Jonas had figured this out all by himself.

He knew which way the river ran, out their way, southwest of town. To confirm it he had asked his father which way the river was and he had jerked his thumb in this direction. Jonas planned to lead his brother and Kyle across the drainage canal and through the brush on the other side. Then, like the picture of La Salle in his social studies book, he would stand atop the little rise and gesture to the territory that would be theirs—long white sandbars, waving stands of cottonwood and willows, clay gulches dug out by recent rains that would be perfect for imagining trench warfare—a territory like the riverside in Little Rock where Uncle Terry sometimes took them but, unlike that beer-can-and-Clorox-bottle-littered place, theirs alone.

He had led Clint to think that he had seen this "surprise" before. But in fact he was being gracious enough to take them with him on the virgin trip. He needed an audience. What would be the point of standing on the little rise and gesturing toward your discovery if no one was there to watch you and applaud?

"Well," said Kyle, "it better be neat."

They rode in silence for a few minutes. Meadowlarks veered away from them, dabs of black-collared yellow against the pale sky. The older boys' tires whispered silkily against the gravel-and sand-stiffened clay. Jonas half-stood on his bike, his breath labored, tilting from side to side as he pumped through the mire.

Finally the road petered out. They parked the bikes and walked single-file. Since Mr. Bledsoe, the substitute teacher, had told Jonas's class that Indians used to walk not heel-then-toe like modern people, but toe-then-heel for silence in the woods, the boy had been trying to perfect the technique. La Salle had adopted Indian ways. The white man had a lot to learn from the red man, Jonas told himself, taking care not to step on any dead leaves lest they make a big noise. Most white men weren't so observant.

Then Clint's voice broke into his thoughts. "What're you walking like that for? It looks queer as hell. You want me to go first?"

"No," insisted Jonas. "This is my trip. Y'all just follow."

At the edge of the drainage canal, as usual, they all took off their pants. Jonas started across, still remembering with shame the first time he had come there, some four or five years ago; Clint and his friend Dwayne—this was in pre-Kyle days—had let him get halfway across, timorously stepping in the opaque, scum-topped water, and then told him there were leeches in it … He hadn't run, he had just stopped where he was and started crying. He could handle all kinds of snakes, frogs, lizards, skinks, and insects, but the idea of leeches horrified him.

Today, however, he strode through the water like the seasoned explorer he was. All three boys reached the opposite side at the same moment. "Where to now?"

"Just follow me."

Jonas put his jeans and sneakers back on, awkwardly teetering on one leg at a time rather than sit down on the wet bank as the older boys were doing. Then he squared his shoulders and starting pushing through the underbrush that lined the drainage canal—cockleburs, beggar-lice, blackberry vines, thistles. Suddenly he held up his hand. "Shh!"

They paused.

"I thought I heard something." It must have been the foghorn of a barge. They would be able to lie on the white, sparkling sandbars and watch the barges go by. The crews would get to know him so well that when he got to be eighteen he could get a job on some barge, easy. Like Jim Ray at the gas station's son had.

"It was just a car horn, stupid."

"A car horn, bull," said Jonas. "From where? I'd like to ask you that."

"From the Old Murdoch Highway."

"Ain't no highway back here. Nosiree-bob."

"Where do you think we're heading?"

Jonas didn't say anything, but his face paled as he lowered it to watch his feet, which he set in motion again. He couldn't be wrong. The river had to be this way. They were almost to the top of the rise now. He was still leading. His moment of glory was at hand. "Clint? Kyle?" he said. "I want y'all to remember I found this place first. Okay?"

25

"Okay, little brother. You got it."

A few more yards, and Jonas gained the ridge. He spread his right arm in a preplanned gesture toward the horizons—and then his eyes took in the scrub land below: sorry land, bush land, with thorns and puddles studding it, and litter showing white in the distance in the swath of weeds that was the shoulder of the Old Murdoch Highway. His eyes filled with tears.

"What's this, kiddo? Where to now?"

Jonas's arm fell to his side.

"I thought we could walk back to town on the highway," he lied.

"That's *it?* That's what you thought was so neat?"

"A trashy shortcut to a trashy nigger highway?" said Kyle. "I ain't believing this."

"And what about our bikes?" said Clint. "Even if we did want to walk to town this way, we'd have to get back to the other side of the drainage canal to get our bikes."

"Of all the stupid—" said Kyle.

"Look here," said Clint. "Here's a dead armadillo. I guess that's something."

"Spent a hour riding back here to find a dead armadillo."

"I shoulda known. I'm sorry, man. I shoulda known better than to believe him."

"Let's get outa here."

"Let's go."

They turned. "We're not waiting for you this time, Jonas. You take too long. You've wasted enough of our day. You get home on your own."

"Stay here in your old neat place," said Kyle. They disappeared down the little ridge, and he heard the faint, slow lapping of their strides through the scummy water.

Jonas sat down where he was. He lowered his head to his knees and wrapped his arms around them. He didn't exactly cry, but after a few minutes some water leaked out of his left eye and ran down his nose and into the faded threads of his hand-me-down jeans. He raised his head and looked again at the scene before him. It looked like the no-man's-land pictured on the

Dogfight board game they had gotten from their uncle. Oh, why had he brought Clint and Kyle with him! If he had checked it out himself beforehand, he still would have had his disappointment to deal with—the loss of the heavenly sandbar—but at least he wouldn't have had the additional burden of humiliation.

Finally Jonas stood up. He'd have to start back soon, or Daddy really would be mad. But maybe first he'd look around a minute. This looked like the kind of place where you might find a cowskull. The dead armadillo had reminded him. Kyle's big brother had this cowskull up on the wall in his room and he hung his ties on the horns; Clint had described it to Jonas. He'd been walking for several minutes—forgetting to walk like an Indian, just concentrating on sidestepping the prickly, trailing berry vines and bull nettle—when he heard the noise. At first it sounded like a kitten—a mewing noise. He halted at once. His ears pricked up and he was an Indian hunter again. "Mew, mew." It came from off to his right. Toe-heel, toe-heel, toe-heel, toward the highway. But suddenly it wasn't coming from in front of him and to the right anymore; it sounded behind him. He turned uncertainly. Maybe it was in those bushes. Behind—before. Then Jonas realized that the bushes masked a gully. Some of the cracks in the chalky mud at his feet had deepened and widened into little ditches. Setting his feet sideways, hurrying as the funny whining noise got louder, he clambered down; young cottonwoods braced him, and kept the sides of the gully from crumbling. Now he was completely beneath the ground level. And closer than ever to the noise.

And then he saw it, sitting on a small ledge of mud at one of the places where the poor earth had cracked and split. It wasn't a cat at all; it was a puppy—speckled all over with all the colors he had ever seen on a dog but never on one single dog, black and gray and brown and white and reddish, sitting like a grown dog and cocking its head at him, but scarcely bigger than a softball, and about as round. Jonas's ears readjusted and the mewing translated into whining. "Oh," he breathed. And then, "But you're *hurt.*" For when the puppy tried to push itself to a standing position, wiggling with eagerness, it would collapse against a rock that seemed to be the only thing keeping it from sliding down the gully, and would lie there whimpering again. "C'mere," Jonas said in a throaty voice, "oh, c'mere, boy, lemme help you." Even in its weak state this puppy wagged its tail. Jonas clambered up the sides of the gulch, bracing his own feet against some saplings that had sprung up there. Reaching out for the puppy, he noticed that the thing it was leaning against was not a rock but a dirty bone. He had found his bone after all—though it wasn't a cowskull. But that could wait. For as Jonas picked up the animal, bumpy-ribbed under its loose coat and surprisingly light, awkward with its big paws and furrowed brow, smelling of something like slightly damp wood shavings or pine straw in the sun, it grunted from down inside itself its notice at being rearranged: at this readjustment: and then it licked Jonas's sweaty collarbone. Something somersaulted high in the boy's stomach, as if he had swallowed a big bubble of air that was lifting him up, pushing up on the inside of his chest and the bottom of his throat and nearly knocking him off balance as he stood on the slanting earth; and he fell in love.

3

HIS BIKE WAS STILL ON the other side of the drainage canal, and with the puppy in his arms Jonas had a long walk back—he had no idea how far up the Murdoch Highway but, he told himself, miles and miles. The puppy kept pretty still, stiller than you would think a puppy should be. So when he finally did reach Groverton, he headed toward the clinic though he had never been inside it—angling resolutely across the huge Piggly Wiggly parking lot and stepping over the concrete border that divided the vet's property from the grocery store's. The sign on the door said CLOSED, but there was a truck in the parking lot that he believed was Dr. Armstrong's, and he hesitated only a moment before knocking.

A couple of minutes passed, the puppy squirmed in his arms, and he was just shifting it to knock again when the door opened abruptly and a woman in a light blue coat over jeans appeared, gazing down at him with an exasperated look on her face.

"Hullo," he said. "I, uh, I got this puppy—"

"Well, come on in," she said brusquely. Jonas handed the puppy up to her and followed when she turned on her heel and marched into the examining room. She set the pup on the Formica-topped examining table, where it lay quivering, too weak or afraid to push itself to a standing or sitting position— splayed out like an oily, speckled puddle. The vet opened its mouth with her finger, quickly, looked hard at its nose and ears, and seemed to be thinking while her hands ran backward along it, one cupping the belly, the other its ribs. "You oughta be with your mama. How'd you get yourself into this fix?"

There was a silence. Then Jonas said, "Oh—*him*. I thought you meant me!" He was relieved. "I don't know what happened," he went on. "I just found him like that. In a—a sort of hole."

"Here. Hold him, please, while I get something." Obligingly he reached up to the high table. Something was a syringe. As Dr. Armstrong slipped the needle into a loose pinch of skin, he flinched and looked away. But on the puppy his hands, grimy and nailbitten as they were, stayed firm. In an encouraging voice he said to the dog, "It's okay, boy. Hang on. *It's* okay."

"You found him in a hole? You mean like he had fallen and couldn't get out?"

"No ma'am, not that kind of a hole. A long hole."

"A long hole, hmm? Here, one more time."

The needle again. "I guess it was more like a big ditch ..." Jonas said lamely.

"Hm." Dr. Armstrong straightened up. "Well—what's your name?"

"Jonas Torbett."

She had stepped over to her counter for a thermometer and another syringe. But Jonas could still see her face in profile and could see that her lips pressed together as if there were something wrong with what he'd said. "Bryce Torbett's son."

"Yes ma'am."

She nodded. When she looked back at him, directly, her dark blue eyes seemed to comb him. He watched them leave his own eyes and scan his chin, his hair, his body down to his shoes for an instant. Then she looked at his face again and seemed to sigh, with the exasperated look she'd had when she opened the door. "Well, Jonas, there are a couple of things that might be wrong with your friend here."

"Yes ma'am."

"He's real dehydrated, he's exhausted, a little bit anemic, and he's just plain hungry. And lonely. He shouldn't even be away from his mother at this age. I think he's only four or five weeks old, even though he's big for his age. He's a Catahoula cur, and he'll be a big dog, if he makes it. See his paws?"

"Yes ma'am."

"I'm gonna give you some stuff to feed him tonight. And tomorrow you get your—someone to take you to the store and get some baby cereal. You wet it up with warm water and stir it up and feed it to him on your finger. The way I'm doing this." She had mixed up something that looked like paste, which she offered to the dog bit by bit. "See how hungry he was?"

"Unh-hunh—yes ma'am."

"And keep him warm. Now the worst possibility, and what I'm afraid of, is that he may have distemper."

"Okay ..." If that was all! He could put up with a puppy in a bad mood.

But Dr. Armstrong went on, "This is a viral disease that attacks the nervous system. You know what the nervous system is?"

Nervous system! He should say so! He made B's in science. "I know all them systems," he said. Nervous system—brains, spinal cord. Circulatory system—heart, blood vessels; muscular, that was easy too. Reproductive, they always skimmed over that; endocrine, they skimmed over that too, said it had to do with your adrenalin running when you were scared; digestive, they skimmed over the ending of that, the waste products embarrassed everyone.

But she had gone on talking, and his mind had wandered, just as everybody was always telling him it did, though his hands hadn't stopped stroking the puppy over his head. "—two weeks for the virus to incubate," she was saying. "So. You say you just found him? How long have you had him?"

"Oh, I just now found him, offa the Old Murdoch Highway. In this place where they wasn't anybody around. I don't think he's anybody's."

"Someone probably just drove out there and dumped him," said Deborah Armstrong. Her voice deepened with disgust. "People. Sometimes I wonder." She looked at Jonas. "Are you going to keep him?"

Jonas squirmed a little, but his eyes stayed round and steady, looking out under a fringe of lashes, over a nose with a couple of small scabs on the bridge. "Yes ma'am."

"Well, over the next two weeks you watch him. If his nose

starts to run, or his eyes, or if he starts to twitch or have any fits, you get him right back to me as fast as you can."

"What does that mean if that happens?"

"That might mean he does have distemper. If he survived at all he would probably have some big problems. If that happened I would suggest you let me put him to sleep."

But it wasn't sleep she meant. Jonas knew better.

"But if he's okay after two weeks he won't get it?"

"That's right. I gave him a shot, so he should be okay once you pass the time where any viruses already in his body take their toll. But there may be other things wrong with him. Or, as I said, if we're lucky he may be just dehydrated and weak from worms and exposure and all. You'll have to feed him real often. Do it like I'm doing now. Okay?"

"One more thing. I have to be sure your daddy'll pay the bill, you know, Jonas." She sounded gentle. "Have you talked to him about this yet?"

"Oh, yes ma'am, he will."

She studied him a little longer.

"How old do you think he is?"

"What? Oh, about five weeks."

"Um, Miz Armstrong? Dr. Armstrong?"

"What?"

"How much is this gonna cost?"

"Forty-five dollars." He must have looked as appalled as he felt, because she added, "Don't you think you should ask your dad about it first, Jonas?"

"I don't really need to. He told me if I ever found a animal that's suffering to go ahead and fix it up and worry about the cost later. He hates to see anything in pain, you know, if there's something he could do about it." Not that Daddy had ever come right out and said this, but the situation had never exactly arisen before, either. Surely this was what he *would* say. "When can I take him home? Are you gonna be through tonight?"

He watched the doctor's face hopefully. At length she said, "Go ahead and take him home. And start talking your dad into letting you keep him." Again she suddenly looked displeased.

"Um-hmh. Then do I have to bring the forty-five dollars, like, tomorrow?"

"No, I can bill your dad."

"Um, can you hand him to me? I can't really reach too good."

Dr. Armstrong settled the animal into Jonas's skinny arms. He rubbed one hand over and over the loose mottled sheen of puppy skin. He suddenly looked up at the vet and smiled—tentatively. "I like the way he smells."

"Okay now, you'd better head home, Jonas."

"Yes ma'am, thank you, one more thing? What kind did you say he is?"

"Looks like a Catahoula cur to me."

"Catahoula. That's a Indian tribe."

"Yes, this kind of dog was bred by Indians. The only dog breed native to North America."

"Wow."

"Night, Jonas."

Outside he saw it was already dusk, and he started to hurry. Dr. Armstrong left the front light on till he reached the sidewalk.

4

WALKING HOMEWARD JONAS was sunk deep in thought about how to introduce his dog to the household. Should he try to sneak him in? Maybe he could wrap him up in his T-shirt—pretend he was hot and had taken his shirt off and wadded it up. Once he smuggled him past his dad he could keep him in his room, swearing Clint to secrecy. But no, that would never work. The puppy might whine and wet and he needed help getting the food for it. Sooner or later they would find out the dog was there, and he might as well get it over with. Besides, just as Jonas was probably in trouble for worrying Daddy by being so late, so was Clint probably in trouble for going off and leaving Jonas. Clint would not be a good ally tonight. In fact it was going to be a bad setting for making a request, period.

But he had never cared about anything as much as this. Not the banana-seat bike, not getting to go on Mikey Rhodes's Methodist camping trip, not the new Levi's denim jacket from Texarkana. He had thought he cared about those things passionately and had pled for them with tears in his eyes, but he now saw how shallow those tears had been. Yearning for those treats was nothing compared to the already painful love for this puppy that had sprung up in him since the instant he touched him. This was something *living*. This puppy *needed* him. If they didn't let him keep him he would run away from home. He and the dog would live off fish and berries and things. He would teach his dog tricks and they would perform for people and earn money that way.

He finally reached the long drive off the highway that led to his house. He stopped to shift arms under the puppy, who felt lumpy and warm against his chest but at least wasn't wiggling to get down. A dog will teach me responsibility, Daddy, he would say. A dog will be—he felt a twisted sob within him just to think it—my best friend! That would do it.

The lights in his father's workshop were on. Jonas knocked before entering and then stepped inside. "Daddy?" he called. The workshop was a long tin building that had once been used as a tractor and equipment shed. Gradually Bryce had made room in it for his Caddo artifacts. He had already excavated two small burial mounds on his property, and a third, the biggest, awaited his bulldozer blade. He called it "excavating," so that's what Jonas and Clint called it too; but it was none too delicate an operation. Finally he had moved all the farm equipment to a new building across the road, and the tin workshop was given over completely to the artifacts. There were long shelves running the length of the building for the arrowheads and beads he had dug out of the mounds, and locked glass cases where the pots sat on crushed velvet. In the middle of the room were worktables where he brushed and cleaned or repaired or added a little paint to the artifacts and pored over catalogs for buying, selling, or trading them. On one wall there was a big map of Wilbur County. There was one corner of the room, with a desk set off by some shelves full of books about Indians, that he called his office, but it had more to do with the Indian stuff than with farming; and he always dealt with his farm hands over where the tractors were now stored and fixed. He didn't like them coming over to his workshop anymore.

"Daddy!"

"I'm back here, son."

Nervously, guiltily, Jonas stood in the "door" of the office— the opening left between the bookshelf dividers.

"Daddy, I got me a dog."

His father was already standing up, not a good sign, and his eyebrows were knotted together, going all the way across his forehead. His eyes lingered on the little bundle in Jonas's arms, with a flicker of interest that made Jonas's heart jump in hope.

But all he said, and sternly, was, "Is that any excuse for being home an hour after dark? Two hours later than your brother?"

"No sir, Daddy, but—he wasn't in good shape—and I had to walk because I couldn't hold him and ride my bike at the same time. I think he's a Indian kind of dog—"

Now his father was talking faster and more emphatically. "What do you think we were thinking here? For all we knew you'd been hit by a car. Did you think about that?"

"No sir, I—"

"Celie wouldn't go home, because she was keeping your supper warm, and she was worried too. I tell you what. You go pick out the widest belt you can find in my closet, and then come back here and we'll have a little *discussion* about the merits of being *punctual.*"

He was already snuffling. "You ain't gonna whip my puppy! You ain't gonna whip my puppy!"

"Oh, for Pete's sake," said his father. "I won't whip your puppy!"

Jonas continued, "I ain't gonna put him down! You'll take him from me! I ain't gonna set him down where somebody could take him away! But I don't want you whipping him when you whip me!" Yet beneath this outburst which he seemed unable to stop, with the words spurting from him along with tears, was the little, crafty thought, *He said 'your puppy.' He said 'your puppy.'*

Then loudly, in a voice getting even louder, Bryce said, "Son, the longer you stand here and make a scene the worse off you'll be. I gave you an order. Are you disobeying me?"

Jonas shook his head wildly, no, and continued to shake it while he clutched the puppy and looked up and said through torrents of tears, "Daddy, I'm going to get your belt but please, I got to know, can I keep this dog?"

His father pried the puppy out of his clinging hands and said, *"Go!"*

Blindly he traipsed past Celie in the kitchen, just starting the dishwasher and shooting a look at his downturned face, blindly he passed his jeering brother, blindly in his father's room he found the closet door, reached back between the age-smooth jeans and the fuzzy flannel and the cool sport shirts, smelling the foot sweat, shoe polish, and leather smells with the clutch of fear in his stomach that he always associated with this place, because he was never here except to fumble for a belt to be whipped with. The widest one. It was braided on the edges. He found it—he could swear his father never wore it, but kept it around only to hurt his sons with—and carried it all the way back through the house and across the carport, still blindly, sniveling.

When he first got near the office he didn't see his father. Then he saw him squatted down, mopping a yellow puddle with a wad of paper towels. The puppy stood nearby on bowed legs, trying to nose at a dust ball. Then he sat down—plop—and looked just the way he had when Jonas first saw him. He yawned, his pale tongue curling out briefly over tiny white teeth, and then he just looked at the two human beings. Jonas's father stood up, dropped the paper towels into his wastebasket with a splat, took the belt, and said, "Bend over, and take hold a my desk."

Jonas endured. Ten licks—that was what they usually got— lurching a bit closer to an ashtray made of arrowheads sunk in clear plastic with every stinging blow, so that by the end, when his butt and the tops of his legs felt like he'd just sat down in a fire ant pile, as Clint described it, his nose was a half-inch from the ashtray. But then it was over, and he straightened up immediately and picked up the dog. Strangely enough he wasn't crying now.

His father laid the belt over the desk and said, conversation-ally, as if the whipping had not occurred, "Have you fed him anything yet?"

"Dr. Armstrong did, and she gave me this stuff to give him."

"Dr. Armstrong? Deborah?" He put the faintest emphasis on *doctor,* as if from scorn. "You took him there?" Bryce did not take his livestock to Deborah Armstrong; he hauled them over to an old male vet in Elmer, twenty-five miles away. He told people he wouldn't trust his vet work to a woman.

"Yessir, I knew he was in real bad shape. That's how come I was even later than I would have been anyway."

"What'd she do?"

"I don't know. She said he might get mistemper but he might not. It's gonna cost forty-five dollars, but I'ma pay for it myself. I'ma see can I start washing people's cars and boats this summer over at Jim Ray's so I can earn it all myself."

"Well, son, that's a sensible plan. At that rate you ought to be able to pay Deborah by the time you're a senior in high school. Where is this dog gonna spend the night?"

"With me in my room."

"Listen here. We're gonna have an agreement about this. That was the last puddle or mess of this animal's that I or Celie or your brother or anyone but you, is going to clean up. Understand? And it's up to you to feed it and give it water. Understand?"

"Yes sir."

"Now let's go see if we can find it something to eat."

His father was weird: whipping him one minute, and the next minute deciding they needed to go up to the U-Tote-M to get baby cereal for the puppy. Jonas waited in the dark, cavernous, hay- and leather-smelling interior of the truck while his father hunted for his wallet inside the house. The puppy lay quietly on Jonas's lap. Clint, who had been excited enough by the puppy to forget "Hawaii Five-O" while he admired it, now came out and offered to play with it till Bryce and Jonas got back from the store. Jonas shook his head no, and Clint went back inside without another comment.

Celie's husband, A.R., turned into the driveway and pulled alongside Bryce's truck. Jonas heard the screen door bang, but it wasn't Daddy, it was Celie coming out, her white uniform glowing in the dark, a paper bag of leftovers in her hand. "Night, now," she said to Jonas, and then he heard her tell A.R., "Got him a little puppy. Yes sir! Found him a puppy-dog!" A.R. tilted his head outside the car and smiled up at Jonas. His gold and silver teeth showed. "Heee! Is'at right!" he said. "Got you a dog to look out for you now."

"Yeah," said Jonas, uncertainly, and then he smiled. They called goodnight again and drove away, their taillights leaning perilously skew to the ground, quivering as the car passed over the cattle guard.

Finally Daddy came. He lit his cigarette as he started the truck. Jonas always loved the sweet scent of that first drag of his father's, the only good-smelling drag, which lasted about as long as the glowing orange circle of the cigarette lighter was in sight. "What are you going to name him?" Daddy said.

"I don't know. I have to think about it."

"How about Spot? He's sure got a lot of them."

But Jonas said no.

"Well, it's about time we have a dog around here. With your mother feeling the way she did about them, I sort of got in the habit of not having one. We had one when we first got married though. Did I ever tell you about that?"

"What, Howdy?"

"Yeah. I called him Howdy. I don't know why. Your mother never did let on she liked him. But when she didn't know I was around I'd hear her, opening the kitchen door, giving him some scraps. 'Howdy? Breakfast time.' Or she'd drop an egg—I'd hear it break—then that screen door and, 'Howdy? Could you come clean this up please? Thank you.' She was always real polite to him."

"Like he was a person," said Jonas, tentatively.

"Yeah."

"There was another thing I found back there too. Only I couldn't get it and the dog too. It was this old bone. Maybe I'll go back and get it and take it to school."

"Where did all this happen?" said his father.

"Across the drainage canal."

"Oh," said his father, "off the Old Murdoch Road. I started to clear back in there last year. Got sidetracked. Haven't been back in there since."

"Well, it was a big bone," persisted Jonas. "I think probably maybe part of a Indian. You might want to go check it out."

"Unh-hunh," said his father absently. "Got too wet to get any equipment back in there and I decided to clear the north pasture woods instead."

Back home, Bryce Torbett took a box that had held two dozen cans of motor oil and cut out one side of it with his pocketknife. Jonas's neck prickled as the blade squeaked through the thick cardboard. "Go get me some newspapers," said Bryce, and when Jonas returned they made a thick layer in the box. "Now," said Bryce, pleased with himself. "We oughta put some rags or something in there. You want a old shirt of mine?" Jonas hesitated for a minute, as the image of his father's closet passed swiftly through his mind. "No sir," he said. "I have a old shirt of my own."

Bryce shrugged. "Suit yourself." They put the box in Jonas's room and sat the puppy in it. Jonas took the shirt he had in mind out of his drawer. It was his Little League jersey from last year, which was too small for him now. He hadn't worn it since the day he broke his arm when the catcher for Greer Chicken ran into him near the foul line, where Jonas was looking for four-leaf clovers in anticipation of going to bat. For several months after he got the cast off it would have still fit him, but he had quit Little League after that. When his father prodded him about it he just stubbornly shook his head. And he hadn't wanted to wear the shirt, the orange-and-blue shirt that was so tough it had once awed him. Now he settled it in the cardboard box, arranging it so that the soft part was on top rather than the stiff vinyl letters or numbers. The puppy padded clumsily on top of it, nestled around for a minute, and then plopped down and put his head on his paws, looking up at Jonas with a tiny ring of white showing around his eyes—as if to say, "Well? What next?" And starting in Jonas's stomach, ending somewhere behind his cheeks, the thrill flowered again.

"Well," said his father, "I expect he'll cry. They usually do. When he does you should take him outside, give him a chance to do his business out there. Don't let him even get started thinking he can do it in here."

Clint went to bed early that night. He was valiantly faking a lack of interest in Jonas's find. After the house quieted down,

Jonas took the puppy in bed with him. For a minute the puppy thought this was a game. He bit the corner of the sheet and tugged on it, shaking his head. But he tired out fast, and soon settled down near Jonas's chest. Jonas lay curled around the animal, smelling its coat and its sweet gravyish breath, and felt that something magic was his. He should have been tired too. He had felt heavy-footed coming home; the walk from his find-ing-place had been so long. Still he wasn't sleepy, but he didn't want to disturb this perfect thing by moving. While the puppy slept he tried to think of a name for it. His dog would have a *tough* name—the cool name Jonas didn't have.

It was Mother who had picked out his name. She had gotten it from a book she bought at the grocery, not in Groverton but in Texarkana, when she was pregnant with him. "It's a good name, it means 'dove,' " she used to say. This was one of the things Jonas remembered most clearly about her, which was sad, because for him it was always an unhappy conversation. "I know, you tole me before," he used to answer her miserably. Other boys liked their names, which never meant "dove." Once in second grade Jonas had realized that if you just moved around the letters in his name it would be Jason. Jason was an infinitely preferable name to his own. He wrote Jason inside all his spiral notebooks and on the outside of the big blue cloth-bound ring binder he had inherited from Clint. His mother saw it and got furious at him and threw the ring binder away, even though she was all weak from the chemotherapy then. That was not long before she died.

Flint, he thought. No. Too close to Clint. Yet he knew it needed to be short and punchy. The good names were like Kurt or Blake or Jed. Gary. Larry. Mike. But he knew real boys with those names, and besides, they didn't sound like this puppy.

His mind wandered back over the day. The moments of shame and disappointment after his mistake about the other side of the drainage canal seemed to have happened a long time ago—at least last week. And then seeing the puppy. He pictured it again. And leaning over to pick him up—a shiver of excite-ment—then he recalled the puppy's grunt as it nestled in his arms, and again he felt that rush, and patted the creature that lay—so trusting, with its nose on its paws—in his arms—as if the puppy had known all along that Jonas would come along and find him. And all at once he had it. *Ace.* Find of the century.

But there was something else to think about: the bone! Who knew what kind of a bone it was? Maybe he could keep it in his room even if it wasn't a skull. Maybe it was even a human bone. Some Indian, and Daddy could dredge it out. But Jonas would have no nightmares tonight. He felt it—in his bones. One of these days he would go back to check it out. As soon as Ace was big enough to run alongside his bike. For the only places worth going to anymore, suddenly, were places where Ace could go too.

5

TRACI MORGAN LEANED FORWARD in her lifeguard's chair and stretched as hard as she could. The shift in her movement stirred the little warm pool of sweat under her bottom. She winced a little, lifting her thighs one by one from the sticky chair, then settled back and sighed.

But the sigh sounded more sleepy and content than exasperated. For anybody else—or maybe, at another time in her own life—this could have been a moment of supreme irritation, when heat and tedium and a lackluster job combined in the low ebb of an afternoon. But for Traci, this summer, lassitude was a blessing. The past school year, her junior year in college, had stretched her to a breaking point she didn't know she had. She had tired of stimulation and tired of enervating cold and the pressure of classes and the press of faces—sharp, ambitious faces electric with ego—and she had dragged herself home to Groverton in exhaustion to heal, to be. Here time slowed down to a crawl, time was the crawl of sweat down your body, and she liked it that way. The less that happened to her this summer, the better.

She settled back in her chair and unbuttoned the old shirt of her father's she was wearing for a cover-up. The faintest breeze, noticeable only to someone encased in sweat as she was, lingered across her belly and chest, where a film of perspiration glittered like dew at sunrise. But she buttoned the shirt again; she had already gotten all the sun she needed. Her legs, for instance, down to her toes, were a nearly solid sheet of freckles. Though she tried to keep them under a towel, the sun managed

43

to sneak in anyway.

The Torbett boy, the only child in the pool at the moment, rose out of the shallow end to readjust the diving mask of his brother's that kept slipping off his face. He gulped and went under again. In a minute his hand came up, a tightly closed fist, searching for the side of the pool. He clapped down the pennies he'd successfully picked off the bottom and ducked under again.

She'd had this job only three weeks now, since June 1, but it seemed like three months. In those weeks she must have watched Jonas Torbett retrieve his pennies a hundred thousand times from the bottom of the Country Club pool. By now she saw him do it as if in a recurring dream: an azure, slow-motion dream that stretched the hours out like spreading skies. Lifeguarding was a wonderful way to make the time pass slowly.

For instance, here came the Dugginses—probably the worst children in Groverton. Even they had an delicious monotony. There was the screech of the metal gate, with its horseshoe-shaped latch that didn't fit over the gatepost quite right. There was Ashlee, with her Goldilocks hair, her tight little behind wagging the yellow frill that suggested a skirt on her pink bathing suit. And there was Trevor, already letting out a yell and running toward the deep end to jump in, and Blake ambling behind, dragging a stick along the fence to set up a metallic humming. Poor Jonas Torbett had surfaced and frozen quite still, like a squirrel who hears a dog approaching.

"Hi, Miss Traci," drawled Ashlee, grinning up at her. Behind the words was a singsong insolence. If Traci had spoken like that as a child her mother would have narrowed her eyes warningly. "What?" Traci, or any child, would have said. "All I *said* was 'hi.' "

And then she would have gotten, "Young lady—watch your tone of voice." No one had ever told Ashlee Duggins to watch her tone of voice, Traci would bet.

How would she explain the pleasure she took from these hours to her college friends? None of them could believe she'd come home for the summer in the first place—to a dinky small town in Arkansas—and when the subject came up, say at the dinner table, Traci always had the feeling they were ducking their heads in embarrassment for her. Her roommate Joan was working for her senator on the Hill in D.C.; Traci had gotten a letter from her this morning. Joan had seen Jeane Kirkpatrick and Dan Rather in the elevator the day she wrote the letter. She was researching legislation about rights of the handicapped and living in a house in Georgetown with two guys from Princeton and a woman from Vassar. Another friend, Millicent, was working as an *au pair* on the French Riviera. "If you're going to be dealing with obnoxious children," she had written Traci when Traci tried to describe the lifeguarding to her, "you should at least be doing it somewhere stimulating and beautiful." Next month Millicent was going to meet up in Paris with a third friend, Claire, who was backpacking through Europe. Already an array of postcards from Luxembourg and the Netherlands leaned against Traci's dresser mirror in her bedroom at her parents' home.

"Quit it!" she heard from below. That throaty, slow voice— Jonas's. "Hey! Quit it!"

Blake Duggins had converted his fence-banging stick into an imaginary golf club and was busy putting Jonas's pennies into the pool. He was a chunky, pug-nosed child who seemed oblivious to anything adults told him, or at least anything not directly pertaining to direct flattery or bribery of Blake.

"Don't do 'em in the deep end!" Jonas went on. "Hey. I can't go get 'em way down yonder."

But Blake continued, his wide face blissful and unheeding. The last of the pennies spurted over the side, skittering into the greater-than-four-foot depths where Jonas would not venture.

"Blake, that was mean," said Traci. "How would you like it if someone did that to your toys?"

"Now I can't get 'em," repeated Jonas, desperately.

"I think you can, Jonas. You swim in the deep end, don't you?"

"Yeah, but I can't go all the way to the bottom down there."

"Give it a try. Try it three times and if you can't get them, I'll come do it for you."

She occasionally caught herself staring at the flashy postcards, pondering them. What was it Claire and Millicent and

Joan were out to do? What did it say about her, Traci, that she had crept back to Groverton instead of doing something similar? What would they learn about the Senate and the Senators or France and the French? Traci didn't even understand Groverton and Grovertonians.

"Traci! Hey, Traci!" That would be Trevor. No "Miss Traci" for him. Maybe that was something that only simpering Ashlee had picked up. "Watch'is! Wanta see me do a cannonball? Watch'is!"

She watched the boy idly, wondered how her attention could mean more to him than a pair of dark glasses, with the impassivity they lent her face, swiveling his way.

She would have to write Joan and tell her what she was reading. "Dear Joan, I know you'll be thrilled" (that was how they talked, always dimly sarcastic) "to learn I'm reading *Catch-22*. I've decided my existence here is sort of like that of Dunbar, who loved to play pool because he hated to play pool and it made the time pass slowly."

The *boing* of the diving-board and its recovering shudder; splash. "I got you wet, didn't I? Watch'is! This-here's a can-opener!"

Back in March when Traci was studying for biochem midterms, Joan had been stretched on her bed, reading *Catch-22* and howling. "Is that for a course?" Traci had demanded. Joan was an English major. "No," Joan had said with an utter lack of defensiveness. "I can't believe that," Traci had said. "I can't believe you have time to read something like that." "So what?" said Joan, starting to rile a little slowly. "Who's stopping you from majoring in English? Then you'd have time to read for fun. Anyway, maybe you ought to blow off biochem and read something like this. You're going to end up like those people Walker Percy talks about who make straight A's and flunk life."

Boing-splash.

"D'I get you wet that time? Traci!"

"Um," said the lifeguard, starting to the present, "almost."

"Miss Tra-aci-i—will you unlock the closet so I can get an inner tube?"

"Yeah, sure," she said. "I'm coming." She stood, ungluing

herself from the chair, shaking off the towel damp with sweat and melted suntan lotion. In the heat she felt dizzy for a second. With her keys she descended the ladder; she opened the closet that smelled of creosote, concentrated chlorine, and bug spray; she reached over a coiled garden hose that was stuck to the concrete floor with some dried-out brown substance, and pulled out a couple of inner tubes and a Styrofoam board that was crumbling at the edges. "Here you go," she said, and locked the closet back.

"Thank you," said Ashlee.

"You're welcome."

"Watch'is!" cried Trevor—"this here's a atom bomb!"

It was amazing how often children could repeat themselves. Jonas went back to his penny-fetching. Trevor continued to jump off the board, swim to the ladder in the same earnest, unbreathing, water-clapping crawl, and heave himself out for the run to the diving board again. Ashlee and Blake were playing some mysterious giggling game at the steps, getting in and out of the pool, exchanging inner tubes. *Boing-shudder-splash.*

A gangly young dog, hideously spotted, showed up at the gate. It cried faintly in the back of its throat and cocked its head this way and that toward the children. When Jonas resurfaced, he pulled the mask off and said, "Ace!" He padded to the gate and reached his fingers through the hurricane fencing, and the pup licked them industriously. Jonas sneaked a look over his shoulder toward Traci, and started to lift the latch on the gate. "Jonas!" she called. "You leave that gate closed. No dogs around the pool." He smiled guiltily at her and said, "Okay, okay." When he was back in the water she said, to be nicer, "Does it know how to swim?" "Oh, yes, *ma'am,*" he said. After a few more minutes of whimpering in the direction of its master, the dog wandered off, nosing for scraps in the weeds under the club-house kitchen window.

In a little while Sissy and D.L. Phelps came, and Jonas's brother Clint, who was getting old enough to prefer tanning and reading comic books to swimming. Mrs. Brandon came at five-twenty to give Traci her check. "Thanks," said Traci, from the top of the ladder. "You could just put it in my bag over there, that striped bag on the chair."

"Oh ..." said Mrs. Brandon, continuing to hold the check up supplicatingly in the air. "I wouldn't want onea those coloreds who works around here to get it ... Shouldn't tempt anybody, the Lord says."

"Well, nobody but me could *cash* it," Traci said mildly, as she climbed down the ladder to take her check. She dropped it in her bag anyway, with its corner sticking out, wishing a white person would steal it; and half an hour later, when she glanced down and saw the Torbett mongrel dribbling the tattered, soggy remains of the paycheck around the pool deck, with his front end splayed down on the ground, his rear end and tail wagging, she couldn't suppress a snort of laughter.

Jonas was in a panic. "Hold still, Ace!" he cried, as he and Traci together fished the last bits of paper out of his mouth. The dog bared his mottled gums and pawed at their forearms with his enormous paws. "He didn't mean nothing by it."

"Oh, it's okay," said Traci. "Louneale'll write me another one. N.B.D."

"N.B.D.?" said Jonas.

"No Big Deal."

The kid's eyes widened and he seemed to chew the phrase over like a Tootsie Roll, as if no one had ever told him *anything* was N.B.D. Sure wasn't to Traci. Nothing was going to get under her skin. It was that sort of summer.

That night Traci met Deborah Armstrong at the Pizza Hut. Sitting over large Tabs with crushed ice, playing with their damp straw paper, they talked town gossip, as usual, and men, or the lack thereof, as usual, though—as Deborah commented—with more humor on Traci's part than the old rancor that used to be present.

"It's hard to explain," said Traci. "Nothing's getting on my nerves this summer. So far."

"Not even your parents," said Deborah.

"Nope," said Traci. "They're fine. They're so happy with each other, and their houseboat. It's like they're on a second honeymoon. They're always at the lake."

A little over a year before, a couple of unexpected financial windfalls had raised Traci's father, owner of a real estate agency, from struggling to quite comfortable status. Traci had been able to cut ties with the financial aid office; her mother had quit the bookkeeping job at the chicken plant she'd always hated; and her parents had moved to a roomy new ranch-style house on the edge of town, innocently giddy in their new prosperity.

"Gee," said Deborah gloomily, "this is bad, when people I used to babysit now have their lives more together than I do."

Traci laughed. Deborah's old-and-despondent state was a constant theme—because she was thirty-two and Traci twenty-one, and she was back in Groverton, struggling, while Traci (as Deborah exaggerated it) had the wide world at her beck and call. Their pizza descended from on high, and after the waitress had gone Traci said, "It's not that I have my life together, not at all. It's just a sensation there's gauze between me and the world right now or something. I don't *want* to be bothered by anything."

"Maybe all that sun has addled your brain," said Deborah, getting up to take some crushed red peppers from another table.

Traci bit into her slice, chewed a minute, and nodded. "Could be. In fact, I should probably worry. Anyone who's too well-adjusted to Groverton life should be alarmed."

Just then a stout woman who had come in a few minutes earlier walked by their booth. Dressed in a mint-green sweatsuit, with lots of gold necklaces and frosted hair, she looked like a large flocked Christmas tree—incongruous on this June night. A toddler with very red cheeks was asleep on her shoulder, and an insistent boy who looked to be about four was tugging her toward the video game terminals near the door of the restaurant.

"How do, ladies!" she said as she passed Traci and Deborah.

"Well, hey, Butter!"

"How you doing?" Deborah said. "Keeping the grandkids, hunh?"

"Yes, Lord," said Butter. "Lemme tell you. Ma-maw's learning all about video games."

"Don't tell me these are Mike's kids," said Traci.

"Oh, no. Mike just has the one, Shawna, who's three. I don't get to see her much; they live in Crowdersville." Butter Mc-Collum hoisted the younger child higher on her hip. "Traci! I meant to tell you! That was just the nicest write-up you did about Bryce and his hobby. I know he appreciated that."

"Oh, well, thanks."

"So you're working at the paper this summer?"

"Ma-maw ..." said the boy, glowering.

"As much as Mr. Walters'll let me. It's just part-time, though. They needed some extra help since Ricky is out with his mono right now."

"Well, good! We'll look forward to that. I sorta thought you'd be working up at the hospital if you came home this summer."

"No, not this summer. I'm over at the *Weekly,* and I'm doing a little lifeguarding—that's all."

"Well, your pizza's getting cold." Also, Butter's free arm was being tugged like a cable by her grandson, who had braced his sneakered heels into the floor. "Good to see you girls."

"You too."

Behind them they heard a video game erupting in bleeps and whining noises. "She's right, the pizza is cold," said Deborah. They ate for a minute and Deborah added, "Sounds like my truck."

"What?"

"That game. All those little popping explosions. I'm constant-ly hearing them under the hood. I don't know how much longer I can drive that thing."

"Can't afford a new one?"

Deborah shook her head. "I can barely afford my rent right now. I don't know why things are so slow. I guess you heard about the layoffs?—"

But Lorene Strait had just come in and spotted them.

Smoothed into white shorts that set off her tan, her bosom nearly swelling out of a jungle-print shirt, she was waggling red-painted nails in a wave that Traci was compelled to return. "Real nice write-up you did on Bryce's relics!" Lorene called.

Traci nodded, smiling. Then she noticed Deborah twisting around to see who it was and grunting her opinion as she faced Traci again. "Poor Lorene," she said.

"She doesn't think she's 'poor Lorene,' " said Traci.

"No, that's part of it. Have you seen the bumper sticker on her car?"

"No."

"I meant to write you about it while you were at school. It says, 'God said it, I believe it, that settles it.' " Traci snorted. "Anyway, as I was saying, Grinson's laid off about—*Now* who are you looking at?"

"I'm sorry," said Traci. "I really am. But there's Stuart Bledsoe."

"Man, I didn't know this would be so distracting for you. How do you make it in the East, where there are *lots* of people to know?"

"I haven't seen him yet this summer."

"Oh, Stuart's always hanging around," said Deborah. "Always planning to do something different, which he never does. Sort of like the rest of us, I guess. Do you want this last piece?"

"No thanks. Why don't y'all see each other?"

"Me and Stuart?" Deborah wrinkled up her nose. "He's not my type. He's a hothead. I want somebody I can—oh—sit with in the shallows at Lake Cooley and listen to Crystal Gayle and not have to talk. Then go home and pick cucumbers."

"That sounds very Freudian," Traci observed.

"You are just back from college, aren't you. Well, you're probably right."

"But that doesn't sound very picky. It seems like there'd be a lot of people in Groverton you could do those things with."

"No, the problem is—" but then Deborah broke off, for Stuart was approaching their table, holding his take-out order. He had intent, deep-set brown eyes and a stolid face that Traci had always thought looked older and more serious than his lean, ropy, track-runner's body—now clad in neat faded jeans and a black cotton shirt. He was like one of those cutout plywood figures whose dashing outline suggests shallow fun and games, only to be contradicted by the real, three-dimensional, human face of the anxious tourist peering through the circle left in the head. His smile came quickly and disappeared at once.

"Hey, Traci—welcome home. Hi, Deborah."

"Hey, Stuart. Sit down." Traci scooted over obligingly, and Stuart set the pizza box on the table as he slid in beside her.

"How long have you been home?" he said, resting his forearms on the table and starting to play with the straw papers she and Deborah had not yet decimated.

"Oh, two or three weeks. What are you doing?"

"Odds and ends. Trying to save money to go to law school in the fall."

Glancing sideways Traci saw Deborah half-roll her eyes. "Look," Stuart continued, "I wanted to talk to you about that article you did in the *Weekly.*"

" 'The real nice write-up'!" Deborah mocked, but either Stuart didn't hear or he missed her satirical tone.

"Yeah?" said Traci, weakly, trying not to laugh.

"You gotta think through stuff like that before you write it. I can't believe you gave a forum like that to—excuse me, but—to an asshole like Bryce Torbett. What are you gonna do next, go over to Crowdersville and start giving accolades to Vaughan Sandifer as a follow-up?"

Traci's smile faded. A few seconds passed as she stared at him. Then, "Stuart," she said slowly and distinctly, "what are you talking about?"

"You are really endorsing activities like Bryce's when you report them so uncritically. What does this guy do? Basically, he robs and plunders several thousand years of native American culture, out of greed, and for these acts of—of *desecration,* he gets written up in the local paper."

"Oh!" said Traci, her mouth twisting in disbelief, offense, and at the same time self-reproach. She had just realized what he was getting at. "But Stuart—"

"I'm sorry. I was meaning to call you and talk to you about it, but I'm just as glad I saw you in person. People here need to know that pothunting is not okay. It's really been bothering me."

"Obviously." Traci spoke coldly. "But aren't you making too big of a deal out of it? This was just a dinky human-interest story about some—some *farmer's hobby,* for Christ's sake, in the dinky little *Groverton Weekly*—this is just a dinky little part-time job of mine—"

"*Everything* in the *Weekly* is uncritical," said Deborah, who had swung her legs up on her bench and settled back in the corner of the booth in an attitude of relishing a spectacle.

"Well." Stuart shrugged. "Maybe it could be a little less so. When I saw your byline—I was surprised."

"Okay!" said Traci. "I'm *sorry. Okay.*"

Stuart slid out of the booth and picked up his box. "Don't take it too hard," he said. "See you around."

"Jesus," Traci said when he had left. She felt her face burning, and shook her head slowly. "So much for my carefree summer jobs."

"I told you he was a hothead." Deborah was sitting straight up again, her feet on the floor, hunched forward over the table. "Are you all right?"

"Sure. I had forgotten he was so big on Indian issues. Now I remember it from high school, though."

"How could you forget all that flap about the mascot?"

"I was still in junior high when that was going on."

Deborah laughed. "He has got a certain style. I remember he appeared before the school board and said, 'What other ethnic group would stand for this? Can you imagine hearing that "the Little Rock Jews take on the Jonesboro Blacks in football tonight"?' "

"And we're still the Groverton Indians," said Traci. "Jesus, he's intense, though. I don't know anybody at *college* who's that militant."

"You know his grandfather always claimed to be a full-blood Caddo. He was the only stable person in his family, really.

Everybody else who had a hand in raising Stuart was half-drunk all the time or scattered out or something. His mother's at the state hospital now. So to him the Caddo bit in his grandfather was the one saving thing in his life."

"Yeah, but *Jesus,*" said Traci. "A lot of people around here think they're one-somethingth Indian. 'My grandmother was a Cherokee princess,' or whatever. You hear it all the time, but they don't act like that about it."

"He got one thing right," said Deborah. "Bryce is an asshole. Though not for the reasons he thinks."

Traci looked up and saw the old bitterness flit through Deborah's sea-blue eyes. It always seemed to manifest itself in a momentary golden color, streaking through. She wanted to say something sympathetic, but Deborah precluded her by standing up briskly. "Come on, let's get out of here. I don't know about you, but any more social encounters are gonna do me in."

After Ron Smitty at the cash register solemnly returned their change, he smiled at Traci and said, "By the way, I saw that write-up you did on Bryce Torbett and those pots last week. That was real nice."

6

MEANWHILE, AT THE TORBETTS' supper table, Jonas was talking to Clint. His face was flushed and sweaty and his voice had risen to the pitch of a desperate whine. His food sat before him untouched, though Clint was eating heartily and did not look up from his own plate. "No, I mean it, Clint, *guess* what me and Ace *found.*"

Only the two of them were at the table, because their father was going out on a date. A year and a half ago he had come to the door of the playroom where they were playing Twister and said, "Boys, I have something to ask you. Do you mind if your father starts to go out with women? Ladies?" They had looked up at him from their twisted, impossible positions like two pretzels linked at the time they were made: Jonas trying to keep one foot on green in one corner and one hand on yellow clear on the opposite side of the mat, and Clint underneath him. Jonas thought, why did he say "your father" instead of "I"? They were breathing hard. Bryce didn't even notice. "No," they said. "Um—" he said, "thank you." And they had heard him going back up the half-flight of stairs toward his bedroom. And now he was leaving in ten minutes to pick up Miss Crumfield, and Celie, having served up the boys' plates, was in the TV room talking to her daughter on the phone.

"Well, what, then," said Clint. "Can I have your chicken pot pie?"

"Sure," said Jonas. "You're not gonna believe this."

Clint let out a belch. Because his own news was going to trump all competition, Jonas didn't mind showing his admiration:

"Wow!" he said. "Celie pro'ly heard that one. So Clint, guess what."

"What!" cried Clint. "I said what. Why don't you just *tell* me? You're so immature sometimes."

"Clint, *this morning we found a human skeleton.* Part of one."

"Sure," said Clint. "And it shook hands and offered you a cigar, too, right?"

"I'm not kidding this time, Clint. I been wrong before but not this time. I been reading about bones in that *Know Your Body* book Grandmother gave me."

"Oh, little brother, little brother," said Clint. "I been on too many wild goose chases with you." He pushed his chair back and went to the fridge. "Want some Coke?"

"You already had your Coke for today, Clint. I did too."

"Well, I'm having another."

"Daddy'll count."

"He'll think Celie drunk it."

The Coke fizzed as Clint sat down at the table again. "Anyway," said Jonas, raising his eyes from the can to his brother's face, "this is really it. I don't have to have you look at it. I'll take somebody else to look at it. Like Daddy. He'll call Mr. Sandifer."

But Clint was not impressed. "So I guess you'll have nightmares," was all he said. "Happens every time you see a skeleton." He sighed melodramatically, as if seeing a skeleton was about as commonplace as going downtown. *"I* won't get a full night's sleep tonight. You'll be screamin'—"

Jonas dropped his head. "I might," he said. "I expect so." His humility on that point may have been what finally piqued Clint's interest. In a low voice Jonas said, "But it was just the leg bone, so maybe not."

"No skull, hunh?"

"No, no skull. Just the leg bone, like right here"—he tipped his chair back (a forbidden act) and pointed at the top of his thigh—"just like in that bone book I got."

They smelled Daddy's aftershave, and then he came into the kitchen. Jonas rapidly eased his chair down flat. Bryce wasn't alert to possible transgressions, though; he was sticking his chin out and wiggling his jaw in an effort to free up more room around his collar. "Ties," he said. "Choking me."

"You look sharp, Daddy," said Clint. "Hey, Daddy"—with a patronizing jerk of his head toward his brother—"Jonas here says he found a skeleton today."

"It wasn't me that really found it, it was Ace," said Jonas.

"Really?" said Bryce, fiddling with his keys. "What kind?"

"Human," said Jonas, with manful casualness. "Mainly the leg bone."

"You'll have to tell me about it," said Bryce. "Clint—"

"I did," said Jonas. "Remember, when I found Ace? I told you about it then. But I didn't go back and look at it till today."

"Well, that's fine, son," said Bryce. "Clint, I want you boys in bed by nine-thirty." Then he was out the door.

"He don't believe you either," said Clint.

"But it is!" said Jonas. "Come with me tomorrow and I'll show you."

"You ever heard of the boy who cried 'Wolf'?" said Clint. "Well, you've cried it too often. You're always wanting to show me this and that and it turns out to be—nothin'. Nothin', nothin', nothin'. Why does Celie buy the kind of these that have pimientos in them? She knows I hate pimientos. You can get the Mrs. Swanson's without pimientos." His pimientos, gluey with whatever held the chicken pot pie together, were pushed together in a little pyramid on his plate. With one tine of his fork he started to pull them into patterns.

"But even those have mushrooms," said Jonas. The pimiento heap on his plate was flanked by one of mushroom pieces. "Clint, I'm telling you, it is a person's leg bone, sticking out of this rock."

"Daddy's right. You've seen those skeletons at Mi-Ka-Do too many times. Now you're hallucinating about them."

"But those aren't sticking out of a rock. Those are in clay or mud or something. I *tole* you, Clint, you're not *listening* to me, this is *different,* this doesn't have skulls or nothing. This is in a *rock,* back in a sort of ditch, over there on the other side of the drainage canal."

"Liar, liar, pants on fire," said Clint. "You can't be satisfied with finding a dog back there. Now you got to make up a skeleton too." But he didn't even seem interested enough for his heart to be in the taunt. He went to the cookie jar and brought it back to the table.

Jonas tried another tack. "Please come see it with me. Please. If it's a waste of your time, I'll mow the yard for you next week when it's your time."

"Mow *and* rake up the clippings?" said Clint.

"Yep."

"And you'll let me pick both TV shows tonight?"

"Yep."

"Okay." Clint let out another, magnificent burp.

"Wow," said Jonas. "Now I *know* Celie heard *that* one."

Two

The hand of the LORD was upon me, and he brought me out by the Spirit of the LORD, and set me down in the midst of the valley; it was full of bones. And he led me round among them; and behold, there were very many upon the valley; and lo, they were very dry. And he said to me, "Son of man, can these bones live?" And I answered, "O Lord God, thou knowest."

Ezekiel 37:1–3

7

As he drove west toward Texarkana, James Donovan yawned, holding on to the steering wheel with only one hand so he could stretch tight everywhere else. He hated interstates. If he had been on a personal trip, he would have used side roads even if they did take longer. But for work that would look as if he were trying to inflate his mileage. He relaxed again at the wheel, groaned, and lapsed into tedious daydreams. He was a medium-tall man of thirty-five, with reddish-brown hair and a short, even beard that was darker and less red than his hair. His eyes were brown and his lashes straight and thick, and his lids at the corners relaxed into a ripple of small, clear lines from the sun and smiling. He was wearing khaki field pants and a khaki shirt and hiking boots.

Suddenly he pulled his notebook off the dusty dashboard and put it on his lap. It fell open to the day's entry and with his right hand James started flipping back, glancing up at I-30 every once in a while to make sure he was still in one lane or the other. The entry he was looking for was a short one between two long ones, he remembered—made a few weeks ago, in mid-June or so—aha, there it was, 6/24. Now to decipher his handwriting. "Bruce (Bryce?) Torbett—NW G'ton—out 23 7 mi. quarry too far—bone stking out of dirt—shale.—" and a phone number. Looking at his scribbled notes made him remember more clearly the voice, young, lazy-sounding, country, laconic but a little self-conscious at the same time, coming over static the way voices from rural areas do, conjuring up images in the hearer's mind of heavy old black rotary-dial phones.

Well, maybe it was worth a stop. He sure wouldn't make a trip down here just for that. But he was on his way to Texarkana anyway, to fool around some more with the mastodon that didn't really interest him. They really needed to get that fellow packed away—he'd have said in a closet somewhere, but there'd be pressure to display it, he knew—but James had not given it high priority. Once enough of the specimen had been recovered to ensure that it was in fact a mastodon, he had put it on the back burner. A big, showy fossil—something to get the state newspapers excited—but so what? What was there new to learn about the mastodons? The university had dozens of them. Transporting and assembling it would be a hassle. It would be like moving a big dull jigsaw puzzle.

And he liked to follow up on these calls from out of the blue; that was one of the purposes of his job, of a state Geological Commission. James knew that it was highly unlikely this would turn out to be anything special—most likely an old cow or mule bone, the way these things went, and loose from the rock rather than sticking out of it as the man claimed.

Still, following through on reports like this one was good for public relations. James urged his younger assistants to do it. It took little enough time and effort. He believed that small visits, small contacts, courteous response, helped the image of scientists in the state, and helped in some small way to educate the public, to keep your average taxpayer from thinking of scientists as "them," big-shot godless experts from Little Rock. Then when you needed public support, when you were in some position of pleading for a rational hearing, you'd be more likely to get it. People remembered that you'd stood in their kitchen and had a glass of tea, that you'd ridden in their pickup truck.

And Lord knew they would need support this winter. As soon as he'd heard that the Creation Science Act had passed—that the idiot governor had approved it—he knew there'd be a trial. Sure enough, this morning before he left the office he had gotten a call from Andy Ropp over at the ACLU. When he'd picked up his desk phone Andy's voice came drawling: "Ready to testify?" Andy started every phone call that way, *in medias res,* making a point of not identifying himself. He liked to see how quickly you could gather your wits and respond. But then he and Andy had known each other for years. They had met in college at Fayetteville, their first week there.

So James had said, instantly, "Of course. Glad you're finally doing something socially useful, Ropp."

"Yep," said Andy. "Got a little lawsuit here. Little school-children-versus-the-state action."

"Scopes Trial revisited, hunh?"

"I hope to do better than Clarence Darrow."

"Do you seriously want me to testify?"

"Well, I'm sure we'll get a lot of out-of-state people here for it. But I'm hoping we'll be able to work you in. Between the preachers."

"Do that," said James. "I'll bring a bag of tricks. Show and tell. Walk 'em through a little potassium-argon dating. Bring 'em some million-year-old sharks' teeth and let 'em pass 'em around. Who's the judge?"

"Bill Overton."

"Is that good? How do your prospects look?"

"Oh, Overton's great. Smart. Serious. Yeah, our prospects'd look great if I believed that sheer stupidity never prevails in a courtroom."

"That's cheery."

"Let's have lunch this week and I'll tell you about it."

"Fine," said James. "When?"

"Ahh—hmm. I'm looking at my calendar. Maybe Thursday. I'll have to check with my secretary."

"I'll be around," said James. "Just let me know. I *don't* have to check with my secretary."

Andy burst into his wild laugh. "You're determined to give me shit, aren't you, Donovan?"

"Ah, you need it," said James.

"I haven't checked on you in a while anyway. Been meaning to, though. You holding up all right?"

He meant with the divorce, now six months old. The last time they had talked to each other was the day it went through.

"Yeah, I'm okay," James had told Andy Ropp.

He was okay. He felt better lately than he had in a while. He no longer turned his truck automatically every afternoon toward the house he no longer lived in. That had to be considered a triumph. He was in something of a routine. He was taking care of himself, grocery-shopping at Skaggs in the middle of the night, cooking Frozen-Pizza-for-One and vegetables bought at the Farmers' Market, running at hours that suited him.

He exited at Hope and went to the men's room at the McDonald's. He considered a snack, but the sight of overweight people chewing without expression as he stood by the napkin dispensers reading the menu turned him off the idea. Junk food, really, and he had gotten so that even when he gave himself permission to indulge, none of it was titillating anymore. And black coffee at these places bore no resemblance to the real stuff. Instead he stepped outside to use the pay phone.

The voice of a black woman, doubtless a maid, answered and gave him directions to the house, saying that "Mr. Bryce" would be back by the time he got there and would show him anything he wanted to see on the place. She sounded doubtful, as if she didn't understand what might be on that place that anyone could possibly want to see.

James headed down the interstate toward the exit that would take him to the winding road to Groverton. The directions were good, and he found the Torbetts' home without trouble. A stocky, square-jawed man, probably in his mid-thirties, greeted him on the porch and asked if he wanted anything before they headed out to see the bone.

"No, thanks," said James. "I stopped for a break at Hope."

A small boy with a dog on his heels came around the house, and his eyes lit up when he saw James. "Can I go too, Daddy?"

"Hop in," said the father. "In the back if you're bringing the dog."

They got into Torbett's truck, a deluxe-model Ford with a bumper sticker on the back that said DON'T CRITICIZE FARMERS WITH YOUR MOUTH FULL. James asked the man questions as they drove down the highway and turned onto an asphalt road between fenced pastures. The man answered monosyllabically, and James eventually quit trying to converse. Once Torbett pulled a pack of Marlboros out of his shirt pocket, shook one out, and fumbled for a book of matches on the dashboard that turned out to be empty. James pulled a lighter out of his own pocket and handed it over. At that point the man said, "Oh. Thanks." He offered James a Marlboro, but James shook his head: "I don't smoke." Torbett gave him a strange look and lapsed into silence again. James considered getting into the bed of the pickup and seeing whether he'd have any better luck visiting with the boy. Or the dog. The boy rapped on the back windshield once, urgently, when they had come to a rolling stop to make a turn. The father let his window down and stuck his head out. "What?"

"This ain't the way, Daddy."

"It just so happens, son, that there's a different way besides your way." Torbett rolled his window back up. "Kids," he said to James. "Only ten and he thinks he knows everything. Thinks nobody was around here all those years before he got here."

"What's his name?"

"Jonas. That's my youngest. I have a thirteen-year-old, Clint. You got any?"

"No," said James. Was this man also divorced, or was he just the kind of chauvinist who said "I" when he meant "my wife and I"?

Torbett didn't reply. They tore on over mud-and-gravel roads in silence.

From where they parked they had a rough hike through an area of gently rolling, partly cleared woodlands, where piles of dead trees and thickets lay like fortifications in some guerilla war, under tangles of second-growth brush already reasserting itself. "Believe it or not there did used to be a road here," said Torbett, "where my bulldozers got through. It'd be worse if there hadn't." James's shirt and pants were soon soaked through with sweat. The few minutes after his heart rate rose and he started to sweat, but before his clothes were drenched enough to attract the slightest current of 98-degree air, were always the worst.

"I wore my high-tops," piped the boy behind them. "Good thing I have them on, because of snakes."

"Doesn't seem to bother your dog, though, does it?" James asked him. The pup kept dashing off into the undergrowth, after rabbits, probably, with his tail curved over his back. Then he would lope back to the humans to check on their progress.

"Ace? Naw. He can go anywhere. He saw a snake once but I called him off it. I think it was a copperhead."

Then they began to descend into a gully that widened and deepened where the earth was cut by rapid washoff. At the bottom was white sandy soil overrun with tough shrubbery and opportunistic trees and vines, poison ivy and trumpet-vine and honeysuckle. Its sides were banked with vines too, seeking out a hold in the gray crumbling marl that had eroded too fast to support much plant life. There were outcroppings of dark shale, still unbleached by the sun—bed upon bed of it, and stretches of gravel—yellow, cream, clay-colored, and purple—that made the hikers' footing a little treacherous.

The boy spoke again. His voice was full of suspicion. "Are we coming from the opposite direction, Daddy?"

"Yep."

"Well, I *wondered.*" He chattered on: "I hope you're not allergic to poison ivy, mister."

"Oh, I am," said James. "I get it every spring and get over it and then I'm immune till the next spring."

"I don't get it," the boy went on. "My mom she used to get it but me and my brother and my dad we don't. Which is fortunate."

"That's fortunate, all right."

Suddenly the older Torbett stood still and removed his cap and scratched his head. His crop of brown hair, damp with sweat, had a dent in it where the band of the cap had been. The boy and James stopped too, breathing heavily. James slapped at a mosquito. Off in the underbrush they could hear the dog rustling around.

"Must be a little farther," said Torbett.

They tramped on for a minute and Jonas said, "That's it."

"No, I don't think the bank was that steep where this was." In a couple of minutes, though, the father admitted, "Huh. You must have been right." They turned around and started up the shale bank at an angle.

"See where we come up here the other day?" Jonas pointed at where some rocks had slid, where some saplings they had grabbed as handholds had been stripped of leaves.

Now the boy darted ahead, up the short slope, planting his feet sideways and starting miniature avalanches of pebbles behind him. The dog, excited by his master's burst of speed, dashed forward too and ran a couple of figure eights and a loop for good measure. But James ignored him; for the boy was saying, "Ta-daaa!"—standing beneath an overhang of limestone from which protruded what appeared to be, in fact, a horizontally imbedded bone.

The two adults joined Jonas, Bryce breathing heavily, James less so. Bryce took off his cap again and said, "Least it's in the shade today. Gotta remember to come see this thing at the right time of day, or you'd just bake."

James squatted down, ran his hand over the rock outcrop and picked up some chunks of marl to examine. Then he reared back and looked at the horizon again, gauging the slight northeastward rise of the treeline beyond the gulch. He returned his gaze to the bed of shale itself for a couple of long, silent minutes before finally moving to the bone itself. He felt it, first with the palm of his hand, then running his thumb over the end of it. He grasped where it came out of the rock and gently tried to shake it, running his thumb around its juncture with the rock.

"How come you got so many pockets?"

It was the boy's voice, startling him. "Oh," said James vaguely, "to keep all my stuff in. As a matter of fact—"

Out of one of the long pockets on his thigh he took a small chisel. He unhooked the flat-headed hammer that dangled from his belt and drew a magnifying glass out of his shirt pocket. "Oh, wow," breathed Jonas.

As James hunched over the outcrop, peering through the

glass, then chipping lightly with the chisel, the dog lunged up the bank again, nudging at Jonas's waist and wriggling between the boy and his father, panting and drooling. Bryce said, "Son, get that dog *away* from here, it's hot enough without him all over me, he like to messed up Mr. Donovan just now."

"Go on, Ace," whispered Jonas, throwing a rock way off into some scrub trees. Ace went bounding off after the noise.

James rocked back on his heels and scooted forward, and leaning forward between his bent knees looked at the bone some more. He drew out his lighter from his other shirt pocket. It made a dry, wispy sound when he flicked it on. He brought it close to the top of the bone and held it there for a moment, then switched the lighter off and brought his nose close to the place he had burned, sniffing.

"Well," Bryce finally said. "What-all can you tell?"

James wiped the sweat off his forehead with his sleeve. His beard and mustache were dark with sweat. "Well," he said, "it's *old.*"

Torbett grunted.

"It's a human bone, isn't it?" said the boy. "Don't you think it's some old Indian bone?"

James looked at him gravely. "No, I don't think that, because I believe this rock it's in is a lot older than Indian bones would be."

They tried to absorb this. In a moment Bryce said, "So what kind of a bone is it, a dinosaur?"

"I don't know," admitted James. "I need to do some reading. My initial thought is that this sort of bone is a dinosaur"—his thoughts tumbled on—"because you're right, it does look like part of an appendage; it's not a rib, not part of the skull or jaw, not a vertebra—though I'd have thought it would need to be more massive up here"—he ran his finger around the top. He became aware of his audience. "Anyway, in a large reptile this sort of bone would flare out more to support the animal's weight."

"But it could be?" said Jonas. "It could be a dinosaur bone? Really?"

"I don't know," said James again. "I need to try to get some pictures." Now he unsnapped his camera case. He took a quarter out of yet another pants pocket and let Jonas hold it near the bone while he took some pictures. "For scale," he explained.

Bryce said, "Oh, like a map scale. So the picture will show how big it is."

"Sure," said James, fiddling with his light meter. "Later on—if this seems to be something exciting, and if we went on and extracted it from this rock—later on I'd take real detailed pictures, with a ruler in them for scale. But for rough field pictures, this'll do."

After a few minutes he said, "That's it. Out of film." He put the camera up and took a small cloth sack out of his pants leg pocket, brushed away the loose, broken bits of rock from the ground surface, and chipped at the earth in several spots around the fossil, putting the samples in the sack. Then he said he was ready to go. Jonas, Ace, and Bryce led the way.

As they edged down the bank of the gully the scientist said, "Now you are the owner of this property?"

"Oh yes," said Bryce. "Have been for fifteen years. And my dad before me."

"And would you mind my coming back to take another look at this, when I get some more information?"

"Nope, I'd just be glad to be in on whatever you find out."

"And to get here—I'll have to pay more attention going back— did you cross anyone else's private property to get here?"

"Don't believe so. All public roads and my own land."

"Good. Well, sometimes people get a little touchy about that. It's always good to know. Another thing," said Donovan. "This rock is soft enough that it'd be pretty easy to collect the specimen, once I decided that was the thing to do. Would that be okay with you?"

"Collect it for me?" said Bryce.

"Well, no. I mean for the state. You'd have to donate it." Instantly he sensed he'd chosen his words wrong. This guy didn't seem like the type who believed he'd ever "have to" do anything. "Hm," said Bryce. "I have a little collection of some old things of my own. And seeing as how this is my property, I *believe* I'd want to keep it myself."

Oh brother. "To tell you the truth, then, Mr. Torbett, I don't know how much more I can do for you."

"But you said you might not collect it. Couldn't you just study it in the ground and tell me its value?"

"Eventually, if it had any value at all, I'd have to collect it. The only reason I'd wait would be to document its position in the limestone bed and to be sure I didn't damage any surrounding bones that might be farther back in that hillside. But I'd like to cooperate with you, Mr. Torbett. I have to admit I'm a little—baffled—by that specimen, and I'd like to talk to you again when I've had time to think about it."

Bryce grunted. "Well, sure. You got my number."

Then they walked in silence. James held a thorny branch so it wouldn't pop back on the boy behind him and smiled at him as Jonas quickened his step.

"Can I ask you something?" said the boy shyly.

"Sure."

"What was that lighter thing for?"

"To let my nose test out what I thought my eyes were telling me. So I could smell whether it was a recent bone or not. Have you ever smelled bone burning?"

"Yes sir," said Jonas, "when my father burns a cow that dies."

"Well, if I had smelled a smell like that when I used my lighter, I would know this bone probably wasn't a fossil. But I didn't smell anything. That's why I said I know the bone is old."

"How did it get to be sticking out of the rock like that?"

"It got washed here along with other stuff—sand, and little particles of crushed-up rocks and shells, and mud—and was buried pretty quickly. Later on the land was uplifted and parts of it were worn away by wind and water and whatnot."

"Did you say shells?"

"Yeah. Arkansas used to get covered by the ocean every now and then. The last time was over a hundred million years ago. Did you know that?"

"Naww." In a tone of wonder. Adding, "Sir."

"Sure. Sometimes I find sharks' teeth, ancient sharks' teeth, all over Arkansas, from those days when the state was underwater. There were probably sharks swimming around right where we're standing."

The boy was quiet, his face lit up. Then he looked up in a flash and said, "You mean the Flood!"

"Well—" said James, conscious of the taciturn father, two steps ahead; of this fundamentalist region; of his need to stay in the father's good graces, to get back to this bone—"a flood of some sort, you might say, sure."

They trooped on in silence for a few minutes. They were back to the half-cleared land. A woodpecker drummed rapidly and then flew its undulating flight to a dead tree farther away.

The boy broke the silence again. "You know that leg bone? That fossil? It was really Ace, my dog, who found it."

"Okay," said James Donovan. "We'll give Ace the credit if anything comes of this."

Now the boy skipped ahead of James. He was so thin that there was air between his legs and the tops of his hightops. But there was a spring in his step.

Leaving town, James was sitting at a red light when he noticed a small, dark-stained wooden building with a neat beige sign out front that said, in Western-style block letters, GROVERTON ANIMAL CLINIC. DEBORAH ARMSTRONG, D.V.M. The light changed but he sat staring out the window, until the driver behind him honked. So this is where she was! He knew it was a small town in southwest Arkansas, but he had forgotten exactly which one. Somewhere in his mind he had thought it might be Prescott. They had been chemistry lab partners for a whole year, and he had asked her out some ... But after a couple of dates she had started turning him down. On an impulse he turned into the alley partway down the block. He circled her clinic slowly—but then bounced out into the street again. He wasn't up for such an encounter. She hadn't liked him too much anyway. She might be married but using her own name. You couldn't tell. No, he wasn't up for it. But he might be back. He knew where she was now.

Michelle, his ex-wife, had complained bitterly, there toward the end, about his tendency to think that way. "You think everything will just *be* there for you when you get ready for it. Just—*moldering* somewhere, *waiting* for you, without ever changing. So that it doesn't matter whether you go look at it today or tomorrow or next year. You think I'm like that, some fossil you can always scratch around at if everything else gets really dull—Well, I may not be here for you like that mastodon at Texarkana. I *change* in the course of a year."

"I do understand change," he had said weakly. "That's all I think about."

"Change that takes place over millions of years, maybe," she shot back. "That's the quickest sort of change you think about. You specialize in catastrophes, catastrophes that take aeons to happen. Let me tell you—just let me tell you this, James—there are catastrophes happening right under your nose and you don't know them when they hit you over the head."

She had floored him when she said those things. It was frightening to marry a smart woman. English majors had to be the worst. She could go on in this vein: "I am not a population of *mollusks,*" was another thing she had spat out during that last sad decline before they separated, "I am a *woman.*"

He thought she was probably right. It was true, in a way, that the oceans of time he pondered in his work were so mammoth, so overwhelming, that he did tend to drift a bit from day to day. What was a day, compared to the Cretaceous Period? What was the point of getting worked up over something that lasted merely a half-hour—a week—or forty-five years? The human time-scale had become much less real to him than the geologic one.

Knowing all this, he sighed, and glanced back in his rear-view mirror at the veterinary clinic on Main Street. He just wasn't ready to look up Deborah Armstrong.

Youngster, Dog Find Ancient Fossil
TRACI MORGAN

Although school is out for the summer, Jonas Torbett, 10, has been learning science anyway. Jonas and his dog were playing on some property owned by Jonas's father, Bryce Torbett of Groverton, when they stumbled upon an old bone embedded in a ditch bank. According to investigators called in from the Arkansas Geological Commission, the bone is a fossil at least 65 to 70 million years old.

"We're not sure what species the bone came from," said Dr. James Donovan, a paleontologist from the commission. "At this point, it's a mystery. But we start with the knowledge that the rock it's in is Cretaceous-aged rock."

Donovan said research is being done to see what animals living in the Cretaceous Period might have had bones like the one Torbett found. He said that in structure alone the piece of bone seemed to be "considerably more advanced in development" than Cretaceous animals.

Asked whether it might be a dinosaur bone, he said, "Well, I wouldn't rule anything out, absolutely. This is a specimen we'd definitely like to have a closer look at. It raises lots of questions."

Asked about his plans for the fossil, Bryce Torbett said, "I don't have any. Mainly I'd just like to find out exactly what it is."

As for the 10-year-old whose discovery started it all—is this a better way to study science than out of a book? "Sure," said Jonas. "It's been the funnest thing that ever happened to me. Thanks to my dog. He just showed me where to look."

8

HE HADN'T MEANT TO SPY. It just happened. He was playing behind the big tool cabinet in the workshop when the drop-in visitor came, and he couldn't help hearing. Jonas didn't announce his presence—he thought Daddy knew he was there—and the longer the grownups had been in their conversation the more awkward it seemed to let them know he was there. For the first time he knew the adult feeling of unintentional guilt; he hadn't really done anything wrong, and yet he had. Thinking about it later he felt dirty, like a piece of paper with something on it you haven't been able to erase right, because your eraser was worn down or blackened or wet with spit or was just one of those too-slick erasers that didn't work, and the paper ended up smeared and sometimes torn, with frayed curls of grimy rubber and paper pulp clinging to it.

He was playing with his army men behind the tool cabinet that jutted out from one wall and partially supported a long work counter set several feet away from the wall. The nooks and crannies there were excellent for playing army. One unit of men could fire from the tool cabinet at another unit set up in an empty one of the shelves for the Indian relics—a bottom shelf, where Daddy didn't like to keep things because he couldn't see them easily and had to stoop to get them. Jonas was crouched on the floor, making soft explosive noises and dying groans as he moved the small, plastic, army-green men around, and Bryce was in the nearby office. Then somebody came to the door.

"Bryce?" Tap-tap-tap. "Yoo-hoo. Bryce."

Jonas was just about to holler *"Daddy!"*—as later he wished he had—when Bryce ambled out of his office, not even looking in his direction.

He opened the door and smiled with surprise, tilting his head sideways as he stepped back and gestured the visitor in with a courtly wave of his arm. "Well, hey, Lorene."

It was Miss Strait, Jonas's sometime Sunday-school teacher at Groverton Church of the Rock. Jonas crawled under the work counter and peered out. Now was the time for him to say hey and be recognized, but he hesitated too long and the moment was lost. Miss Strait was dressed in a perfectly consistent color scheme, like that of a new car or a football team: a snug white jumpsuit with a red belt, red scarf, red open-toed pumps, red hoop earrings, red nail polish and red lipstick, and red-rimmed sunglasses pushed up on her head. Bryce, in Jonas's opinion, looked sadly dull beside her. He had on jeans and a plaid short-sleeved shirt with pearl snaps for buttons, a package of cigarettes pushing up the flap on one of the breast pockets. He was tanned dark from the summer sun and his hair was disheveled, as if he'd just been running his hand through it. "How you doing?"

"Just fine. How about you?"

"Can't complain. This air conditioner's so loud I like to not heard you. Got the kids let out for the summer?" Miss Strait also taught regular school: eighth-grade science. Clint would have her next year.

"Oh yes, I can have me a little peace and quiet now."

"About the time us parents lose ours." Jonas thought of coughing to save his father the embarrassment of hurting his feelings, but again somehow he didn't.

"It doesn't look too wild around here," said Lorene. "What are yours up to?"

"Hell, I don't know. They're off swimming, I reckon. Let's go sit down." Bryce paused at the opening to his office and again made the courtly gesture for Lorene to precede him. God, Daddy, thought Jonas, you're not supposed to say Hell in front of a Sunday-school teacher.

But she was lingering by his display cases. "Isn't all *this* interesting. You know, I read in the paper this was a hobby of yours but I hadn't ever seen it before."

"Um-hmm." Then they went into Bryce's office, but it had no door, and Jonas could hear them clearly. He continued to play as they talked. He wasn't really trying to listen; but his falling-hand-grenade noises got quieter and quieter, and the imaginary anti-aircraft guns quit making any sound at all.

First his father: "I have to admit I'm surprised to see you."

"Bryce—you know better than that! How come?"

"Like you say, you never have been out here. Now, did you come to save the old backslider or what? Come to tell me the real story on something one of the boys did at church?"

"No, I'll tell you what." Miss Strait's voice got serious, the way it did in Sunday school when she was winding up, just before she said, "Let's bow our heads": "I had to come see you because I'm concerned." There was a little pause, and she went on, "I'm concerned, Bryce, about this human fossil that everybody's talking about, that was found on your place."

Human fossil! Pause from Daddy. "Well, it's not necessarily— but what about it, Lorene?"

"I don't know if you know what-all they're saying about it. You saw the article?"

"Sure, I saw the article. I was *interviewed* in the article."

"So, Bryce, you must have thought about the effect this will have on Jonas, as far as—well Bryce, you're right, it *is* a religious issue I've come about. Didn't you see where that scientist from Little Rock said the fossil is seventy million years old?"

"I read it. Guess I didn't pay too much attention to the numbers."

"It's people like that who are a thorn in the side of the Creator God Himself. Bryce, I realize most people don't think about this too much, but I am an educator as well as a Christian, and I know there are other ways to explain a fossil than to say it's seventy million years old. The Bible tells us that is simply not so. Either we believe the Word of God, or we don't."

Daddy didn't say anything, and Miss Strait's voice became more joking. "I didn't come here to preach, now," she said. "I just thought I'd remind you ... Did you know I'm going over to Waylon College this fall to take a mini-course?"

"Why no, I didn't. What's it on?"

"It's on this very issue, creation science, and how we Christians have to work as hard on our godly science as the evolutionists do on their atheism. It's just a little workshop for teachers, really. We're going to do some lobbying at the Capitol at the end of it. This is very timely, Bryce. You know there's been a suit filed against the act that was passed this spring that allows creation science to be taught in the schools. And when *this* came up, right here in Groverton, I thought, well, what an opportunity to put our words into practice. I was telling Daddy." Her father was the preacher at Church of the Rock. "Especially since the finder of this fossil is a member of our very own church."

"What do you want me to *do,* Lorene?"

Throughout the conversation her voice had been high and singsong, as carefully sweet as a beauty contestant's. Now it fell in pitch and became more neutral as she answered, promptly, "Well, for starters, you could forbid those scientists to trespass on your property."

"Aw, I can't do that. They're just about to find out what it is."

"I thought you knew already. I thought it was a fossilized person."

"It might be a fossil person. That's what Jonas thinks it is, and that's what he told my mother, who has told everybody she knows. Hell—excuse me—for all I know they're right. But there seems to be some time problem. Too old to be a person. They don't know for sure yet what it is."

"Don't you see? You've been brainwashed like the rest of them," she said. "The earth is only two days older than man. Don't *listen* to them. There are other scientists I could get to come here and look at that bone. I could get my teacher at Waylon to invite his friends from the Creation Science Headquarters. *Or* from this place at Glen Rose, Texas, where there are human footprints intermingling with dinosaur footprints. Intermingling, Bryce!" Pause. "You may as well at least get both viewpoints."

"Both viewpoints?" he laughed. "Like there're only two? Hell, there are, what, four thousand people in this town? I think I could get four thousand opinions as to what it is, if I tried, just by standing on Main Street with a clipboard and a pencil."

"But I mean scientific viewpoints."

"Lorene, I'm just not sure I side with you on this one." There was a pause. Jonas heard the scratching of a match, and sure enough, in a minute he smelled cigarette smoke. Then his father's voice again, quiet and boastful: "I've got artifacts out there in those glass cases that are four thousand years old."

"That's okay. The Bible says the earth is that old."

"It's not for you to say it's okay or not, Lorene; it's a fact." She started to say something but Bryce went on, interrupting, just as Jonas would have been reprimanded for doing. "So you think I shouldn't let the Little Rock people come back?"

"Right. And then you could let the creation scientists come take a look."

"This guy from Little Rock not only wants to come back, he wants to take the bone with him. He wants to collect it for the state."

"Now he's sounding like a communist as well as an atheist! He's just sounding more and more charming all the time! Bryce, of course you're not gonna let him do that."

"Well, I don't know. I want to find out what it is. I guess I get that from my Indianology. I like to have answers."

"We all do." Lorene's voice got soft again, and she sighed. "We all do that." Chairs scraped, and she said, "I want you to just think about what I've said. Okay? And think about how your actions will affect your boys. They're good, churchgoing boys and I know you've worked at that even though you don't come yourself and I know you do it at least partly because it's what Marianne wanted—she wanted them to be as strong in their religion as she was."

No response from Daddy. He don't work at it, thought Jonas, he just drops us off there every Sunday and picks us up two hours later.

"So just think about it—'kay?" Lorene was saying, now

brightly as a schoolgirl again—"'kay? Do that for me?"—smiling. Now they were out in the main part of the workshop, walking toward the door, and Jonas stuck his head out from the shadows very cautiously. At the door they stopped, facing each other.

"I'll do it," Daddy said, "for you." He stepped close to Miss Strait, coolly and blandly as a man in a Sears sport-shirt ad, and reached toward her neckline and tucked her scarf in with gentle, tugging movements that let his knuckles brush a couple of times against her collarbones; then he patted the scarf and the neckline smooth, as matter-of-factly and patiently as if she had been an untidy little girl. "You were sort of coming apart at the seams there, or something," he added.

She blushed. "Good! I'm sorry," she said. "I've got to go." But she didn't move. "Oh."

"Thanks for coming out," Bryce said, unperturbed. He patted her arm with one hand and opened the door, very slowly, coolly, with the other, so that the bright afternoon light streamed in. "You know you're looking real good, Lorene."

"Thanks," she said, wobbling a little as she stepped over the threshold.

"I'll be thinking over your visit!" Daddy called after her.

And Jonas heard her voice, trailing back like a scarf, like the red scarf itself: "I'll count on it." By the time her car started up in the driveway, he had pulled back into his corner like a turtle drawing back into its shell, his army men forgotten in his general, blurry dismay.

9

ALL SUMMER LONG, JONAS had been riding his bike to Jim Ray's filling station to wash cars and boats. He did cars for three dollars and boats for five. Though all types of people stopped and fueled up at Jim Ray's before heading on to the lake, mostly the ones who wanted their boats washed were skiers; fishermen didn't much care whether their boats were clean. One day a man came along with a big houseboat and paid him ten to wash it. It took Jonas two hours because it had algae stuck to all the pontoons. Normally he made eight or nine dollars a day, but that day he'd made sixteen. He never worked all day long; Jim Ray would shoo him along after two or three hours, saying, "All work and no play makes Jack a dull boy." Jim Ray didn't make Jonas turn over any of his profit, which astounded Jonas's father.

Gradually Jonas was making money. Even though the Windex and paper towels and soft soap had to come out of his earnings, and even though he worked so few hours, he was still making enough to pay his father back for the vet bill. And it was a good thing, because he had just gotten a postcard from Dr. Armstrong saying it was time to bring Ace back.

"Son, I want you to start taking him to Dr. Hanks at Elmer," Bryce said. "We shouldn't have our business split up like this."

"Please, Daddy," said Jonas. "I really liked Dr. Armstrong. She was nice to me." He liked the way she had talked to him without changing her tone of voice. She looked straight at him without smiling or widening her eyes. And he liked the way her thick, dark hair swelled up under the neat little clips she clipped it with back over her ears, and the way the rest of it billowed just over the collar of her light blue doctor's coat, which matched her eyes. "And I'd lose time working," he added cunningly, "if I had to go all the way to Elmer. I'd have to get you to carry me over there. We'd both lose time working. But if I use Dr. Armstrong, I can just go myself."

His father just grunted. "You have her bill you directly from now on," he said. "You see if she'll let you pay *her* piecemeal. I don't want any more dealings with her myself."

Ace always came with him to the station, and Jim Ray didn't even mind that. It was a good time for Jonas to teach him to stay out of traffic. Ace, for all his spunk, was a little scared of loud noises like engines starting, and he usually stayed back from the cars and trucks pretty well. He would sometimes lie down inside the garage where it was cooler, but always at the very edge of the shade, so he could see Jonas. He liked to get in the way when Jonas was hosing things down. Sometimes Jonas would get carried away squirting Ace, watching him leap and dance and twist in the water, opening his mouth to catch more spray. Then Jim Ray would holler from the office, "Boy, I'm giving you my water to wash cars, not to wash that mongrel of yours."

Later, when Jonas went in to get water, stepping on the stack of old parts catalogs Jim Ray kept there so he could reach the drinking fountain, he would say earnestly to Jim Ray, "He ain't a mongrel, though, he's a purebred Catahoula cur."

The water had a metallic taste, like the way a car smelled under the hood. It was so cold you had to drink it slow, or it would make your teeth and forehead ache. While he was drinking it Jim Ray would answer, ritually, "Sheeut, boy, I don't know who sole you that billa goods. 'At dog ain't nothing but a mutt."

And Ace would pant in the shade of a stack of tires.

One Friday in mid-July, Jonas was sitting on an upside-down wooden Coke crate, scrubbing on the bug-plastered front grille of a Ford LTD. He reached behind him for the roll of paper towels he had just set down, but it wasn't there. When he looked around he saw Ace halfway down the block, with a long, long white banner of unfurled paper towel stretched out behind him. Jonas ran down the street yelling, "Ace! Come here! Ace Torbett! You come here!" A note of hysteria came into his voice as Ace got near the highway fork. He reached the end of the paper towels and stepped on it, but Ace only found the tension intriguing, and pulled backward with the roll till the towels tore. Then Jonas advanced, pretending to be holding a morsel of food. "Acey, Acey, come get it. Want a snack?"

Ace put the towels down and eyed him doubtfully. Jonas had tricked the dog this way only once before. Standing on the curb of Main Street, just where it became Highway 23, Ace looked around, panting. But he hadn't forgotten Jonas; he eyed him again. Jonas pretended to nibble at something in his palm. "Come on. Want a snack?"

Ace came forward hesitantly on his oversized paws. "Aha," said Jonas, swooping him up. "Gotcha." He could just barely still carry Ace, and had too much of an armful to reach down and get the paper towels too. He'd have to come back for them. "Bad dog!" he fussed. "Bad, bad Ace." Ace wriggled impatiently and wrinkled the skin on the sides of his nose, baring his teeth and gums. The outright ugliness of this move always shocked Jonas. "Bad boy!" he said in an even more terrible tone of voice, and Ace gnawed on his arm in irritated retaliation. Jonas didn't think he meant anything by it, but his teeth were sharp, and it hurt.

Back at the station he stooped and let Ace straggle out of his arms. Shorty, the mechanic, was shaking his head and grinning. Jonas went back for the strewn paper towels and Ace scampered alongside, biting the towels and shaking his head as Jonas tore successive pieces of them out of his mouth. Finally Jonas had the bulk of the paper off the sidewalk. The two arrived at the station a second time. "That stupid dog," Jonas said crossly. He was digging in his pocket for change.

Shorty laughed. "He ain't stupid. He just wants a little attention. And he got it, didn't he?"

"Yeah," said Jonas grudgingly, "but he wouldn't come when I called him. I had to bribe him."

"*I* wouldn't come to you if you'uz hollerin *my* name like that. He knowed you'd whip him if you caught him."

"No, no matter how mad I got, I wouldn't whip him," said

Jonas, putting money in the snack machine.

"Ohhh," said Shorty. "Come on now."

"I wouldn't!" insisted Jonas. He pushed 5 for Cheetos. "He might hate me then. I just holler at him."

"Yonder comes your pa," said Shorty.

"Where?"

"Ain't that Big Bryce's truck? Yeah, that's him."

Jonas watched his father roll up to the self-serve pumps. "Acey," he said. "Come here, you want a snack?" But Ace hung back, near a windshield-wiper dispenser.

"What are you doing now, buying food for that dog?" said Shorty. "He over here, Mr. Bryce!—Your dad's calling you."

"I've got to show him I mean it at least *sometimes*. Come here, boy, come get you a snack." And hearing the crackling of the bag being torn open, smelling the cheddar-dusted puffs, Ace finally came forward and ate what was offered him, happily.

"Jonas!"

"Sir! I'm coming!"

The boy and the dog crossed the stained concrete apron. Jonas dropped Cheetos on the ground and Ace followed a step behind, snuffling them up. Jonas turned and grinned back at Shorty. "Hansel and Gretel!" he called, pointing at the trail of Cheetos. And Shorty just shook his head.

"Hi, Daddy," said Jonas to Bryce. "Can I put the gas top back on for you?"

"Sure." Bryce hung the nozzle up on the tank again. "How's business?"

"Oh, okay."

Bryce went and paid for his gas and then, slipping his billfold into his back pocket, said, "What are you gonna be doing this afternoon?"

"After I finish here? Reckon I'll go swim."

"You got your bathing suit with you, or are you coming back by the house?"

"I got it with me. How come?"

"I'm just trying to keep tabs on you boys. What about Clint?"

"He's baling hay at the Nestersons'."

"That's what I thought. Now listen. If it gets to be suppertime and you're still at the Club, you just order you a cheeseburger or something and eat there, okay? Celie's off this afternoon and we aren't gonna have a hot supper."

"Yes sir."

"Bye now."

"Bye."

Celie had packed Jonas's lunch—a sandwich made of vienna sausages, a big dill pickle, and a package of Oreos. Just as he was finishing it with his last swallow of a strawberry Nehi a customer pulled up: someone with a dirty old Plymouth, Jonas's expert eye saw, and moreover a dirty ski boat on a trailer. He was so engrossed in speculating on whether this person would want the wash he needed, or just gas, that he didn't notice till the driver got out that it was Mr. Bledsoe. He had never seen him in shorts, and they made him look even younger and nicer. Jonas jumped up, started to run across the concrete to him, and then, realizing that wasn't cool, cut his gait to a sort of loping skip instead. But he didn't try to temper his smile. "Heyyy!"

"Hey, Jonas. What's up? You working here this summer?"

"Yes sir. You saw my sign?"

"Sure did. You think I'm a candidate for your business?"

"Yes sir."

"You're probably right. I'm taking a lady out skiing. I guess the least I could do is have a clean boat for her to ride in."

Jonas craned his neck. It was hard to see through the dirty windshield of the car. "Where is she?"

"Oh, I have to go pick her up."

"Well, just pull your car right over here."

"Sure. Just a minute. Lemme get some gas first."

While Mr. Bledsoe gassed up Jonas lingered beside his car and boat. The boat had a shiny stripe like sunken blue glitter or sequins that would be real pretty once the dust was cleaned off it. Jonas ran a hand down the stripe. "Is this yours? I didn't know you had a boat."

"No, a friend of mine loaned it to me. A man I work with who had a heart attack a few weeks ago, and can't get out in it this year."

"That was nice. For you, I mean."

"Sure was. Here, you want to put that on for me while I go pay?—Thanks."

Mr. Bledsoe came back and let Jonas direct him over to the washing-place, out of the way of the gas pumps and garage doors. Jonas waved and semaphored grandly, holding up his hand at the last in a firm command to stop.

While Jonas washed, Mr. Bledsoe squatted in the shade and patted Ace. He said, "I read where you found something interesting this summer."

"Yes sir, I guess so."

"How'd you find it?"

"Me and Ace—Ace and I were going back to the place where I found him, found Ace, because I remembered seeing the bone that day, which was a long time ago, but we went back around there and Ace he just run up on it and there it was."

"And it's a fossilized bone?"

Jonas nodded and scrubbed. "This scientist from Little Rock came to look at it. I think it's a leg bone, a fossilized Indian's. *Maybe* from a dinosaur," he allowed judiciously, "but probably a Indian."

"Is that what the scientist said?"

"Naw, he hadn't exactly said yet."

"Well, that's pretty neat. Pretty neat stuff," said Mr. Bledsoe, but he looked real serious. "So is the bone still on your dad's place, back where you found it?"

"Yes sir. If you'd like to go see it, you know, I could take you." Oh, to lead Mr. Bledsoe, adored substitute, on the hike to his find!

"I might like that. I'll let you know."

Jonas worked his way around to the far mud flap, his last one. Then he straightened up and said, "You want me to rub it dry or are you gonna let it air-dry?"

"I reckon I'll let it air-dry. I gotta go get my friend."

"I hope y'all have a nice time."

"Well, thank you. How much do I owe you?"

"Eight dollars."

"Eight dollars well-spent."

"Thank you, Mr. Bledsoe."

"Thank *you*, Jonas. Good to see you again."

10

CYCLING TO THE COUNTRY CLUB, with Ace alternately trotting beside him and making forays into a ditch choked with day lilies, Jonas mused over his teacher's appearance. That was how he thought of him—"my teacher." Much more so than he ever did the real fifth-grade teacher, Mrs. Peters. Mr. Bledsoe was the most wonderful man and the only Indian he knew. He hoped he could be just like him when he grew up. What other grown-up looked so playful and slim and energetic in shorts? Or would have a date to go waterskiing? Or would even go waterskiing? Not Jonas's dad, for sure. When he had dates he took them out to eat in Texarkana, at dark restaurants where you had to wear a sport coat, the sort of restaurant where Grandmother took him and Clint on an occasional birthday, the kind that had heavy menus. Where every time he said what he would like to order, Grandmother shook her head, saying, "Hon, I don't think you'd like that," and slid her bent spotted finger down the page looking for something he *would* like. Daddy also sometimes took his dates to places like cookouts or pool parties, or Razorback games, or the race track. But before or after these outings, when he brought his companions by the house to meet Clint and Jonas, he never seemed to be having much fun. The lady would make loud friendly talk with the boys, and Daddy, uncomfortable in his necktie, would jangle his keys impatiently.

He never went out very long with just one person. Sometimes he got a sitter and left home with no particular date that he told the boys about and didn't come back till late. He would call from Texarkana around eleven or twelve to check on the boys. He always sounded happy and tired then, though his voice was faint under the static of all the miles from Groverton to Texarkana. And they knew he was with women on those times because Celie complained about the makeup on his shirt collars. "Cattin' around," she said fiercely once as she squirted the pre-wash.

"What?" said Jonas.

"Never you mind, little pitcher."

When Jonas got old, he planned never to go out on miserable, boring dates. Like Mr. Bledsoe, he would go waterskiing or do something really fun. "Hi," he would say to the most beautiful lady he knew, "I am Jonas Torbett and I would like to take you to Wild River Country, over in North Little Rock. We will ride my motorcycle to get there. Would you like to go?" Or, "I am Jonas Torbett. May I please take you up in a balloon? Okay. Wear blue jeans, please." That was the kind of date he would have.

He wondered who Mr. Bledsoe's lady friend was. He could picture them waterskiing. Mr. Bledsoe would be a strong, excellent skier. He would be good at it because he was an Indian. Indians had a good sense of balance. That was why they got all those jobs working on skyscrapers. He would slalom, leaning far back in his own spray, happy and smiling, and the big muscles on his thigh would stick out. His girlfriend was probably an Indian too. She would turn the boat in a wide curve, looking back at Mr. Bledsoe with a big smile, the wind whipping her dark hair around her face just as it did Sacajawea's hair in the social studies textbook. "You're doing great, Stuart!" she would call.

He turned into the Country Club and pedaled beneath the double row of old crape myrtles up to the dirt parking lot. The soft ground wouldn't support his kickstand so he let his bike fall against the fence. Ace watched him enter the gate and then trotted off on his own business; there were dogs in most of the yards that backed up to the golf course, and he liked to touch base with them.

On his way to the men's room, carrying the plastic sack with his bathing suit and towel in it, Jonas glanced toward the pool, expecting to see Miss Traci in the lifeguard's chair. But it was

Brian Cowley instead. Aw, he thought at first. But that was all right. Sometimes Brian could be talked into playing Keep-Away Frisbee. If there weren't too many big kids around it could be fun. In a way it was a relief that Miss Traci wasn't there. Jonas liked her but she made him nervous. He could never talk to her easily, man-to-man, the way he just had to Mr. Bledsoe.

Yes, this was a great summer—better than he could ever have expected. He had been waiting and waiting for something to happen, and here without his even really doing anything to bring it about, a discovery had fallen in his lap; that day had seemed like any other, but it had turned out to be quite different. He was famous: Jonas Torbett, Great Discoverer.

Coming back out to the pool, walking as fast as he could to minimize the blistering concrete on his feet and still not be called down by Brian for running, he reached in his bathing suit pocket for pennies. They were there. As the afternoon wore on he dove and surfaced, dove and surfaced. The shadows of occasional big fluffy white clouds and of droplets cast by moving hands and feet and of the ripple rings thrown by those droplets moved slowly underneath him, silvery on the smooth white plaster bottom of the pool. His hands, groping for the shining spots of copper, made shadows too. Then he would shoot up from the turquoise gulfs and suck lungsful of air and wipe his face before flinging the pennies wide and ducking under again. Hello! he said in his mind. I am Jonas Torbett! Would you like to go scuba-diving with me? Good, I will pick you up at four. Please wear a bathing suit. We will be hunting treasure.

On one of his trips toward the surface he became aware of a noise. He went to the side and pulled himself out and sat there, rubbing his stinging eyes.

Brian kept blowing his whistle. "E'body out!" he commanded. "E'body out—I seen lightning over yonder."

Jonas looked anxiously at the sky. There was only one small patch of blue left, but you could see which cloud the sun was behind—a blaze behind a film of whitish-gray.

"Aw, Brian," said Heather Martin. "I don't see any lightning."

Slowly the sides of the pool filled up with kids, heaving themselves out of the water like seals on Wild Kingdom. Their bathing suits were accents of color—orange, pink, bright yellow, blue—against an afternoon that now was a dull gray-green; the group's attitude was dejected, belying their bright garb. They trailed their legs in the water. The girls' ponytails dripped little slow, persistent rivulets of water down their backs. The smallest ones' teeth chattered.

Sean Watson, who was Clint's age but almost a head taller, was standing by the ladder. "I really don't think it's stormy, Brian," he said seriously, appealing to the lifeguard as one mature person to another. "I think it's just shady."

But Brian just shook his head. "Wait five minutes. If I don't see no more lightning, y'all can get back in."

The children waited quietly and watched the surface of the pool turn calm. Now they could sense one of those stillnesses that does mean rain; they could clearly hear exclamations from a knot of golfers who they knew were far away, way off under the pine trees by the seventh hole. Jonas sniffed. He tasted chlorine and snot in his throat.

Trevor Duggins, squatting over the drain overflow, must have been counting to himself, and now he chanted softly aloud. "Fifty-eight Mississippi, fifty-nine Mississippi, *four* minutes," he said, raising his head long enough to shoot a triumphant look at Brian. "One Mississippi, two Mississippi—"

Then lightning struck—a white bolt close enough to make them all blink, with a crash of thunder following quickly.

"Aha—see there?" said Brian. "This pool is closed. Y'all get on inside. This may even bring the golfers in."

Already a few fat drops were splatting on the hot pavement.

"When are you gonna let us get back i-i-in?" said Tara Watson.

"When it quits rai-aining," Brian mimicked in a high-pitched voice, as he herded the kids toward shelter.

Already, from outside, Jonas could hear Mrs. Brandon starting to fuss at them: "No wet bathing suits over on this carpet, you know that, Blake, now y'all stay over here on the linoleum.

If you want some cards or checkers ask me and I'll bring them to you."

The air conditioning seemed really cold on his wet body, and once inside the paneled, noisy room Jonas felt suddenly sad. He didn't want to stay here and play games to wait out the rain. He went to change clothes, and then slipped out the door. Sure enough, there was Ace, wet and humbled and turning in half-circles with gratitude at seeing Jonas. Ace was a little bit scared of thunder. But the rain seemed to have slacked off—it was mostly just drip now—and Jonas decided to ride on home anyway. He was tired of being out. Maybe Daddy would be in a good mood and make grilled-cheese sandwiches. He would let Ace in the kitchen and they would all be together with the smells of sizzling butter and cheese.

Daddy's truck was in the carport and Jonas coasted in beside it expertly, jumped off and kicked the kickstand down in one smooth motion. He and Ace padded into the kitchen and Jonas shut the swinging door on Ace as he went on into the hall. The TV was off and Daddy wasn't in the living room, but at the end of the hall, past the boys' rooms, the door to his bedroom was ajar, and Jonas thought he heard noises coming from there. It was hard to tell. The rain had started to beat down hard again. "Daddy," he said as he pushed open Bryce's door, "Dadd—?" and then "oh."

Someone was in the bed with Daddy. They were all tangled up with each other like they were playing Twister. The moving shapes were indistinct and gray, like dolphins underwater, because the rain outside made heavy silver curtains at the windows, and the room was very dim. Jonas had an idea that they froze when they saw him, and that his father half rose from his odd position, but he didn't stick around to find out—backing out of the room as soon as he'd said "oh."

All the way back down the hall, as he burst out the kitchen door and jumped back on his bike and fled into the rain, the bedroom stayed with him—not just as he'd seen it in that one quick glance, but fleshed out over and over with wild new dimensions of sensuality: added details like smoothness and murmurs and warmth and sleek skin and cradle rhythms and summer-weed-like, rank but attractive smells. There was no way he could have absorbed all these details in his split-second at the threshold, but he was as certain they belonged to that scene as he was of his own name. And deep, deep down, this sense of pre-knowledge, of not being surprised, was as shocking as what he had seen itself—like facing a monster and realizing he'd dreamed and loved it all his life. He pedaled madly down the road, with Ace running alongside, gray dolphins playing at Twister in his mind.

11

JUST AS JAMES DONOVAN was leaving his office, he saw the mail clerk heading toward the boxes. "Hey, James," she said sunnily. "I've got yours here on top. You want it?"

"Sure, sure," he mumbled, flipping through it quickly. Notice of conference—notice of conference—notice of a parcel waiting for him in the Map Room—two identical envelopes from the state employment office, they were still convinced there were two James Donovans working here—a thick envelope from the Corps of Engineers, probably quadruplicate forms on that minerals project they were doing jointly—postcard from Davidson in New Guinea, he could read that later—aha—and here it was, an envelope from Sanchez at Montana. Great scholar. A horse's ass personally, but still a great scholar. Comparative paleo-vertebrate anatomy. "Wrote the book," he said, "he wrote the book." The clerk cocked her curly head at him and continued filling the mail slots. "Great," he said. He walked a couple of steps to stuff the rest of the mail in his pigeonhole. "I'll leave this here till I get back."

"Oh," she said. She took a pink message slip out of the pocket of her blazer. "I almost forgot. I caught the phone on my way up here and it was Dr. Gertsch. Says he's coming up this afternoon and he'll drop in to see you. He said he wanted to know if you had any plans for dinner tonight." She smiled at James's grimace. "I know!" she said. "But at least you have time to think up an excuse if you want to." Gertsch used to work for the Commission, and the entire staff disliked him as much as his colleagues. Now he was at a college in Texarkana; as a matter of

92

fact, it was he Donovan was supposed to be working with on the mastodon, and he was another reason James was dragging his feet on that project.

"Okay," he said. "Oh brother. Did he say what time he'd be here?"

"No sir."

"Well." He shook his head vaguely. "Maybe I'll miss him. I'm heading out to—um, to lunch now."

"Okey-doke." The clerk smiled. Who else but James would feel compelled to explain his actions to her? Or would start out the left-hand hall door, which was permanently bolted shut for some reason nobody knew, when he had been going in and out by the right-hand door for almost ten years now? She just hoped he could still remember where he was planning to go when he got in his truck.

And Donovan did. He was meeting Andy Ropp at Zeke's Barbecue. There was one table left, which he took after scanning the ranks of white-shirted, light-blue- or tan-suited men for his friend, in vain. He faced the door so Andy would see him right away and ripped open the letter from Sanchez.

"... left a little puzzled by the specimen .... undoubtedly from an upper limb bone. The shape of the upper end suggests that this appendage was attached underneath the torso rather than at the side. Oddly enough the joint, though it has deteriorated somewhat, does suggest the ball-and-socket arrangement associated with erect bipedal stature in the primates. The muscle and tendon scars would seem to support this. Their points of attachment also suggest a much larger muscle mass than is surmised to have attached to the reptilian femur, or its equivalent. In short I would suggest that you question your premise of a Cretaceous-age outcrop as the authentic source of this specimen, as all discernible evidence points to a much more recent origin ...."

"But I know it's Cretaceous," thought Donovan. "Damn. I *know* that."

"One?" said a white-aproned woman who suddenly towered above him, sliding a plastic glass of water and crushed ice across the formica tabletop. "Something to drink?"

"Iced tea, please." James moved the letter away from the trail of ice water near the glass. "And oh—there's my friend."

She slid another water glass across like a shuffleboard puck and said, "Okay, I be back in a minute to take y'all order."

Andy came in, small, rumpled, and grinning. He always looked like he'd just won a case. He had on the light blue seersucker version of the Southern lawyer's summer uniform, with a white-polka-dotted blue tie to redeem it, or possibly as a symbol of Andy's last-ditch stand against conformity. "Hey, man. You been here long?"

"Nah. Just a few minutes." James half-stood and shook his friend's hand.

"Well, sorry I'm late. But it's heating up around here."

"Yeah, every year I forget how bad it is."

"Oh, not the weather," said Andy. Just then the waitress came back. "Iced tea," said Andy, "and ribs."

"Ribs," seconded James, and the waitress stalked away.

"No, I mean all this stuff I want to talk to you about. We're doing discovery for this creationism trial. Actually, I'm not doing it; it looks more and more like the New York firm's going to do all the hands-on work for the case. But I've had access to the documents and I've been helping with some of the administrative shit. It's fascinating. It's like doing intellectual history, only it's the real stuff."

"Science versus religion?" said James. "And who's winning?"

"Well, that's not really it. The sides aren't that clear-cut. That's what I thought before I got into it. I mean, *personally* I believed that they didn't have to be at odds, science and religion"— James was nodding—"but I thought that in the public arena they were still fighting it out. But it turns out everything's all mixed up, with the plaintiffs arguing religious and philosophical reasons for their case, and the creationists trying to persuade us how 'scientific' they are. The plaintiffs are mostly theologians and ministers—I mean we've got some scientists testifying, of course, but you'd be amazed at the religious people who are stepping forward. And in the meantime, come to find out most of the creationists have Ph.D.s in science from, you know, reputable schools. So in that respect the sides are blurred."

Two beige plastic plates, with their partitioned compartments aswim in reddish sauce, landed in front of them. Tucked under two slices of white Wonder bread, the ribs steamed provocatively.

"But anybody can get a Ph.D.," objected James, "if you hang around somewhere long enough and crank out enough bullshit. Some Ph.D.'s mean something and some of 'em don't."

"True," said Andy. "But you and I are prejudiced. We're snobs about fundamentalist Christians. Where the hell's my tea?" he complained, looking around, and then went on with scarcely a breath: "So you have these creationists, who you think of as this bunch of fundamentalist religious zanies, going to elaborate lengths to convince us that their ideas are science. Listing the things point by point that they think make it science—'observable facts that fit the theory' and all this shit. Thanks," he lifted his eyes and smiled his cherubic smile upward, at the tall, cold-sweating glass of iced tea that was descending from the even taller, browner, cooler figure of the waitress. "It's like everybody in today's society thinks people will listen to them if they claim their particular deal is *science.* I've started noticing. Of course pop psych has been that way for a while. And now you have, oh, diet books doing it, and even shampoos, women's makeup, talking about their pH, their 'chemically balanced formula'—so even religion can't just be itself, but it's got to try desperately to disguise itself as science."

"And not very convincingly at that," said James slowly. "Because they miss the point most of the time. They don't know what science really is. What rules—limits—scientists accept about their studies before they even begin their research. We don't deny a supernatural power, we just don't think it can be studied with our methods. We stake out a certain realm, the realm of natural, demonstrable laws that are assumed to be consistent throughout the universe. And within that realm scientists are open-minded. Whereas these guys, these *creationist* people, start with a priori ideas. They never look at any interpretation of the so-called observable facts but their own. Don't get me started."

"Right, right," said Andy, now hunched over his plate. He had taken advantage of James's expounding to attack his ribs. Now he pulled some extra napkins out of the dispenser and wiped his fingers rapidly before starting to gesture and talk again. "Of course everybody *is* biased to some degree. Right? Not even science is purely objective. That's one of the myths. One thing is, you scientist guys need to study up on all this, so you understand what the *issues* are when you get attacked. I mean, as this one theologian was telling me—somebody on our side, understand, this guy from Chicago—what other discipline can you belong to without being required to take courses in that discipline's history or philosophy? Could you graduate with a degree in English and not take some literary philosophy? Or be an art major and not take art history?"

James was laughing. "Yeah, I can tell you a few places in this state where that's quite possible."

"Well." Andy mopped up juice with his white bread. "Arkansas aside." He chewed. "I mean, let's be *real.* But my point is—"

"Yeah, yeah, I get your point. Scientists don't have to be versed in the ideas behind what they're doing. You don't have to take the history of biology to be a biologist."

"Right. And then you don't even know how to *talk* to these people who are so wrong-headed about what you're doing. The rift just widens." Andy pushed his plate away, sighed. "The rift widens, man."

"That's the story, isn't it?" said James. Despite the stimulation, it was always slightly exhausting to see Andy Ropp. No one else he knew said things like "The rift just widens." It made James feel as though he'd stepped back into one of the late-night bullshitting sessions in the dorm where he first knew Andy.

"So how've you been?" said Andy abruptly. "What are you working on?"

"Oh." James grinned. "That rift, man. The widening rift. It's getting me down."

"Yeah?" with interest.

"Oh no, no." James waved away sympathy and pretended to look around for the waitress. A man always disclaimed problems. Michelle used to say that too. Once they spent a weekend with another couple who were having marriage trouble—long before their own—and on Saturday the women went shopping while James and the man played tennis. At the end of the weekend, when James and Michelle were discussing their friends, Michelle knew the entire terrain of the other, straining marriage—all the ups and downs, the arguments, the bedroom pleadings, the salient points of dispute and of the wife's despair. James, in contrast, knew nothing of what the husband thought. "Well, what did y'all *do* all day Saturday?" "I told you. We played tennis." "But what did you *talk* about? I can't believe you didn't even talk about *anything.*" "We did talk, okay? We kept score. This is what we said: 'Good shot. Two-one. Two-two. Was that on the line? Three-two.' God*damn* it, Michelle." "Well," Michelle had said, "I guess that's the difference between women and men."

As these sad memories washed over James, his blank gaze had fallen on the waitress. Now she approached their table. "Y'all need anything else?"

"I'll take some more tea," said James.

"And the check," said Andy. "Yeah, sure, that's fine."

The woman set the pitcher down, propped her small receipt pad on her stomach, and scrawled phlegmatically. She put the check down between them, where it clung to the table in a puddle of water left by the sweating tea glasses and quivered in the mild damp breeze from the fans. "Thank you, gentlemen, you can pay the cashier."

When she was gone James looked up again. "I just liked that about the rift," he said. "It sounds like your feet are in a boat but you're trying to hang on to the pier with your hands and the boat's drifting away. And you look down and all you see is water underneath you. Or like you're Wile E. Coyote, stretched across some big old canyon ..."

"Yeah, yeah, I know the feeling." Andy nodded vehemently. "But you said on the phone you're doing better?"

"Oh, yeah, sure."

"Now where is it you're living?"

"You know those apartments off Wildacre Road? Pretty bland out there."

"Yeah, it is." Andy was quiet for a minute. He and his wife lived near where Michelle and James had lived, where Michelle still lived. In an integrated neighborhood of modest old houses. The sort of neighborhood where Dick and Jane went to the Safeway together on Sunday afternoon and washed the golden retriever or strolled the baby when they got back and sat on their porches drinking beer and never, ever thought about divorce.

"Singles city, out where I am," said James.

"Hmm." Then Andy said, "What about work?"

"Oh, I've got this one thing going on that's sort of interesting. This kid out in the country found a fossil bone. I'm not real sure what it is yet, but one thing's for sure, it's a hell of a lot older than the kid's father thinks the earth is. It sort of fits in with *your* deal."

"Sounds like it. Fundamentalist family, hunh? Where they from?"

"Groverton."

Andy rolled his eyes. "Oh, Jesus."

"I never thought of that as a fundamentalist haven before."

"No, it's not, really—not that—it's just politically real draconian. I don't think of 'em as particularly *religious* fanatics."

"Well, I may find out," said James. "When I told the kid Arkansas used to be covered with an ocean, he said I must mean from the Flood."

Andy snorted. "What are you gonna do? You're still having a lot of dealings with the family?"

"Well, yeah; I don't want to collect the specimen till I have some evidence to prove its location and the way it's oriented in the outcrop."

"So what's the law on this? I have to admit I'm not up on it. Does the state have a valid claim to fossils or are they the property owner's?"

"Or the finder's," said James. "That's not always the same

person as the landowner."

"Oh yeah, you've got him mixed up in there too."

"Well, it's blurrier than we'd like it to be. The best thing for us to do is to maintain a good relationship with the landowner. That way, once we collect the specimen, there are no hurt feelings. The thing is, to us these fossils are extremely valuable. There's no replacement for the information they can yield. But once we use the word 'valuable' to these dirt farmers, the dollar signs start chinging up in their eyes. Of course they have no *monetary* value. If the landowner kept the specimen he'd end up sitting it on his mantel and striking fireplace matches off it a couple of times a year."

"Why don't you just barge in there and yank it up? Worried about me and my ilk?"

"Yep." James grinned. "Well, also that's something you never want to do too early. The interpretation of a specimen is always just that—interpretation. Like you were saying, science is subjective. Paleontology especially. There are always two things that are hard and fixed, though: the specimen itself—I mean it's tangible, you can hold it in your hand—and its location where it was found. So once you remove it, you'd better be sure you have all the data clarified about that location." He drank some tea. "That's why I'm proceeding with kid gloves right now. But it doesn't look too good. When I mentioned to this landowner that I might eventually want the bone for the state, he drew up and 'lowed as how he didn't know about that. So I don't know. I need to go back down there."

"Hmm." Andy nodded. "I like it, I like it, Donovan. You guys can't insulate yourselves from these humanities problems any more than the rest of us can."

"Come off it, Ropp," said James, laughing as he scraped back his chair. "You're not telling me anything new."

In his absorption in what he was saying, he had failed to notice that Andy picked up the check. He argued for it but Andy held firm, kidding that the ACLU would pay for it; James had given him salient background for the creationism case. So James had to succumb, and be treated to lunch. "Lawyers," he said. "So that's what all those fees were for in my divorce. So Jerry Beal could take some friends of his out to lunch, when they were talking about things 'salient' to my case."

"Ah, quit bitching," said Ropp in the parking lot, before they shook hands good-naturedly. "You *chose* to be a poor geologist."

James was back in his office late that afternoon, examining some nautiloids he had scooped up when the city was laying a big water main near the library downtown. He did not expect anything remarkable among them, and had not been surprised so far.

Suddenly a massive shape filled his doorway, and a booming voice followed it almost immediately. James turned his head to greet the face that was, if anything, more florid and contorted by loud speech than usual.

"Donovan! Working late, no less! The taxpayers don't pay you to work overtime, you know! I remember the days! But you've missed the most important thing you should be working late on!"

He rolled back his chair and stood up, a little less than eager. "Well, hey, Fred, how you doing."

"Got over to Groverton to look at your find."

"Oh yeah?" James was still regretfully shaking out of his mind the nautiloids—those dear nautiloids and the splendor of their tiny, modest, silent dignity.

"Can't believe what the hell you missed. You're slipping, man, slipping."

"Yeah?"

"Yeah. Either that or you didn't tell me about the most interesting thing on site"—and here Fred Gertsch held out his fat fist, and slowly unfurled the fingers from around the objects he had been clasping—"Arrowheads, as they say. Projectile points."

12

IF JAMES DONOVAN'S MOTHER had been in the nightclub off Reb-
samen Park Road that night (which, of course, was impossible;
at that hour of night she was always at home several miles to
the west, in her immaculate peach bedroom with her thermo-
stat set precisely at 72, Estée Lauder smoothly applied to her
face, and her body curled slightly into the fetal position inside
the peach nightgown), and if, once there, she could have seen
her son's face (which would have been equally unlikely, given
the way the lights over the dance floor alternated from purple
to red to blue and blinked dimly, and a haze of smoke curtained
the room)—but if she had been at his table she would have
laughed with recognition at her son's expression. This look had
first showed up in his toddlerhood, when he was confined
somewhere he did not want to be and all his escape ploys had
failed. It had appeared off and on since then, coming into its
prime when James was a teenager. The exasperated twist of his
mouth made his cheeks puff out, warping his jawline, which
even under his beard was normally lean; the glare of self-disgust
in his eyes was veiled only by balefully drooping eyelids.

He sat with his arms folded, his eyes fixed stonily on the little
stage without really seeing it. Projectile points, he was thinking.
Arrowheads. How could he have missed them? He had gathered
up some gravel from beneath the ledge where the bone was—
unremarkable flint gravels. He had scanned the ground for yards
around. How could he have missed projectile points?

*You miss what's going on right around you. How could you not
tell I was seeing someone else? I left clues **hoping** you'd find them!*

As plain as the nose on my face!

Damn, damn. Do too much office work and your powers of field observation get bad. Maybe he really was in the clouds, as Michelle had said. But how could this fat slob do better fieldwork than he? How could Gertsch even climb that embankment, for Christ's sake? He had thought about not even telling Gertsch. But the St. Louis conference was coming up this month and it would have been politically bad for Gertsch to hear about James's find there, from the people James had written with his questions, rather than from James himself. Also he had been on the defensive about the stupid mastodon—had rushed to flesh out his excuse to Gertsch about why he hadn't beat it on down I-30 to do *that* jigsaw puzzle lately.

And now what would happen? The implications of human activity at the fossil site were staggering. He would have to call in archaeologists, with their persnickety ways and their own barrage of methodology and paperwork. Of course if something—something new—came of it, it'd be worth it. But to a paleontologist, it was a dreary bore to have to consult his colleagues in the ancient history of life, the archaeologists. Also, now the landowner needed to be warned against Indian pothunters: once the word got out that artifacts were on his land, those guys would come swarming, and they could get rough, mean, in their efforts to get their hands on good relics ... Oh, this news complicated things, all right. And what did it say about this femur-like, mammalian-looking bone? *Now* what would Sanchez say? Could the arrowheads have been left later? Would there be any other signs of Indian life at the site? *Could this bone be human?* And what the hell would a human bone be doing in Cretaceous marl?

"You didn't tell anyone this, did you?" he had asked Gertsch.

"Well, just the landowner, just Torbett. Of course."

"And you told him not to spread it around?"

"Well no, Jim. Who do you think we are? Haven't we been talking about public relations? He was going to have it put in the local paper. Indians are his bag. He got real excited about that, more than he was about the bone."

James just groaned and fumed.

He needed to get down to Groverton first thing in the morning. He would leave at—let's see, at five-thirty, and be there by eight. He would go back to the site, inspect for any other evidence of human history involved, ingratiate himself with Torbett some more—why had he been putting that off?—and stop to see an archaeologist buddy at Henderson State on his way back. And he wouldn't be getting much sleep tonight. No, it didn't look likely that he'd get his seven hours. His head would have that tinny, hollow feel, he would have that super-consciousness of his eye sockets that he always got when he had too little sleep. The expectation made him even grimmer and madder.

Thank God, their waitress was coming around again; James recognized her huge frizzy mat of hair in silhouette against the lights of the dance floor, and her thinness, the way her pelvic bones pushed against her shiny-smooth cocktail dress. "Would you care for another? Now, this'll have to be the last round." You couldn't be positive she was saying that; you had to guess and fill in the missing syllables that the blaring music drowned out. Last round—good! Surely that would make Gertsch realize how late it was and how many he'd had; surely he would decline; surely his wife looked sleepy.

But no. He saw Gertsch's big bullet head pumping affirmatively. Then he leaned toward Marla and said something.

"Why not?" James saw her mouth move. "Another white wine."

"Jim?" yelled Gertsch.

When would he figure out that James never went by "Jim"? He shook his head vehemently. "Oh, nothing for me," he said, looking ostentatiously at his left wrist—but he had left his watch on his dresser after showering, though God alone knew why he had been in a hurry. And it wouldn't have done him any good anyway, for it was not as if they were the most sensitive people in the world, not likely to change what they wanted to do because they picked up on his discomfort.

As the cocktail waitress swept away he reached up to touch her elbow, but missed. "Excuse me, could I have some ice water?" But she didn't hear.

Marla and Fred sat with their chairs cocked to the tiny table, facing the dance floor and band. Marla jiggled her head and shoulders along to the music, and her earrings flipped to and fro. Fred as usual looked bland and complacent. As if noise at the volume of a jackhammer weren't pounding into his ears. As if he hadn't consumed four drinks of his own and the combined cigarette smoke of a dozen people over the last hour and a half. James sucked at his glass, straining to swallow even a cubic centimeter more of melted ice in the bottom of it.

It was his run that had nailed him. The excuse had backfired. When Fred had asked him to go out to dinner—"Marla's shopping; you know these women; we'll pick her up at the mall and go get a steak"—he had cleverly answered that he had to run that evening, that he was in training for a road race (not quite true—he had the entry blank but had not decided whether to sign up) and never, ever missed his nightly six miles.

But all that did, instead of getting him out of spending time with the Gertsches entirely, was make Fred say, "Well then, you can go barhopping with us after dinner! Come on, you need some fun! We'll meet you at Jimbo's at ten!"

Barhopping? He didn't know anyone even used that word anymore. But the more industriously he declined, the more insistent Fred became. And after all, they were still colleagues in some sense; the mastodon loomed. At last, grumpily, James had agreed. Dinner would have been infinitely preferable.

He would have liked to be home reading Stephen Jay Gould, or better yet, sleeping. He had a headache from the smoke and Marla's perfume and the efforts of smiling and conversing during the band's breaks and shouting and wincing during their sets. The taste of his one wine cooler was sour in his mouth. Who would have thought Little Rock had such a night life? Was this the life he would have to adopt in order to meet someone? He saw The Pickings, lined up at the bar, women with hair either poofed out farther than their collarbones, or cut shorter than a man's, with earrings so big and dangling they threatened to dip in their drinks; women with fingernails so long they clicked against their glasses. Would you want a woman like that in bed? James wondered. Those nails! those earrings! that sprayed hair! How would you make love with all those armaments in the way?

But he saw the writing on the wall; he saw what he would have to do to get paired up again. He saw the men, standing as though in cigarette ads with one fist on their hip, pushing back their sport coats. Yes, he would have to stand and push his sport coat back like that, and wear those tieless shirts, and laugh, and drink, and get a poofy hairstyle himself, and grind and hop on the dance floor. He would have to buy pants with pleats and no back pockets and go on first dates and say ha-ha to women's jokes and wonder—God, like a high school kid again—when he was supposed to kiss them goodnight, pay their way, bed them. It was a nightmare. He felt a sensation in his chest he had not felt even lately, a crawling cold misery. He had never realized what a nightmare the social life of unmarried people was. He refused to call it the singles scene. He should have taken this whole thing more seriously in college. He should have paid more attention then. But how was he to know how everything would turn out? Was there something even then that should have tipped him off that he and Michelle were doomed, like mutant genes pairing? He *had* loved her—not in the tangled aching complicated way she called love, but simply, the way he knew he loved canoeing, or, say, sugar maples. Was there something wrong with that? It had been so easy to meet her, to love her that direct way, in college. There were classes and good movies to go to. You could study together for hours and think of that as a date. They hadn't had to go to smoky nightclubs and track each other's pelvises on the dance floor. They could wear jeans and drink beer on the library steps. Now what would he do? Where would he go?

He didn't even think he wanted to be with someone as badly as all these people lined up at the bar must want someone. He wasn't that lonely—yet. He didn't miss sex. Yet. It was a while since he and Michelle had had real fun making love; the stretch of bad times must have dampened his desire. Sex seemed like so much trouble.

He sighed. Alcohol, he thought, not a stimulant for sure, a depressant all along.

So why was the matter even on his mind? He might believe he were destined to be single, if it weren't for occasional longings that took over at odd times. Like when he was running on the levee a couple of weeks ago and saw a fat, brown old man and woman out in a johnboat, fishing. She had a wide-brimmed straw hat held down by a scarf tied under her chin. He had on one of those sleeveless white undershirts. They had tied up by some willows near the bank where the river had risen and as James went by, looking their way because he had just seen the woman's pole bending, had seen her drawing something out of the water as he approached, they looked at each other and started laughing. The man laughed in isolated rolling bass syllables, the woman in a high chitter of giggles like a bunting's song. The fish swung crazily in the air between them, and the woman made sporadic attempts to catch the line and hold it still. Finally the man got the fish and wrested it off the hook and was in the motion of flinging it back in the river as James ran on and they slipped behind him, out of sight. But he became aware of a pooling in his chest that had nothing to do with his running—an accumulation of desire and loneliness. To be fishing or laughing either one with someone else, at sixty, seventy, he thought, you'd have to be pretty fortunate.

Suddenly he realized that the awful band was stopping. "And—thankyouverymuch!—ladies and gentlemen—for coming out to hear Freddie and the Stingers tonight—" A few lights came on dimly; already the Stingers were casing their guitars and sliding mikes and wires across the small stage; the waitress's hair appeared again by James's elbow, and her face after it. "You can just pay me when you're ready," she said. She had one of those mincing, gushing voices that would have put James in a gloomy cast of mind about the female sex even if he weren't already disposed that way tonight, and her voice sounded abnormally loud in the relative quiet after the band's last number.

You pay for this, you fat sucker, James was thinking, you

talked me into going. He was glaring at Gertsch already, though under the influence of his Scotches the man didn't notice. He was checking his wallet. "Geez!—no cash!—Do you have any cash, honey?"

Of course she didn't.

"Do you mind, James, if I just put this on my Visa card, and you pay me?"

Criminal. It was criminal. Now he wouldn't have cash for the morning's trip. Glowering like a fifteen-year-old, James got out his wallet. "Of course not," he said.

The next morning he was up at a quarter to five and was showered, tanked with coffee, and dressed by ten after. He picked up Mary Cavendish and Dietmar Frierson at the office, gassed the Commission's GMC Suburban and hit the automatic teller machine, and by five-thirty-five was rolling out of town on I-30, heading west along with the morning's eighteen-wheelers.

Shortly after eight his vehicle was bouncing along the muddy tracks of Bryce's road. Scissortail flycatchers were soaring from tree branches above, their fringed appendages swooping behind like tails on a conductor's coat. A skunk waddled across the road. James was in the middle of an enthusiastic discussion of shoreline ecology when he rounded a brushy bend in the road and slammed on the brakes. In front of him, stretching completely across the road and padlocked to new fence on either side, was a gate welded of silver-painted pipe. On it hung a sign about six feet long and four feet wide that said, in big block letters: THIS PROPERTY CLOSED TO PUBLIC TRAFFIC. NO TRESPASSING. And beneath that, in curlicue letters, *Trespassers Will Be Prosecuted.*

"What the—?" James's mouth gaped open.

Mary, always one to have the obvious spelled out to her, said, "This wasn't here before?"

"No," said James. "No. I had no idea." He was slowly putting the big Suburban into reverse—a change of direction the vehicle did not take lightly. "Come *on*, baby," he mumbled to it. It was more like a dinosaur than anything James had ever dug up. He floored the accelerator and after a minute the Suburban lurched back down the road they'd just driven.

"Where are we going?"

"To the landowner's house," said Dietmar, "I reckon." He had had all his higher education in the States, and he used American idiom with just the faintest trace of a German accent.

"Right," said James. "I reckon."

At the Torbett house nobody answered the door. James felt sure someone was home, for there was a car in the driveway as well as Bryce Torbett's pickup. But he beat on the kitchen door for a while and then went around to the front door, and still no one came. He walked despondently back to the Suburban, got in, and despite the heat sat without starting the ignition. He noticed that Mary and Dietmar were giggling.

"Check out those bumper stickers," Dietmar said by way of explanation.

"That's the mentality of this whole state, once you get out of Little Rock," said Mary.

DON'T CRITICIZE FARMERS WITH YOUR MOUTH FULL.

GOD SAID IT, I BELIEVE IT, THAT SETTLES IT.

"Oh yeah," said James. He was too discouraged to find them very amusing. At last he started the Suburban.

13

JONAS KNEW HOW THE VERSE WENT. "Men shall persecute you, and utter all kinds of evil against you falsely, for My sake ...." And Jesus Himself had been persecuted by the bad people, the Jews and Romans. It always seemed that the bad people were the ones doing the persecuting and the good people were being persecuted. Why, then, had Daddy put on that sign that he would persecute trespassers? Jonas resolved to ask him.

There were things he never understood. Like when they said Jesus was crucified for your sin. How could that be? Jonas wasn't even alive when Jesus was crucified. So how could it be his fault? He could see why the Jews and Romans were burning in eternal hellfire, but why did *he* have to take the blame for what they did as well? Once at Sunday school he had asked Miss Strait that and she had stared at him, appalled. Finally she said, "If you had been there, Jonas, you would have stood by and let it happen. You might have driven in the nails." Well, that was a pretty bad thing to think about him. And could she prove it? "Might have." Maybe he *wouldn't* have just stood there and let it happen. How did anybody know? Jonas didn't ask Jesus to be crucified for him. Maybe he would have rushed out and said, "Hey, you can't do that, you can't persecute my Lord and Savior Jesus Christ." But maybe Miss Strait was right. Would he have been such a big fan of Jesus at that time? What if he hadn't *liked* Jesus? Jesus was supposed to love little children, but He sounded like a pain. "Suffer the little children." If He loved boys and girls why did He want them to suffer? There were many questions Jonas could not ask in Sunday school. If he did, he might be persecuted.

So, as a matter of fact, Jonas was *not* glad-when-they-said-unto-me-let-us-go-unto-the-house-of-the-Lord. In the first place Bryce never said, in the midst of the Sunday morning array of Cap'n Crunch boxes, milk cartons, and glasses of Tang (Celie did not work on Sundays), "Boys, let us go unto the house of the Lord." He said, "Get your damn coats on now and I mean *now.*" And not only was Jonas not glad when this was said unto him, but he would get a knot in his stomach that seemed unique to Sunday mornings and would suddenly feel he had to go to the bathroom, not just to pee either. But if he went Daddy would be beating on the door saying, "Damn it, Jonas, son, don't set up camp in there." Which was a form of persecution in itself.

Why had Daddy even put that gate up? To keep out the guy from Little Rock with all the pockets—the scientist? Jonas had sort of liked him. To keep out curiosity-seekers from town? Mr. Bledsoe and his lady friend might have been among them, before the gate went up. Jonas would have bet that Miss Strait had put his father up to it. She was at their house all the time now. Talking church business, Daddy said. Ha. Jonas knew better than that. He didn't know for sure that she had been the other twisting dolphin, the lady in bed with Daddy that day not long before, but he could guess. They probably took off their clothes and lay very close and felt loving, as *A Doctor Talks to 9-to-12-Year-Olds* said. It was in the chapter after the one about your voice changing. Jonas was not sure why you could not lie close together with your clothes on in order to feel loving. He had a few suspicions, but they were utterly ridiculous and surely could not be true. He had broached the topic with Clint, and Clint had told him to take a good look at Terry Bradshaw the next time he humped Vernal Equinox. Terry Bradshaw was the Torbetts' Charolais bull and Vernal Equinox was one of their cows, who had been born on the vernal equinox the same week Jonas had been studying it in school (Jonas and Clint took turns naming the farm animals as they were bought or born). All Jonas knew about the violent humping of the mammoth Terry Bradshaw was that once his father, glancing sidelong at Jonas and seeing, probably, his misery as he watched the act, had said to him kindly, "Terry Bradshaw is fertilizing her eggs." And after a pause, as if he realized more explanation was needed, he added, "To make a calf." Fertilizer was a white grainy substance that was spread on plants; eggs were fist-sized things with shells that could be scrambled; who would have thought they were life-producing?

Maybe he would understand when his voice changed.

In the meantime, his father was doing something with Miss Strait that had an intensity of pleasure, secrecy, and shame such as no other relationship Jonas observed. Jonas could never have described this relationship—and no one discussed it anyway—but he felt its difference vividly. The household had internalized it, Celie knew it but did not talk about it, and they were all revolving around its weird heat, around the giddy joy it gave to Bryce, like planets around the sun. He did not like Miss Strait. He could not quite articulate the reason for that, either. When she noticed Ace the first time she said, "That must be a fine dog, it's so ugly." His father answered, "Good guess, Lorene, but no, it's a mutt." Jonas would bet that Miss Strait had even gone with Daddy to hang that gate. She wanted to persecute people like the man from Little Rock.

When he had seen his father with her that day in the bedroom he had felt strange. It was not that he saw any of their private parts, exactly. The light was grayish and dim and mostly he saw their pale sides: the swell of the lady's breast but not the nipple, the side of her flank and hip and thigh, a glimmer of white under Daddy, but not the crucial middle of either. When he remembered the scene, he seemed to hear the rain again, drumming, strumming all around, over the roof and the room, under the moans and the startled silence. But it was not so much the nudity that disturbed Jonas, nor the fact that this had been his mother's room too (the bed he now associated only with Bryce, and the only temple that another woman's presence could desecrate, for Jonas, was his mother's closet, with its long swishy fragrant nightgowns, her soft velour robe, the cloved orange he'd made her in kindergarten hanging between her

Sunday dresses). It was a hurt that later in his life he would identify as jealousy. Pedaling home in the rain he had been thinking about having Bryce all to himself, in the coziness of waiting out a storm. He had pictured—expected—that kitchen full of crisp hot sandwiches and his father in a good mood because the crops needed rain, squeezing the back of his neck, slapping his bottom playfully, raising an eyebrow, maybe, as he joked about something before he bit down into his sandwich; the two of them giggling over the hot orange strings of melted cheddar stretching away from their mouths. But when he had stood on the threshold of the bedroom and had seen his father oblivious to him, absorbed even literally in somebody else, he had felt—real bad. Like a fool for thinking about grilled cheese in the yellow kitchen light. And this fooled, hurt feeling had driven Jonas back outside and as far away from the house as he and Ace could get. They had stayed in the tractor barn that day until the rain quit, and then had gone back to the bone-site to hang out until dark.

It had become Jonas's favorite place to be alone. He and Ace could sit on the limestone ledges there and make up games and scenes for a long time. Sometimes he brought pieces of cardboard and slid down the embankment. Sometimes he brought his army men and set up battle scenes. Sometimes he brought his arrowheads from Mi-Ka-Do and played Indian, and he even left a few of those there, on purpose. The poor old ancient fossil Indian, whose leg-bone was now miraculously uncovered, would want some artifacts around, like the Indians at Mi-Ka-Do. He needed company too. And Jonas's play in the special place took his mind off the odd, hot, never-mentioned throb that was dominating things back at the house.

Fossilized Indian Bone at Center of Controversy

TRACI MORGAN

Arrowheads have been found at the site of the fossil bone whose discovery by Jonas Torbett, 10, was reported in the July 21 issue of the *Weekly.*

Dr. Frederick Gertsch of Texarkana Community College held a press conference to disclose the find. Gertsch investigated the site with the permission of Bryce Torbett of Groverton, who owns the land on which the bone was found.

"No question about it, this means there was human activity tied in with these remains," said Gertsch. "Anytime you find projectile points near a burial site, you assume you're looking at part of an old Indian community. And given the age of the rock the bone was embedded in, we are presented with some very intriguing questions."

Asked what those questions might be, Gertsch refused to comment. "We're hoping to get in there and do an exhaustive study," he said. "Till we get more bearing on this case, I'd better not say."

Although the Arkansas Geological Commission was originally called in to identify the bone, Gertsch said that they have delayed their investigation and that an academic institution like his, being closer to the site of the find than the Little Rock-based commission, is a more appropriate group to carry out the study. James Donovan, the Commission paleontologist working on the case, said there are "apparent contradictions" in the facts which need to be studied further.

Stuart Bledsoe, a Caddo Indian who lives in Groverton, is angered by the research. "If projectile points were found near old human bones, they were probably my ancestors," he said. "This should be treated as sacred ground." Bledsoe said he hopes that Torbett and all investigative groups would give the bone to the Caddo tribe.

Bledsoe noted that the Caddo tribe is not organized in Arkansas and that official contacts with Caddoes would have to be made with the Council based in Oklahoma.

Bryce Torbett has reportedly closed the site to access from visitors and could not be reached for comment.

Letters from our Readers

To the Editor:

As a Christian preacher of the Word I am very concerned about your coverage of the fossil found by a Groverton youth. Doesn't your reporter or her editor know that there are more ways to interpret this fossil than the heathen claim it is 70 million years old? The Bible tells us the earth was created roughly 4 thousand years ago. Even your scientist from Little Rock was boxed into a corner by this one. There is no "apparent contradiction." The human bone and the earth it was found in were created by our Lord at almost the same time, during the seven days we read about in Genesis, not during the ridiculous amount of time the evolutionists think happened.

Fortunately, thanks to our legislators, Darwin and his kind have suffered a blow, and our Arkansas schoolchildren will no longer be brainwashed by a one-sided, evil, secular humanist doctrine that contradicts the Bible. That is unless the ACLU (and we know what a fine moral bunch they are) wins its lawsuit. But must the adult public in Arkansas still be denied a balanced view by members of the media like yourself?

I hope Mr. Torbett will do the only right thing with this bone—give it a decent Christian reburial that we can all be thankful for, Indians and whites alike. Thus we may celebrate how far Arkansas has come in her battle against the evil forces that would weaken our children's minds.

Say—you could even cover the reburial and try and rectify your recent sorry journalism.

The Reverend Jarred Strait

Three

... Life
matters if or

when the your- and my-
idle vertical worthless
self unite in a peculiarly
momentary

partnership (to instigate
constructive
        Horizontal
business ...)

            e e cummings

14

IT WAS LATE AUGUST, and the summer was drawing to a close. Lately Traci and the other lifeguard, Brian Cowley, had changed their schedule; Brian now worked afternoons to accommodate his night job at the drive-in, and Traci took the shorter evening shift. She made a little less money, but recently that was offset by bigger checks from the *Weekly,* since Eddie O. had been giving her more assignments.

She liked the evening shift better anyway. Between six and seven the shriveled, insistent, unsupervised children bailed out of the pool to nibble cheeseburgers and fries at one of the umbrella-shaded redwood tables on the patio nearby. The sun became a little mollified. Its light softened and deepened into something solid and amber like a block of resin. Gradually, as they got off work, fathers and mothers would join their children in the pool; the children, made ecstatic by this company, would call in pleasant, soft, charged voices over the languid sounds of their parents' unpracticed sidestrokes. Teenagers in love would arrive for nightfall, treading water endlessly in the deep end, wrapping themselves around the pool ladder to rest. The surface of the water would gleam for a few minutes with pink and flame-colored lights borrowed from the sky over the golf course. Fireflies would start to blink, near the ground at first, and then rising higher and higher into the oak trees as the darkness settled in. The lights over the little tennis court would come on, and the whapping sound of the ball and of running feet would accompany the splashing and lapping sound of water.

This late summer period had something bittersweet about it,

an underlying pang. Traci saw it in the children. One by one, lately, they had been seized and taken into dressing-rooms to try on crisp new-smelling clothes, jeans stiff as cardboard and tight-collared dresses, bought too big so they would last a year; they rode their bikes past football and cheerleader practice, schoolyards being mowed, buses being serviced; and they wanted none of it. Everywhere they went grownups asked them when school was starting. They would get absolutely still, and answer gravely, "Coupla weeks," "Week from Monday," then "Monday, I reckon ..." Released by the grownup's nod, they would throw themselves more wildly than ever into their play.

Traci, too, was being queried at every turn, and she had a more surprising answer to give. "When you going back to school?" people would ask. "How much longer you got at home?"

"I'm not going back this year," she would say. "I'm taking the year off."

They usually backed away with scandalized faces then. The only pigeonhole they had for such an action was labelled DROPOUT. Traci didn't try to defend herself anymore. It had been hard enough with her parents. "It's no big deal," she had said. "I'm just taking time off. Lots of people do it. Look here, in the college administrative handbook it says that approximately thirty-eight percent of the student body will take time off before graduating. That's over a third."

"But what are you going to *do?*" they said.

"I'm trying to figure that out."

Their faces were stricken. How happy they had been, blithely oblivious to this ugly decision working itself out in their child. How promisingly their rosy, well-earned-but-still-serendipitous early-retirement years had started to unfold, expanding and glistening around them—houseboat, new camper, plans for a fall trip to the Smokies—until this ungrateful daughter, whom they had thought was all taken care of, stuck a pin into the bubble! Maybe they weren't thinking such thoughts, but Traci, still peevish in the choppy emotional wake of her decision, assumed they were. She had such a hard time explaining her year off to her parents that she'd quit even trying to defend it to others in the town.

Only a few people seemed to understand. She had run into Ken Wainwright, her high school biology teacher, at Wal-Mart, and he had nodded as she tried offhandedly to say she wouldn't be at college this year.

"I think that's a good idea. I understand the pre-med stuff gets to be a real rat race."

"Yeah, it does," she said gratefully. "It really does."

"And even though you're through the worst of the course work, this is the year you'd have to start your applications."

"That's right—Med-CATs, and interviews, and all that."

"Are you going to stay around here?"

Traci had nodded. "For a while. As long as my folks'll put up with me," she said, only half-joking. "Eddie O.'s going to keep me on at the paper, so I'll have a little money."

"Well, that's fine. We'll be glad to have you around."

"Thank you, Mr. Wainwright."

Maybe it was a little silly to stay around Groverton. But she didn't have a better plan, and she could live here more cheaply than anywhere she knew, especially if she got another part-time job to replace the lifeguarding, which would be over soon, and to supplement her fling at the *Weekly.* The articles about Bryce's bone and all the stink it had raised were proving to be fun, and other assignments she was given were, at worst, harmless, at best hilarious—they would make great dinner conversation when she did go back to college: "No, no kidding, so like this pickup truck carrying this huge tank of bull semen was in a wreck, and it spills all over the highway, and this was like *major* news ..."

Her social life was not great, of course; Deborah was the best woman-friend she could ask for, but there weren't many men on the scene she wanted to see. Almost all the guys Traci had gone to high school with had married, some more than once. A couple of divorced men she knew from church had asked her out, but she never had fun with them. There was always Stuart Bledsoe; she had gone out a few times with him. Conversation with him was always lively, his sense of humor was more of the cynical sort she knew from school rather than the Groverton cornpone kind, and she'd grudgingly come around to seeing his point about respect for native Americans, but in the long run his intensity put her off. Sometimes when they were alone a brisk desire for him—or at least for his jawline, his chest, lean muscled legs, the cocky punch of his butt moving under his Levi's as he walked—wafted over her, and she wanted to say, "Oh, Stuart, quit talking and let's just go to bed." The closest they got was some intermittent tangling; the current between them sputtered.

She wanted somebody different from the glib city men she met at school, with their short blow-dried hair and their subscriptions to *Esquire*. Stuart *was* different in some respects, down-to-earth and unaffected in ways Traci liked, but he would have been surprised at how ho-hum his native American sentiments were to her. Maybe no one else in Groverton could relate to his relentless, polemical hammering on the subject, but for three years on the East Coast Traci had gone to class, eaten, slept, and argued with ideologues on El Salvador, South Africa, the arms race, Hispanic rights, gay rights, women's rights, civil rights, animal rights, and finally, as part of her burnout last spring, she could care no longer about any of that. It had embarrassed her when Stuart pointed out her insensitivity to the Indian issues in that piece she did at the beginning of the summer on Bryce Torbett's hobby. How provincial, how gauche that was of her, in some East Coast sense—but she was tired of sensitivity. And in some ways, beside Stuart she felt worldly-wise, superior. Sin though she might, she had been baptized in the waters of political awareness just by *existing* in the liberal Northeast, and as smugly as a fornicating Baptist she knew she was saved by the one immersion there—no matter how far she might err from its doctrines henceforth.

Sometimes when Stuart was off on one of his native American tangents, Traci would break in and seemingly change the subject, rambling on and on about some torchlight march or demonstration or rally or hunger fast she had watched in

Cambridge. She knew perfectly well the maddening effect this had on Stuart: he listened with a peculiar light in his eyes, angry that she was ignoring his train of thought but magnetized by the picture she painted of a world where such passionate involvement was commonplace, where everybody cared about such things.

Everybody. It was that "everybody" Traci had tired of so thoroughly last spring. "Everybody" pushing and grappling so for this letter of recommendation, that fellowship—*insisting* on his or her opinion, his or her right to this or that. In late March Traci had become so irritable and lethargic she thought she might have mono. She went to Health Services for a blood test. The nurse obligingly drew blood, and then said, "I'm sending you up to the fourth floor."

"Fourth floor?" Traci had said. "Mental Health?"

"Yes. Give them this paper."

Standing in the elevator, Traci started to look over her shoulder, wondering for a moment whether anyone was observing her, noting the lighted "4" on the panel of buttons. Then she shrugged. Who cared?

The counselor was an attractive woman in skirt and boots and a wedding band, with diplomas on the wall. Pleasant as she was, she had done her share of battling and conniving and insisting, Traci would bet. And now she had won a fourth-floor view of the teeming, compressed little city, the brick buildings crowding over narrow gray streets, the bright, self-promoting spires thrusting up like hands on the first day of class.

As if from a great, foggy distance, Traci heard herself drone on about her life. After a while the woman said, "It sounds to me as if you're rethinking your options right now. Maybe you're questioning whether you really want to go to medical school. Depression is usually a sign of great change taking place within you. Also, sometimes, of anger.

"Who is it that wants you to become a doctor?" the woman continued. "Is it really Traci? I'm glad you're paying attention to your depression, because it can be a great learning experience." She had made Traci an appointment for three weeks later, which

Traci called and cancelled. She was too busy studying for a biochem test, she explained on the phone. She had hung up and stared at her unread lab notebook from which half the experiments were missing and then went out for a walk.

So naturally, instinctively, she had come home this summer. Her parents were happy to have her; she hadn't told them about her depression, didn't show them her dropped grades. No, she didn't want to work at the hospital, no, she didn't want to take the Med-CATs early just to see how she'd do. She hadn't wanted to worry her parents by seeming too changed, but she'd told them firmly, I'm *tired.* And then, I'm *fine.* And the other folks she knew in Groverton, from friends to acquaintances, were happy she'd come back too—as if her return, even for a season, vindicated them. "Seen the light, hunh?" Since she'd gone East to college there was always the idea hovering around, rarely spoken, that she had rejected everything here. "Oh, Arkansas wasn't *good* enough for you, eh?" People didn't come right out and say it, but you could tell it was on their minds. In fact she had longed for home. If only those people had been with her every minute she'd spent looking out of her square gray window at the square gray days of New England's April—they would have seen her humbled, all right. Seizing the *Groverton Weekly* from her mailbox and poring over it every week as if it had been some precious tablet, some modern Rosetta Stone, bearing encoded all the secrets to life itself.

Gradually, slowly, in the drowsy heat of the place she had once chafed to leave, she was unfolding: just simply being again, like the big, dark, velvety butterfly she had seen one day the week before, sitting on a half-formed eggplant in the garden, soaking up sunlight in its wings. Maybe that image, more than any conscious rationale, had spurred her to write last week's letters. To her senior tutor, formally: "This is to inform you that I have decided to take the academic year 1981–82 off ... You can take me out of the housing lottery ..." To her roommates, matter-of-factly: "Would you guys please get my stuff out of the squash courts when school opens? You can ship the clothes to me, C.O.D., and use anything else you want ..." And to her thesis advisor, flippantly: "Sorry, Bill, but I haven't sketched one rough outline or done one inter-library search anyway. It looks like the fruition of genius is going to have to wait a year. Hope you'll still be wanting to advise me in '82–'83. I know it's a long time off. If you get any burning inspirations on short-chain organic compounds, I'd love to hear them. Academic discourse on the same in Arkansas is in short supply."

So here she was, open to whatever happened. Maybe she'd save some money. Maybe her parents would get over their disappointment and go blissfully off to the Smokies in their camper. Maybe that Donovan guy would come dig her up like a fossil while Deborah went after Ken Wainwright, as she should've done years ago. Maybe Groverton would get so deliciously boring that twelve months hence Traci would gladly head back to college.

15

"TRACE," SAID EDDIE O., coming out of his office and rubbing his hair, with his eyes fixed on a legal pad in his hand, "I've got an idea for you."

"What's that?" said Traci. She was sitting on the edge of the layout table drinking a Sugar-Free Dr Pepper and talking to Kelly Divers, the staff photographer.

"It's another angle on all this stuff about the bone, the creation science stuff and all that."

"We just got six more letters about it," interrupted Renée, the secretary.

"You're gonna run out of room to print all of 'em, Eddie O.," said Kelly.

Eddie O. nodded. "Well, so be it. Keeps readership up, that's for sure. Look here, Traci, what I'm thinking is, you can do a story on how the Groverton schools are impacted by this. How are the origins of the universe, the origins of man, currently taught here? How will they be taught if Act 590 stands up in court or if it doesn't? It's a great back-to-school story as well as capitalizing on all this controversy."

Traci laughed. "I can tell you how it's taught. Lorene Strait tells the students God made 'em in fixed kinds, black and white, poor and rich, and there's no changing the Almighty. Then they move on to the six simple machines and that's that."

Eddie Ray stared through his crooked, black-frame glasses. "No."

"Sure! Renée—don't you remember that? She doesn't even use the textbooks for that unit."

Renée looked doubtful. "I'm not sure. I remember her telling us about the Flood. We saw some film about how Noah's bones and part of the Ark have been found somewhere over there in the Middle East."

"Brother," said Eddie O. "What grade is this?—I'm trying to figure out how long we have to straighten this out before Heather has her."

"Oh, it's okay," said Traci, gulping Dr Pepper to cover her glee, "because two years later she'll get Mr. Wainwright, and he teaches evolution.—This is a great idea, Eddie O. It'll be a fun story."

Eddie O. stared at Traci a minute, and then fixed on his notepad again, pondering, while his staff idled patiently, waiting on his next move. He was a lanky man whose parts were handsomer than the sum. In someone else the hawk nose, tall build, ice-blue eyes, and tousled hair might have combined into striking good looks, but in him they were strung together so disjointedly that the result was more Ichabod Crane than Clint Eastwood.

"Listen to this," said Renée, reading. " 'I am sick and tired of every time I open the damn newspaper I see all the damn liberals including you, Eddie O. Walters, trying to run the country in a conspiracy to weaken our children's minds. What a man does with his own private property is his own business and it shouldn't belong to the state or the government or anybody else which is the problem with this country right now and if you don't like it you can leave it.' "

"Who's that from?" said Kelly.

"They didn't sign it. I guess we can't run it."

"We can't run it anyway, because of the profanity," said Eddie O. mildly. "Well," he finally said, looking at Traci again. "I think if you call the principals first you should be able to sit in on some classes. Use your judgment. Call Bill Duggins"—the Groverton state representative—"if you want to bring in the balanced-treatment bill, I know he voted for it, or call somebody in Little Rock about the lawsuit, I don't care. Let's just see what you come up with."

"When do you want this to run?"

"Next week, if we can—while the letters are still coming in hot and heavy."

Traci sat in the teachers' lounge at Groverton Junior High, talking to Lorene Strait, and marveled that so little had changed. The school seemed just the same, down to the smells of cut grass floating in on hot breezes, green beans cooking in the cafeteria, sweat and pencil shavings; Mr. Taft walking down the hall snapping his fingers and hitting his fists together softly in front of him, then in back (there was not a child who passed through the school who couldn't imitate him); bitter Mrs. Dole poking her pale head into the door and giving a sarcastic greeting. It gave Traci a weird feeling, as if she were still thirteen years old and didn't belong in the teachers' lounge at all—this inner sanctum of empty Coke bottles and doughnut boxes, laced with smoke and mystery—as if any minute some authority was going to loom in the doorway and chase her back to Language Arts.

And Lorene herself looked not a day older than she did when Traci knew her as Miss Strait and had her for girls' gym and eighth-grade science. Even her makeup looked the same. Traci and her friends always figured she must have learned from magazines how to apply it. On her eyes she put three colors: the main color (Teal or Lilac) on most of the lid, shadow (Midnight or Smoky Ash) in the creases, and highlighting (Moondust, Golden Shimmer) up near the browbone. You could count the three areas. On each cheek, over the dewy foundation and beneath the "pearlescent" powder, she applied a rectangle of powdered brick-red blush. The rectangle was intended "to contour the face," the magazines said, creating the semblance of hollow cheeks. She also outlined her lips in a darker tone than the color she filled them in with, before adding the layer of gloss. But Lorene had not learned the art of blending all these colors and disguising shades together. Maybe the magazines had failed to stress that. The outlined patches of color on her face made her look in some lights like the subject of a child's paint-by-number set.

Otherwise she was attractive. She was petite, shaped in firm curves, with those firm, widely-planted, slightly bowed legs that are always recognizable at a glance as a gym teacher's, especially when the woman wears skirts or dresses, which Lorene did—always youthful fashions, junior size 5 or 7, in pretty pastel colors, "perfectly accessorized," as the magazines also said. She had brown hair coiffed in a puff around her small, pert head; she moved briskly—she liked to stay active, she would tell people—and she smiled and laughed with a droll, fetching, down-to-earth forthrightness.

For Lorene was a woman of conviction. And in her convictions, whether they were moral or political, intellectual or simply personal, she allowed as little blurring or shading as between the areas of makeup on her face. Lorene made up her mind quickly about things. She did not go through the times of indecision that most people did. One phrase she was never heard to say was, "I don't know."

Lorene was in her mid-thirties now; she was not long out of college when Traci had been in her class. As Traci had told Eddie O., she remembered the way Lorene taught. When her students finished the first six weeks on the scientific method and physical properties and were ready to start their unit on the solar system and the universe, Lorene had said, dramatically, "Okay, people, close your books." Which they did with dispatch in what was, in its own right, a big bang. Then she went on: "Now I need two volunteers to take up the books. Okay, Ricky, over here, Sandra, over here. Now people, that's the last you're going to see of that book for six weeks." The students gave a cheer, of course, that lapsed into groaning and sighing as she passed out a packet of freshly mimeographed worksheets instead. Talking to Ken Wainwright yesterday, Traci had asked him about those worksheets, and he shook his head. "She uses those every year. They're distributed by the Creation Science Headquarters."

"Isn't that a church group?" said Traci. "One of those fundamentalist groups?"

"To *me* it's a religious group," said Ken. "I don't know how you can postulate a creator of the universe and not have that creator be divine."

"But isn't that illegal?"

Wainwright smiled and shrugged. "We'll see. I think it is. We'll see this winter if the federal courts agree."

The students would pass the still-damp pages back over their shoulders, sniffing in deep wafts of the purple ditto ink, and thus every year they began their learning about the special creation of the universe and life.

"Special creation." Traci suspected that Lorene even liked the *sound* of it better than Big Bang, which to Lorene would sound so uncouth: a big, graceless, heaving ejaculation of matter. It probably threatened her in some way—and the idea of evolution was worse.

"Were you, yourself, ever taught the theory of evolution?" Traci asked now.

"Oh, yes. I was exposed to it at college." Exposed. Again that indelicate connotation: a flasher's open raincoat ...

"And where'd you go to college?—I know I should know."

"I went over to Elmer. I hated to leave Mother and Dad."

"Did the theory of evolution always rub you the wrong way? Did it ever strike you as plausible?"

"Oh, no. I always knew it ran counter to the Word of God. It frustrated me, because I always knew it didn't have to be the only scientific explanation for—things—you know? But I couldn't really pull all my thoughts together. It wasn't until the past few years that I ran into the literature, the teaching materials, of creation science, to show that alternative viewpoint."

"I remember that," said Traci. "You used those worksheets for my class." She refrained from saying that the "alternative" viewpoint was the only one her class had been taught, that she hadn't learned who Darwin was until she got to Mr. Wainwright's class.

"Yeah, what year was that? Seventy—"

"Lemme see. That would have been seventy-three–

seventy-four."

"Yep, I believe that was the first year I taught creation science."

"So you really feel that in good conscience you can't teach evolution?"

Lorene tapped her tongue against her teeth. "Let me think, Traci. How can I put this to you?" She was silent a minute. "Rather than a daughter of God, it makes me feel like some— some *clown*—trying to nail Jell-O to the wall: everything slipping and sliding and emerging, one thing out of another and into another—nothing clear and fixed ... I don't know what your church teaches you about God, Traci, but God is more organized than that, I'm sure. *My* God is!"

Organized, thought Traci. It's not the first attribute I'd look for in a God, if there is one. She pictured God in Heaven, with "to do" lists and cosmetic cases and drawer dividers. Well-organized.

"And the bearded communist types, like a certain Charles Darwin"—Lorene was warming to her subject—"they don't even have a God, all they have is their apes, their Jell-O. How can the cracked theory of somebody like that—for even the evolution scientists call it just that, a 'theory,' and Traci, you know what a theory is, I taught you that, you were a good student: a theory is something *unproven.* How can a godless theory suddenly take over the classrooms of America? I don't know, but it's not going to take over mine. Education has gone downhill since I first set foot in the classroom, but I haven't gone downhill with it. Not that far."

So the interview went on, straying so far afield that Traci had long since quit taking notes. Or maybe it wasn't far afield, she thought later; when you were talking about these questions, of beginnings and becomings, was anything far afield?

It was this integration that had messed things up, Lorene went on. Not that all the blacks were bad—she had some who did all right, you'd hear her admit it, say, "Yes, she's a real good little black student." Lorene was fair. Lorene was color-blind. She knew how to talk to them. In her gym classes she would sometimes say, "Okay, all you little chocolate girls go over there and all you vanilla girls come over here," and the girls would giggle. This year there was one black girl named Vernilla and somebody always made a joke about her. Yes, Lorene knew how to communicate with them, for that was the name of the game: communication.

But Lorene would also tell you one thing: there was some behavior that would make her label you a nigger, black *or* white, it had nothing to do with your skin color; and that was why the word nigger was still in her vocabulary. And it just so happened that the worst of this behavior, the worst sass and rudeness and disrespect and truancy and obscenity, came from black students. What did you expect? It was what they got at home. "Face it," Lorene would say in the relative privacy of the teachers' lounge, when there were no black teachers in there, *"they* do not start from the same moral basis *we* do." Yet they were always wanting special privileges. Look at Lorene's own people, just two generations back—white country people with scarcely a dollar in the bank, certainly not in the days of the Depression; self-sufficient, made their own soap, had a big garden and a little livestock. But proud? Lord. And did they consider themselves poor? Never. Never would have occurred to them. And when the time came to pull themselves up, up they did. Not with all this lollygagging and making excuses like the blacks did. So what if the blacks had been slaves? How long did the whites have to keep making up to them for it? Why didn't they just snap to it and catch up? Instead they went on welfare. Lorene knew that the welfare system was grossly abused. Drive around in Little Rock or Pine Bluff and you could see the welfare mothers cruising in their Lincolns and Cadillacs. How else would you explain blacks being able to have those things?

"Well," she finally said, "I've been talking a blue streak. I'm about to wear you out, I can see. But you tell Eddie O., Traci, that I am real glad he's sending you to find out all the points of view. I really respect that. I think that's what a newspaper is all about. I don't know if I've been able to help you at all—I've probably gotten way off the subject—but it's good to talk to someone who knows the schools from the inside. Bird's-eye view, right? And who's really listening. You'll have to come by the house sometime and have some tea. I want to hear all about what's going on with you."

16

ONE REASON TRACI WAS enthusiastic about her latest assignment was that it gave her an excuse to call James Donovan again. As soon as she got back to the *Weekly* office after interviewing Lorene, she dialed the Geological Commission.

She didn't know exactly what it was about Donovan that appealed to her. He seemed so—peaceful, so obliging. And, refreshingly, a little absent-minded. But friendly to her, so animated whenever she steered around to the subject at hand that she believed he was attracted to her as well. He was probably glad to meet someone like her. There were few women he could talk to about these matters. When Traci's articles came out, Deborah had said something about having known James in college, but when Traci pressed her about him she waved her hand in evasion. "Ah—it was during that time when I was all screwed up."

"Meaning you were so worked up about Bryce you didn't even notice James. I'm surprised you even remember his name."

"Ah," said Deborah disgustedly, waving the subject away. Traci hadn't been able to get anything more out of her.

So on the phone today she'd apologized for bothering him yet again but said she'd like to discuss Act 590 and how it would affect science education in the state. "Or," she hinted, "are you coming back to Groverton any time soon? I could interview you in person here, if you'd prefer." This would give him the entrée he needed to see her again.

"Oh," he said, "gee. I don't know whether there's any point to my coming back down there. You think I could change this

Torbett guy's mind and get some access to the bone again? Do you know this guy?"

"Um, I know him a little bit," said Traci. "He's sort of a wild card. But sure—it's worth a try, isn't it?"

"I guess what I'm saying is, I don't have any *plans* to come down to Groverton. Maybe we'd just better talk on the phone now. If this is a good time for you."

"Sure, it's a good time for me," said Traci. "I'm the one who called you, remember?"

"Oh, right, right." Adorably bumbling.

James made such a contrast—and a favorable one—to Stuart. But as these things went, of course it was Stuart who pursued her. His latest campaign had been to take her skiing. The last time they had planned to go, a huge thunderstorm had descended before they even got to the lake. They had gone to Stuart's little rent house and sat on the porch drinking sangria and listening to Joe Ely and watching it rain till they both grew melancholy, but not in a way that turned them toward each other: that day too, under the influence of the wine and the potentially cozy rain, Traci was nursing a wistfulness for the company of some sweet, uncynical man, while Stuart brooded over she-knew-not-what, probably the thousand-year decline of his people.

Today the weather was in their favor, and as they turned off the highway onto a pine-shaded road that led to the boat ramp, Traci tried to pay kind attention to Stuart, without dwelling on all the things he was not.

"It's a great example of how we've been dumped on," Stuart was saying. "Where this lake is now was sacred ground of the Caddoes. My ancestors are *buried* under here. But because the people weren't organized when the lake was proposed, they did nothing. I don't even know if anyone protested. So, whoosh, here comes the water, there goes a major center of a civilization—the Washington, D.C., of the Caddoes at one time, I guess."

"Mmm," said Traci, feeling a vague guilt.

"It's like this bone the Torbett boy found—"

"Now Stuart," said Traci firmly, "you can't rant to me about that bone. I quoted you in the article. I gave you whatever forum you have on that subject."

"I know that, I'm not ranting. Brother. But it's just such a good example of what I'm talking about." He kept talking as he backed down the boat ramp, craning his neck, glancing in the rearview mirror, easing them backward and down. Then he threw the car into park. "Look—who's in a tug-of-war about it? The Anglo landowner and the state government. Gimme gimme. Maybe it should belong to *neither* of them. Do they think of that?"

"No," said Traci wearily, "of course not." But today Stuart did not really pursue his indictments anyway. He pushed the emergency brake and started whistling as he went behind the car to the trailer to unhook the boat.

Traci got out and went around. He gave her a knot to undo while he fiddled with some chains and wires. They scooted the boat off the trailer and Traci took the skis, life jackets, towels, and rope Stuart passed to her. While he went to park she held the boat, standing ankle-deep in water on the bumpy concrete incline, enjoying the warmth of the water lapping over her sneakers, the slight tug of the boat against the rope, the sun on her arms. She yawned. It wasn't that she was bored, by any means. But the surroundings made her feel lazy ... The lake was a deep greenish-brown, rimmed all the way around by low clay banks, ranging in color from bright orange to gray, interrupted here and there by wads of tangled gray roots and stumps. Farther back were wooded hills, their green turning darker and more muted in the middle distance, a soft blue smear at the horizon. Out on the lake Traci saw just one sail and two boxy houseboats. A couple of fishermen floated in a small army-green boat in the cove adjoining the boat ramp. Stuart rejoined her and followed her gaze. "After Labor Day the crowd really drops off out here," he said.

"You can see some trees already turning. See? Every once in a while there's a red one, a yellow. Unless," she added, "they just have some disease or something."

"No, it really is getting to be that time. The water's still warm, but can't you tell a difference in the air? It's a great day."

"A lot better than the last time we tried to come skiing," said Traci.

"That's for sure."

He held her elbow briefly while she climbed into the boat. Then he pushed off and scrambled in himself and started the motor. Soon they were heading toward the middle of the lake, where Stuart stopped and killed the engine. "Why don't I ski you first," he said.

"Great."

While he attached the lime-green ski rope Traci put on the life jacket. It and the skis were also lime green, with yellow accents. "Shoe size?"

"Seven."

"Jump on in. I'll throw this to you. You gonna try to slalom?"

"I don't know. Go ahead and give me both skis, and if I feel real confident I'll drop one."

The lake barely closed over her head—brown, tepid, with its smell of the underside of piers, quilted with algae—and then Traci popped back up to the surface, her ski jacket rising up to her ears. She started to swim awkwardly toward the rope, but Stuart said, "Don't worry, I'll bring it to you." He added, "Now here you go. Look out." The ski smacked the water and glided right to her. Waiting for the second one she looked up at him—his neatly muscled figure articulated against the blue sky, clad only in a pair of blue shorts and a waterproof watch; the tendons in his forearms working while he readjusted the plastic shoe on the ski. He suddenly raised his head and looked at her and smiled. She smiled back. A feeling of warmth washed over her—and, curiously, of thirst, and pleasure.

"Here it comes," he said, lobbing the second ski her way, so that it spanked the water briskly and slid toward her too.

"Check the fit. I wasn't sure about it."

"I think it's all right."

"Okay. Then just nod real big when you're ready. And when you want to quit, give me a hand signal, or else just drop." Stuart went toward the front of the boat.

She was crouched in the water with the rope between her

skis, watching how fast it spun by at the surface of the water once it tautened, though the boat seemed to be only idling. And now she caught the handle; there was the jerk of tension. She adjusted herself all over—feet in their loose plastic pouches, skis close and parallel, arms ready to extend, hair tossed back—and gave a big nod.

With the roar of the boat's acceleration, struggling up into noise and gasoline fumes and spray, she realized she had forgotten how big that force was; she had forgotten how to balance against it, use it and not be dragged under. She fought to rise but felt herself losing, didn't let go until it was all but over, and fell forward, the top of the water hard as dirt. She brought her head up instantly, feeling sheepish, and started flailing toward the right ski, which had come off in her fall. "You almost had it," called Stuart, circling back toward her. Waves from the boat had reached her by now, and she bobbed in the deep troughs.

"Yeah," she answered, "I'd just forgotten what it feels like."

"Here comes the handle." It went zipping by, she almost missed it.

"Take your time," said Stuart. "How's the water?"

"Warm. Feels like bathwater." She nodded. "Okay!" There it was again, the acceleration—massive, feeling solid as rock. "Let the boat pull you up, let the boat pull you up," she remembered her aunt saying. And this time Traci's thighs caught on, her arms straightened gradually as they used to. She was up. And it was easy. Her ski jacket finally settled around her waist, the wind pushed her hair behind her, out of her face. She smiled. She loved this. She remembered why she loved this. Oh—Stuart was turning, and there came the right wake. And she was over. No sweat. She pulled out far to the side, leaning, watching her skis cutting and hissing over the smooth water—much better than the choppy surface inside the wake. She let herself drift back in, over the two wakes this time—she had a little trouble with the left one; did it one leg at a time, clumsily—and back out in an arc to the left, grinning. She was wonderful, she was invincible. The world was speed and cleanliness and color. Suddenly she adored Stuart; here behind the boat, safely across water from him, zipping along in her magical stance, it was all a sort of lust, the speed and the tension and the dazzling light, and she could admit her infatuation with him, with James Donovan, with any y-chromosome-bearer, with life itself. She laughed, her teeth in the wind. And smashed down hard, backward, on water that at the speed she was going felt like concrete, like ice.

When she came back up she heard the lower whine of the engine circling slowly. "You all right?" Stuart called.

"Yeah." She tugged at her bathing suit underwater. The crotch had been pushed so hard by the force of her fall it threatened to cut her in two.

"You hit pretty hard."

"Yeah." She heard the engine sputtering off.

"You were doing great there for a while," said Stuart.

"I love it. It's so much fun."

"What happened?"

"I don't know."

"You ready to go again?"

"I think I'll let you take a turn."

Stuart took the skis back into the boat and then extended his hands toward Traci. "I'm sorry, we don't have a ladder." But he held his forearms rigid enough that she could pull up on them— brown, hard, with big knobs at the wrists—and clamber in. There was nothing suggestive in his touch. It was a practical measure of assistance.

She gave him the ski jacket and they went over the controls of the boat. "It's really pretty easy," he finished. "I don't think you'll have any trouble."

"We're gonna have to turn pretty sharp as soon as you get up. Is that okay?"

"Yeah. Also you'll have to accelerate a little more than you think for me, to get me up." And he was over the side.

Traci waited till she saw his head nod vigorously behind the bright tip of the ski, then eased the throttle up. She glanced back. He was partway up, leaning back into the spray, cutting across the wake already. She looked forward again, to make her turn toward the middle of the lake. No sweat. They were cutting a wide swath across an open expanse of water. She looked back again: he was jerking his thumb up. She pushed the throttle wide open this time and he gave her a big grin and a nod, and zipped across the wakes again, far out to the side of the boat, his thigh muscles standing out, the wind blowing his short hair into a ruff. Traci looked forward again: all clear. The sun was off to her right, beginning its change from a blaze of yellow to a fiery thumbprint—still nothing you could look at directly; instead you had to focus on the sky around it, just turning pale pink. On the opposite side of the lake the shore was bathed in a deep golden light. She could see piers and boathouses and long flights of steps ascending the hillsides, up to camphouses mostly hidden by trees, revealed by the glint of the sun in their big windows. She looked back at Stuart, poised on the ruffled surface of the water, balanced on the balmy air—skiing over the bones of his ancestors, a hundred tons of water below. She began a wide figure eight to take them toward the middle again. Around the arc, toward the stumpy end of the lake, sweeping again toward the moment when she had to blink out the glare of the reddening sun, sweeping back toward the softening outlines of the east shore—she glanced over and over at the man on the other end of this see-saw of speed. The roar, the spray, the coves she veered from, the open expanse she zoomed across, it all repeated; Stuart's hypnotic glides from side to side, the blink of the sun, the turn of her head, Stuart against the red ball of the sun, the dropping sun, the tilt of the turning boat, the silhouette of Stuart's spray, over and over. With a start Traci realized she had no idea how long he had been skiing. She glanced back over her shoulder again and made the sign her uncle used to make, querying whether the skiier wanted to stop—a spiraling motion with her hand. Immediately Stuart dropped the rope and she decelerated. When she looked back he had glided several yards unaided and was sinking neatly into the lake, with the spray from his ski subsiding behind. Traci circled and came slowly back to him and cut the motor. The boat bounced hard on its own intersecting waves. She peered over the side at Stuart.

"Was anything wrong?" he said.

"No! I was just trying to ask if you were ready to stop. I thought maybe I had missed your signal."

"I was getting a little tired."

"I had no idea how long you'd been skiing. I lost all track of time. You're a *beautiful* skier. You looked like you could go on forever."

"Oh, well, let's not go overboard." But he grinned. "Are you gonna go again?"

"You don't think it's too dark?"

"Nah. There's still some light hanging around. You'll be all right."

This time she got up right away. It seemed different. She was not a knife-blade anymore, slicing into yellow-white air, inserting herself into a perfect balance of tensions; this time she was hardly aware of tension. For one thing she was chilled. The water she rose out of was warmer than the air by now, and the wind cooled her off. Despite the roar of the boat's engine she had a sensation of silence. Rather than sensing Stuart nearby she felt alone. The lake had grown dark and glassy-smooth. But where motion stirred it up, the waves were burnished hot-pink. She felt like an explorer, darting into new, fire-colored realms, and pulling back again. Beneath the sun, now one-third sunk, now half, a long flame of orange lingered across the water, like the sensation of touch lingering where a finger has brushed across skin. She suddenly dropped the rope.

It took longer than usual for Stuart to come back around. He must not have been watching her. And this time he didn't say anything as he took her skis and helped her back in the boat. She found her towel, slightly damp from being wadded on the floor so it wouldn't blow away, and pulled it around her shoulders like a cape, perching on the vinyl seat and shivering a little. Stuart had cut the motor off and was bringing the ski rope in. He coiled it over one arm. The boat slapped heavily against its own waves. Traci could see how far out their waves extended around them, getting smaller and smaller till they were only ripples, still looking molten at every crest. Nothing stirred on the lake but them and what they had set in motion, for no other boat was in sight, and the water was still motionless with the quiet that had overtaken it at sundown. Overhead the sky was a soft gray-blue. Some small birds were wheeling around in it, dipping down to the water and zooming back up again.

"Are you cold?" said Stuart, turning around.

"A little." Their voices sounded unnaturally loud. He started walking back to the driver's seat and Traci stood up, thinking she was moving to balance out their weight, but they looked at each other by accident. The instant Stuart touched her Traci's arms flew up and gripped him. The towel slid off her shoulders. He was warm, his skin was so smooth and warm, and through either side of his chest she felt his heart thudding. His kiss was light, unhurried, probing; she followed his lead in it. She sagged in a sense of relief so great it surprised her. She hadn't realized what tension there was before. She slipped her hands around his ribcage, down across his warm, flat belly, and felt him breathing faster now—felt each little push of his belly through her palms, and left her hands where they were, innocent, as snugly tucked in the waistband of his shorts as if they were in her own jeans pockets. He withdrew his tongue and closed his lips; she still felt him breathing hard. He rested his cheek against her head. Something scratched the back of her legs and she heard a thud and realized that all this time he'd still been holding the coiled rope; he'd just dropped it.

Now he was leaning back from her a little, saying oh. He eased her to the floor of the boat. He reached toward the steering wheel and touched some switch. "Lights," he explained, drawing close to her again, for the first time smiling, with humor in his eyes that she mirrored when she grinned, picturing their small craft bobbing in the dusk.

They lay like the dead on the bottom of the boat until mosquitoes finally penetrated their consciousness. Then the corpses rose up, slapping, plucking up their clothes and towels and covering themselves in a hasty, twitching dance.

"Come sit by me, behind the windshield," said Stuart. "So the bugs don't smash against your face."

Traci obeyed silently. They shared the seat behind the steering wheel, and Stuart slipped a warm hand inside her thigh and drove one-handed, slowly, peering into the darkness behind the boat's feeble lights.

"It's a good thing you know this lake well," said Traci.

"I'm looking for the reflectors by the boat ramp," he said, almost absently. "I'm sure there are some."

"That's them." Traci pointed.

"Oh, right." He veered slightly, toward the red chips of light Traci had spotted.

They landed, and Stuart disappeared into the darkness to get the car and trailer. They hitched up the boat in silence, using light from inside the car, deflected back by the open doors. The woods around them were rocking with the noise of insects and tree frogs, sound so dense it seemed palpable, like skyscrapers around them. When they finally piled into the car to leave, Traci suddenly felt how tired she was, a wet-sneakered, stringy-haired, sunburned, damp tiredness. She slid into the middle and leaned on Stuart's shoulder. "I don't think we need the air conditioner," she heard him say.

"No."

Her dozing was bumpy for a few minutes, as Stuart kept glancing into the rearview and sideview mirrors to check the trailer. Then they pulled onto the highway and he was able to relax his right arm enough to be her pillow.

She dozed lightly for some time, whether two or twenty minutes she wasn't sure, and then felt him lightly hitting her leg. "Hey. Traci."

"What?"

"Wake up a minute. I'm going to think of all kinds of things to talk to you about and you might not be around. Sit up. Are you going back to your parents'?"

She struggled upright, squinting and tousled like a child. Then she laughed. "Well, I don't know," she said. "You're driving."

Now he was annoyed. His eyebrows drew together briefly.

"C'mon."

"Well, where *else* would I go, Stuart?"

"You could come to my place." He turned his head and glanced at her. "What are you doing?"

She was shifting around, twisting, and feeling the car seat behind her with both hands. "Aren't there any safety belts in the middle?"

With instinctive manners he started helping her, jamming his right hand into the gritty crack where the upholstery divided. Then he pulled it out and caught her hand and said, "Traci."

"What?"

"Cut it out. I asked you a question."

"Well, I'll have to scoot over, and wear this one," she said, edging into the passenger side and clicking the old lap belt together with a little air of triumph.

"I think I have my answer," he said darkly.

They rode in silence for a while before Traci said, "What do you think my answer is?"

"I'll run you back to your folks' place."

Several more miles of the dark road passed by, several rising and dropping series of curves, and then Traci spoke, surprising herself: "It's my place too." Crazy—she had no idea what she meant by that.

He nodded. "Fine. I'll take you back there."

After several more minutes Traci said, "I'm a little confused." Again, once she had spoken she realized how belligerent her tone was. The statement stood in the darkness between them, with a curl, a sneering tail, on the end of it.

Stuart nodded.

A long time passed. Finally they were passing the church that marked the edge of Groverton, and they bumped over the railroad tracks and came to a stop under the red light at the main intersection in town.

"I mean, I don't know what you think of what happened," said Traci, "but this is not like me. I don't believe in casual sex."

Behind the steering wheel Stuart seemed to grow taller. He turned his head and looked at her. "I don't do *anything* casually," he said.

Traci kept a meek and startled silence while he headed out the road that led to the fancy new subdivision where the Morgans now lived. At their house he started to get out and she said, "Oh, good grief, don't walk me to the door."

"Sorry."

"Um—thanks," she said, and heard a little sarcastic explosion of a laugh in return.

"You're quite welcome."

"Goodnight."

"Goodnight, Traci." When she took her eyes away from his she just shut the car door, closing him in darkness. But she heard his door opening, and he stood up, formal-looking, on the other side of the car—as if he couldn't bear to be seated while a woman rose. "Let me hear from you," he said.

She hurried up the steps and slipped inside.

17

WHEN JONAS WALKED IN THE DOOR he saw his father taking three big potatoes from the découpaged wooden potato bin one of his girlfriends had given him, and carrying them to the sink.

"Where's Celie?" Jonas said.

"Now how'd you know Celie isn't here?"

"You always cook baked potatoes when she's gone."

"Well, she wanted off."

Daddy sounded grumpy. But no matter how much time off Celie demanded, Jonas knew his father would never fire her. She had worked for his grandparents years before, and Mama and Celie had loved each other, and Jonas sometimes heard people say, "That Celie is a treasure you know she practically raised those boys after Marianne died," though he didn't think it was true.

"How was school," said Daddy.

"Fine."

"I want that dog out of here while we eat. And you better wash your hands after you fool with him."

"Yes sir."

It was amazing, too, what Celie could get away with telling Daddy. The night before, Jonas had been sneaking up on her from the den, planning to say *boo* and then while she was laughing and grabbing her heart and fussing at him to wheedle for another Fudgsicle, when he was stopped in mid-sneak just inside the kitchen door by a conversation she started with Daddy. "You looks tired lately," she had said. "Kindly peaked." She was letting water out of the sink and wringing her dishrag hard while her eyes looked out the window with an innocent, mild expression. Daddy was at the table writing her check.

"Well, I am a white man, Celie," Daddy had pointed out. "I'm bound to look peaked compared to your people." *Rip* went the check coming out of the checkbook.

She had clucked her tongue. "Gonna wear yo'self out," she said, turning, still not meeting his eyes, but wiping the countertop with a vengeance. "Gonna wear yo'self out, one way or the other."

"I don't know what you mean," Daddy had said.

"People are talking, Mr. Torbett. That's all I know. What I hears."

"Well, I hope you set them straight when you 'hears' whatever it is," was all he had said, lightly.

She was re-wiping the stovetop now. Her face was set, downcast, her jowls and lips and the flesh on her upper arm quivering from the effort of her scouring. "Sure hope them boys don't hear it. That's all I pray when I lay down at night."

"I hope not too," said Daddy. "I always hope they don't hear ugly talk." Then he strode toward the den, to close the conversation.

"Boo," said Jonas weakly, on all fours on the threshold.

"Son? What the hell're you doing?"

"Um, coming to ask for a Fudgsicle."

"Well, get up on your feet like a man and ask for it. I'm tired of all this sidling around, feel like I'm living with J. Edgar Hoover."

Why does this keep happening to me? thought Jonas. Used to, when he set out deliberately to spy on grownups, just as a game, nothing of interest ever happened. Now every time he turned around he was running into something he didn't especially want to see or hear. Sometimes he really did just want a Fudgsicle, plain and simple.

At noon today he and Clint had seen Miss Strait on the news. She had been gone several days to some teachers' workshop at Waylon College, but here she was suddenly in their den, wearing sunglasses and a lime-green T-shirt, looking barely older than a teenager, holding a big poster that said, GIVE GOD EQUAL TIME IN

THE CLASSROOM!

"That's Miss Strait," said Clint. "Hey, turn it up."

"Daddy!" Jonas hollered. "Miss Strait's on TV!"

"—themselves the Christian Teachers Association, were demonstrating in favor of the Creation Science Act and in opposition to the suit pending against it: that suit will come to trial later this fall in Little Rock. Meanwhile, Marcia has a little action for us on the weather scene—"

Daddy rushed in trying not to look like he was rushing, but all he saw was the announcer, which didn't improve his mood any.

Now, as he stood at the sink poking holes in the potatoes, he still seemed preoccupied. The door slammed, and Clint came in, in his muddy football pants and ripped net practice jersey, his hair matted to his skull. "Where's Celie?" he said.

"I don't know," said Bryce. "At any rate, she's not here. You got any greetings for us, other than asking for the maid?" He put the potatoes in the oven, took a package of fish sticks out of the freezer, and started to read the directions.

"Oh, *hi,* Dad. Jonas."

"Hey, son. What happened at school today."

"Nothing."

"We're fixing to eat in a little while, so why don't you close that door before you let all the cold out? How was practice?"

"I don't like fish sticks. Could I just have cereal?"

"Yeah, eat the Froot Loops," said Jonas. "There's a invisible ink pen I'm trying to get with proof of purchase."

"If I finish the box, it's mine," said Clint.

Daddy shrugged. "Suits me. You're not gonna gain weight that way, but it's up to you."

"I thought we were having pot roast tonight."

"If Celie was here we probably would be having pot roast. But she's not, and we're not. You could at least wait for your brother and me, no matter what you eat. How was practice?"

"This is just my first bowl. I'll have another when y'all eat."

"You starting Thursday night?"

"Probably not."

"Gee, when are they gonna let you play?" said Jonas. "I went to these games all last fall and you're always on the bench." Clint shot him the bird behind their father's back. "It's because you're too skinny," Jonas went on. "That's what my friends say. Hey, I hear somebody driving up. We expecting anybody?"

"No," said Daddy, going to the window over the sink and pulling the curtain aside.

"Texas plates," said Clint. "I saw 'em poking along the highway like they didn't know where they was going. I passed 'em on my bike."

It was not just one car but two that pulled up behind his truck—a gray Mercedes and a dark red Lincoln. "Hnh," said Daddy, curiously, putting down the fish sticks and starting for the carport door. But the visitors, three men in suits, were walking in front of the house toward the little-used front entrance, and Jonas beat him to that door, just as the doorbell rang. Daddy walked to the opening door behind Jonas, wiping freezer frost onto his pants.

"Hello there!" said the gentleman in front. He had neatly trimmed silver hair and a florid face, and was wearing a navy suit with thin stripes in it, a white shirt, and a maroon tie with a silver tie tack. On his lapel was a teeny gold cross.

"Evening," said Daddy, cheerfully but slowly, belying his caution. "What can I do for y'all?"

"Are you Mr. Bryce Torbett?"

"That I am."

"We'd like to talk to you, Mr. Torbett, if you've got a minute."

"Well," said Daddy, "sure. Come on in." He led them to the real living room, the one they never used. Clint seemed to disappear. Jonas plopped right down on the armchair next to the couch, pointedly conspicuous so as not to offend anyone by seeming like J. Edgar Hoover; but Daddy cut his eyes at him anyway and motioned him toward a straight chair against the wall. The silver-haired man took the seat Jonas vacated and the shorter, chunkier man, with brown hair brushed back and up from his forehead and temples, sat on the end of the brocaded couch. The third man was thin, with brown, concerned-looking eyes behind tortoise-shell glasses, sparse auburn hair combed carefully over a bald spot, and a wrinkled high forehead. He sat in the nubby mauve armchair flanking Daddy's. When everyone got settled Silver Hair said, "I understand, Mr. Torbett, that you have unearthed an interesting—uh—fossil specimen on your land here."

"Apparently so," said Daddy. He was lounging in a chair by the fake fireplace, with his khaki-clad legs extended far out in front of him, crossed, his big work boots looking incongruous with the other men's dark patent-leather slip-ons. Despite his easy posture his body was very still. "That's what they tell me."

"We understand that the state scientists think it's a human fossil, with arrowheads all around it, and are perplexed because with their understanding of the geologic time line they cannot account for its being found here, in this particular soil, at this level of deposition, and so on.—Even when the Lord makes it easy to see, secular humanism tries to keep the blindfold on!"

"Well," said Daddy, "they haven't clued me in, completely, on what-all they think, or exactly what this confusion of theirs is."

"Is that why you blocked them off from going to see the bone?"

Bryce was silent a moment and then said, "Gentlemen, may I ask what it is you've come to see me for?"

This time Fat Face cleared his throat. "We're from the Creation Science Headquarters in Rourke, Texas," he said. He took a card out of the inside vest pocket of his jacket and handed it to Bryce. As if on cue the other two men produced cards and turned them over, too, each one murmuring his name as he reached across and put his card in Bryce's hand. Daddy looked up at them questioningly till they took their seats again.

"We are here to make an offer on your fossil bone, Mr. Torbett," said Fat Face. "It would be of great value to us in our program of study. And we know a fine Christian man like you would be glad to see it being used to support, rather than mock, the Word of the Lord."

Daddy was silent. He seemed to be studying the cards in his hands. Then he put them on the table and Jonas peered at them but didn't pick them up. *Dr. Alvin O'Malley, Ph.D.,* the top one said, with a little design with a cross in the middle beside the name, *Executive Director, Creation Science Headquarters, Rourke, Texas,* and a phone number. "How'd you hear about this?" his father said suspiciously. Something *-bert Heiskell, Ph.D.,* was all he could see of the second, and he couldn't see the one on the bottom at all.

"Through a church friend of yours, your pastor's daughter. Miss Strait. She attended a seminar we gave a couple of days ago at Waylon College and was most receptive to us. And she did us the kindness of telling us your, uh, exciting news."

"What are you offering?" said Daddy.

Now it was Silver Hair who cleared his throat. "Let us just take a few minutes of your time, Mr. Torbett, to describe exactly how your specimen would fit into our exhibits. We would use it to show that God did in fact create the world in a short amount of time, four thousand and four years ago, that human life coexisted with the age of reptiles and oceangoing creatures, that the reason rare fossils like yours confound the agnostic scientists is that they give a true, accurate account of Creation, of the way things were when our world was real young, before Noah's Flood. Picture this: in our main exhibit hall"—he gestured toward the balding man, who held out a ring binder, opened it on the coffee table, and slowly started turning the stiff glossy pages that had photographs of the Creation Science Headquarters—"have you ever been to our headquarters?" said the man suddenly.

"No," said Daddy, looking up with his most disarming smile, "don't believe so."

"Well, next time you're *in* the Dallas–Fort Worth area, you might make it a point to stop by." He accented funny words when he said this, as if he were rattling it off by heart. "You'll see our excellent facilities, outdoor amphitheater, Living Garden, interdenominational chapel, auditorium that seats sixteen hundred, and, *of* course, our museum, which eight thousand people, mainly school and church *groups,* tour every year. Picture, *in* our main exhibit hall, a display of your bone"—now his voice slowed—"with your name in a permanent plaque beside it, and the bone explained and put into context by our professionally written Words of Illumination. Your name could go down into posterity, Mr. Torbett; *into* posterity."

"How much are you offering me?"

"Aha, a true businessman in the best tradition of business, wants to know the bottom line," laughed Silver Hair. But he was already relaxing back into the couch, and apparently it was Baldy's turn to take over.

"Mr. Torbett, we're in a position at the present time to offer you two thousand dollars."

Daddy laughed.

No one responded.

"I'm sorry, gentlemen, but that's not acceptable. I could get more for it than that on the artifacts market tomorrow."

Fat Face's eyes had narrowed. "We're aware that this bone is not in particularly good condition. It's going to require a great deal of time-intensive labor for it to be in any shape for public viewing. Any prospective buyer will have to take that into account."

"Plus," said Daddy, "I've got the State of Arkansas as a prospect."

The Texans laughed harshly. Baldy said, "I'm afraid the State of Arkansas could barely afford the stamp to *mail* you a bid."

"Plus," said Daddy, "I'm going to unearth the rest of this guy. I'll have more than just a femur to sell. I'll have his skull and all his bones and all the stuff he was buried with. And if it was a multiple grave, a mass grave, I'll have all those folks and all their artifacts. Gentlemen, in short, I have no interest in selling my find to Texas, to the Creation Science Headquarters, whether the Lord has a hand in it or not. Thank you for your trouble. Now do you need anything before you go?"

"I can't believe you told them that!" flashed Miss Strait after Daddy told her this whole story. Jonas and Clint were in the TV room and couldn't help overhearing, but they had also turned down the volume on "The Dukes of Hazzard" so they wouldn't have to strain.

"Why not?"

"After all the trouble I went to! I really went out on a limb for you, and now you made me look like a fool!"

"You don't look like a fool, Lorene—I just rejected the offer they made me. A sensible rejection of a not too sensible offer, that's all. You didn't have anything to do with it."

"I'm the one who told them it'd be worth their while to stay in Arkansas two extra days, to make all these phone calls back to Rourke—"

"Honey, I'm sure they can afford it."

Clint and Jonas exchanged glances at the "honey." Clint made gagging gestures. Clint didn't like Miss Strait either. He made up songs about her that he and Jonas sang privately: "Lorene, Lorene, your skin looks like Visqueen" and "Lorene, Lorene, go screw a Marine" and "Lorene, Lorene, she don't drink milk, she drinks gasoline."

"Bryce Torbett, will you quit trying to get me off the *track!* You have made a stupid decision and you're now trying to blame it all on me, is what's going on here. I can read the writing on the wall."

Daddy's laugh sounded incredulous. "I made a smart decision, and you're mad about it."

"You'll be sorry. I don't know who else you think is going to offer you two thousand dollars for that ratty old bone anyway."

"Vaughan Sandifer, for one."

"Oh, has he made you an offer yet? Is the check in the bank?" said Miss Strait archly.

"No, I'm waiting. I'm waiting till I can excavate the rest of the bones in this skeleton, and the other artifacts that might be around it. Who knows? This might be the corner of a mass grave. Two thousand dollars is just not that much money. It's chicken-scratch compared to what I might make off this thing. Those guys know that.

"I'm studying on it now, Lorene; as soon as I can figure out how to get in there and dynamite, or bulldoze, or something, to uncover the rest of it without hurting what's there, I'ma do it. I may let Vaughan in on it so he can help me with the whole thing, or I may not. Like I said, I'm studying on it. See—no, calm *down*—see, to me, I don't really care about the religious implications. You say it's someone who died in the Flood. Fine. I don't dispute that. But to me it's more important that it's a *Caddo* who died. I really don't care too much whether he died during the Flood or not."

"I can't believe what a selfish, greedy person you are, sitting on something that would help the Lord so much, and turning it to your own ends!"

"If the Lord can create the whole universe, He shouldn't need that much help from me in this one instance, should He?"

"I knew you didn't go to church, Bryce Torbett, but I have thought all this time that you were at least religious." And Miss Strait slammed the door, so she couldn't have heard Daddy saying, "Aw, can't you take a joke?" Then the boys heard her car start and heard her roar down the driveway.

"Wow, she peeled out," said Clint. "Peel out, Lorene."

"Yeah," said Jonas. "Peel out, Lorene, with the voice like a sirene." He actually got Clint to giggle over that one, while they watched their father walk despondently across the back yard to his workshop. There were times he almost liked his brother.

Oh Lord, he prayed that night, forgive me for spying. Lord, I don't mean to spy like J. Edgar Hoover. I'm not even trying to find out all these things. Please save me soon, Lord, so I don't have to go to Hell for spying when I don't even mean to.

He kept wondering when it would happen to him. He felt very uncomfortable these days and Clint said that was a good sign. Clint had been saved two summers ago at a revival. Jonas could still picture his flushed, tear-stained face as he went down to the altar with several other kids at the end of the service—the only time he remembered seeing Clint cry. And just this month it had happened to Jonas's best friend, Gary Shaffer. Jesus came in and sat down on Gary's bed and talked to him before Gary went to sleep and the next Sunday Gary was baptized and now no matter what Gary did, whether he meant to or not, he would not go to Hell. Jonas slept toward the middle of his bed and kept Ace on the side nearest the wall, so Jesus would have plenty of room to sit down if he wanted to. It was not a pleasant prospect, having your Lord and Savior perched on the edge of your mattress. Even Gary got a little vague and subdued when the subject of being saved came up. But pleasant or not, the way things had been going lately, with each day that passed Jonas needed it a little bit more.

A couple of nights later, just as Jonas was falling asleep, Ace suddenly stood up on the bed. Jonas opened his eyes and saw him silhouetted in the faint moonlight, the hair over his shoulder blades starting to rise in a ruff like a lion's. He stared at Jonas's window, starting to growl, and then a bark squeezed out of him. Oh, God, thought Jonas in panic, it's Jesus. He felt a sudden urge to move his bowels and thought of an expression Clint used—scared shitless. Then Jonas heard the gravel scrunching under tires outside. He peeked out the window and saw Mr. Sandifer getting out of his van and coming to knock on the front door. He heard Daddy walking heavily down the hall to answer.

Allowing the men two or three minutes to get settled, Jonas sneaked down the hall and nearly cracked heads with Clint, who was doing the same.

Bryce hadn't invited Sandifer to sit down. They were standing in the entrance hall. The door between the entrance hall and the hall that led to the Torbetts' bedrooms was a slatted, folding door like the kind some closets have. Behind it, by standard procedure, Clint and Jonas stashed themselves, surreptitiously moving the slats to their advantage. Ace sat behind them, occasionally shoving his muzzle between them to get some attention himself. They could see how Mr. Sandifer towered over their father, although Bryce was a big man; they could see Sandifer's big belly and iron-gray sideburns that swooped out toward the corners of his handsome, level, thick lips.

"—been keeping this to yourself, haven't you?" Mr. Sandifer was saying.

"How can you say that?" said their father. "Of course not. It's been in all the papers. The whole county knows about it. Little gal from Channel Nine even came up and interviewed me. I've never been in the public eye so much."

"Oh." Mr. Sandifer was nodding. "It's just that *I* haven't seen you in so long, I reckon. Started to think you were trying to avoid me. Didn't want me to know too much about this find of yours."

"Why hell no, Vaughan," protested Bryce.

"You haven't taken me to see it. I sort of thought you would. Me being your best adviser on Indian matters and such. Of course, now you've got all those state geologists coming, you've got the archaeologists warmed up on it too, you not only got bones, I hear, you got projectile points out there. First thing I know, you'll open you a museum and go into competition with me."

Bryce laughed. "Oh ho ho ho. Come on now, Vaughan, sure you don't want to sit down? What'd you come see me about?"

"Naw, I can't stay. I just wanted to make you a proposition, Bryce. Fifteen hundred gives me exploratory rights back there where that bone is, then we split anything I find."

The boys saw their father looking at the floor, shaking his head.

"You know I can do it right," said Sandifer. "You know I can get dynamite from the gypsum mines, if we need it, I got labor used to handling a pickaxe. We've talked about how you busted a third of the pots in that last mound you did on your own, Bryce."

Daddy looked up at the taller man and smiled sweetly. "But I've already turned down a better offer than that. I turned down two thousand dollars from these church folks over in Texas, wanted just that one leg bone for their creation science museum."

Sandifer's eyebrows went up. "Oh?" For the first time he seemed at a loss for words.

"So as you know, Vaughan, first and foremost I'm a businessman. I've got to look out for myself, not do anything rash, when a better offer might come along any time."

Mr. Sandifer was quiet, and so was Bryce, so that Jonas was afraid Ace's panting would be audible or his knee would creak when he shifted his weight to sit back on his heels. Then Sandifer said, "So when are you going to get into your other mound anyway? Ever' time I drive by I wonder if it's still in one piece."

"I don't know. I reckon this comes first." Sandifer nodded. "You sure you don't want to sit down? I could make a pot of coffee."

"No. No, thank you, anyway, Bryce. I've learned something from my visit, and a man can't ask for more than that, can he? You come see me, now. Don't think you've got to avoid me."

"Vaughan, I'm telling you, I haven't been avoiding you."

Mr. Sandifer was sticking out one hand and opening the door with the other. Bryce shook with him.

"Take care, now."

"Bye bye. Sorry to get you up at this hour."

But Jonas and Clint didn't stay for any more formalities. They were speeding back down the hall to bed.

18

JAMES DONOVAN COULDN'T concentrate. Not that concentration was all that important to him. He suspected it was one of the more overrated intellectual qualities. Probably more breakthroughs in science were caused by daydreaming than by focused concentration. But maybe that was just an excuse he made for himself, for his own lack of mental discipline, of tunnel vision ...

He was spending hours, literally hours, in his office not getting anything done. Sometimes he would have the microscope on, and he would be in his rolling chair behind it, but with no eye to the lens. Once at the end of the day he found the bulb had burned out—it must have happened hours before, and he didn't notice. He would just sit while the butter-yellow sunlight, fashioned into long diagonals by his venetian blinds, crept slowly, slowly across the walls, across his bookshelves, his framed photographs of the Badlands, across the antique display counter from his grandfather's pharmacy that his mother had given him for his collection. Slowly, bar by bar, it edged along the rocks and fossils within, touching some of them for the millionth time—the solar radiation so unchanging, the planet's spewed artifacts so rough and variegated: cream-colored, gray, and salmon, nubby, silk-smooth, and jagged; granite, as richly and subtly patterned as a good suit; glinting feldspar; gypsum, flaky and white like some fancy confection, nearly glowing with a pinkish inner light; the crinoid stem fragments, like a petrified slab of that Cheerios-and-Rice-Chex snack mix James's mother made at Christmas, or like a bas-relief made of bolts and washers by an eccentric sculptor; a small hunk of rock, nondescript except for one bumpy surface that spelled algae remnants and meant it was 500 million years old; and the coiled nautilus, its surface pocked and pitted with age like a dirty cast.

But James had seen these things over and over, so many times that it was rare for them to make an impression on him anymore, and he was not pondering their secrets when he sat staring for hours while his scope light burned. Later he would try to reconstruct what he did think of during the day. He honestly didn't believe he was brooding over Michelle, or his career, or any professional project he had underway. He thought occasionally of those things, and of Deborah Armstrong, and whether he should call her, but they did not occupy him all the time, and he didn't know what did. If anyone interrupted him during these days—if a colleague stuck his head in the door to ask him when the deadline for some grant was, or Andy Ropp came by and plopped down to talk about the upcoming trial, or his mother called inviting him to dinner—he had no trouble at all picking up whatever thread they wanted him to pick up and responding appropriately. Though he seemed unable to initiate action, he could react to others with no problem. Still he wondered if he were, as the saying went, "losing it." If he should "see somebody." He consoled himself that if he were cracking up, at least it seemed to be happening safely and quietly. He didn't think he'd be buying a machine gun and terrorizing people from the top of a Days Inn. He wasn't drinking or taking drugs to get into these trances. But who was he to say what they meant?

So the days went by. Automatically, without noticing it, he tuned into football as well as baseball on the radio, and then the World Series, and then football almost entirely. He took his jacket out of the closet and wore it to work as the mornings got cooler. There was one day when he could see his breath in the morning air, and another when he had to wear sweats instead of shorts on his run. On some Saturdays the crowds dressed in scarlet poured down Markham Street toward the stadium, and when he forgot and drove too near the bottlenecked area he

looked at them incuriously, as if he were a traveler inured to strange sights and they the worshippers of some red god. He had the antifreeze checked in his truck and, noting the first plaintive whistle of a white-throated sparrow for that year, wrote it down as he always did. Yet, somehow, none of it made a real impression.

Then one afternoon—he never could say, later, what day or time it was, or what made the difference—he reached for his phone, and slowly punched some numbers.

"Groverton Animal Clinic," the voice said. "This is Sherry."

"Um," he said, "um, may I speak to Dr. Armstrong?"

"She's in surgery right now; can I have her call you back?"

"Um, no. She doesn't have my number," he said gravely and illogically. "I'll call her back."

There was the question, of course, whether he really would. He wondered it himself after he hung up. But apparently, whatever emotional sediments and fires and leanings and upheavals had been going on inside him were ready to surface now; the developing motive, inscrutable as it was, was not to be denied. An hour later he called back.

"Here she is. Just a minute."

And then, "Dr. Armstrong here."

"Deborah," he said, "I don't know if you remember me, but"—what a stupid way to begin!—"but this is James Donovan. We were at Fayetteville together."

"Oh yeah," she said. Surprised? Pleased? Irritated? He couldn't tell. "Umm—physics?"

"Organic chemistry."

"Oh yeah," she repeated. Then she did seem to get a little more enthusiastic. Her voice got a little clearer; maybe she had shifted the phone from under her chin, or to the other ear or something. "I thought about you this summer. I heard you came down here to look at a fossil, and your name kept ringing a bell. As a matter of fact a friend of mine is the one who interviewed you for some of those stories."

"Yeah, that, what's her name? Traci? Yeah. She's a friend of yours?" Well, at least they were talking about something. "That turned out to be sort of a fiasco. Not the interview, I mean," he corrected himself, "that was fine, she seemed like a bright girl"—oops, they didn't like to be called girls, she would probably think he was being patronizing—"um, woman, but I mean the whole fossil thing ... Do you know this guy Torbett?"

"Slightly," she said.

"You know, or maybe you don't, that he closed that fossil site off to scientists—didn't like what we might conclude about it, I heard."

"Yeah, there's been some talk about that around here."

Now her voice was definitely getting that so-what'd-you-call-for edge. He'd better hurry up. Some smushed cat could come through her door at any minute, and she'd have a good excuse for hanging up. Calm as he'd been when he dialed, now he was sweating profusely, like a teenager asking someone to his first dance; he couldn't seem to get out of this bumbling, clichéd mode. "Well, anyway, I saw your clinic when I was down there once, and I just thought I'd give you a call"—thank goodness he didn't say "for old times' sake," but he stopped himself just in time. He asked her about vet school, about her practice, about a couple of vague mutual acquaintances. Then he blurted out, "Are you married?"

She almost seemed to be laughing. "No."

"Oh. Well, I was going to offer to take you and your husband out for a hamburger or something next time I'm in Groverton. But ..."

"You and I can still go out for a hamburger, even though I'm not married," Deborah told him, but wearily, without much zest.

"Oh, really? Sure. Good. Well, I'll—let's see. I've run into problems with that project, actually, as I said, and I'm not sure when I'm coming back. But maybe I'll come down and try to talk to this guy again. And even if I don't get anywhere with him, I can give you a call and see if you'll have lunch with me. If you'd *like* to, I mean. Because he was the one who called me, he showed me back to look at the bone, he seemed interested in having me take an interest in it."

"Are you asking me or Bryce Torbett to have lunch with you?"

Ha-ha. "You," he said.

"Great," she said. "When?"

"Um—what's today?" He realized he had no earthly idea. He glanced at his desk calendar and saw it was still on August. "How about if I come tomorrow?"

"Great. You have my number. Call me when you get here. Or just stop by the clinic, since you know where it is."

"I'll look forward to it."

He hung up and stood for a minute staring at the receiver. Then he picked up his keys and wandered down the hall, right past his surprised secretary, downstairs and out of the building, and got in his truck. He drove around for a while. There were some new stores in town that he hadn't noticed before. New restaurants. He poked along, angering drivers behind him, who blew by glaring. He drove out the freeway and veered onto Highway 10. Pumpkins were for sale at roadside stands along the way, and those bundles of Indian corn women liked to put on their doors. How late in the year it must be. He drove to Pinnacle Mountain, climbed the lookout platform, and stared down at the river, leaning folded arms on the splintery wood railing. A marsh hawk was flapping and soaring far beneath him. Its white rump patch gleamed at all this distance, like a fleck of alabaster—like the kernel of something—something to focus on. God, it must be late in the year.

Four

Full fathom five thy father lies;
Of his bones are coral made:
Those are pearls that were his eyes:
Nothing of him that doth fade,
But doth suffer a sea-change
Into something rich and strange.

Shakespeare, *The Tempest* I.ii

19

RATHER THAN MAKE COFFEE at home, Traci waited to have it at work every day. She lived so close to the Waddle N Cafe that her car heater never warmed up by the time she arrived, and between the chilly mornings and her sluggish, caffeine-less blood, she was usually shivering and yawning in her thin blue-jean jacket as she banged at the kitchen entrance and waited for Nelda to let her in. Six twenty-nine, she thought, was her absolute limit. If she had to be here a minute earlier she'd have to look for some other job. Fortunately Nelda was the one who arrived a little before six to start the coffee and heat the grill. All Traci had to do was be ready to wait on the first six-thirty patrons, whose pickup trucks often beat her to the parking lot, whose chairs were usually scraping into place while she was clocking in and tying her apron. They were easy to wait on, though; they were the same men always wanting the same thing, and probably no one had written their orders down in years.

The Waddle N, formerly a realtor's office, was a low tan brick building surrounded by a poorly drained gravel parking lot. Outside, on its front wall the silhouettes of three large ducks were profiled in neon over the name of the restaurant and a big arrow pointing to the door. Inside were two large dining rooms lined with booths and filled with tables, a cashier's stand, a line for buffet service, and, behind one paneled wall, a kitchen and a club meeting room adorned by an American flag and Rotary and Optimist Club banners.

When the lifeguarding season ended, Traci had been left with only about twenty hours a week of work at the newspaper. Ricky

Thompson, the other staff reporter, had recovered from his mono and was back at the paper, and it was really probably out of kindness that Eddie O. kept her on at all. Then in early October she moved out of her parents' home, more for her own pride's sake than because her parents minded giving her room and board. But they were still mystified as to why she was in Groverton right now at all, and the most well-intentioned conversations Traci had with them tended to blow up into arguments. To prove her self-sufficiency—to herself if not to her parents—Traci decided to move in with Deborah, who had a spare room and welcomed help on the rent. Then Traci faced Groverton's meager part-time job options in earnest. She was left with either being a teacher's aide at the day-care center, which would have interfered with her best hours at the *Weekly,* or taking the late-night shift at the new convenience store, which her parents plainly thought was dangerous, or waiting tables early at the Waddle N. So here she was. "My hair smells like hash browns," she would grumble to Deborah at night, as she bent over and brushed it upside-down. "I finally broke down and got some of those ugly shoes like teachers and old people wear. I'm standing up so much, I'll have varicose veins by the time I'm twenty-five. And the *gossip,"* she went on. "You wouldn't believe."

"Oh yes I would," said Deborah calmly. "How long have you been away from here anyway? Had you forgotten?"

"But they're so sure of the conclusions they draw," said Traci. "And they're so damn nosy."

"Concerned," said Deborah. "That's how they'd put it."

Gossip, Traci was beginning to think, was the real lifeblood of the town, the healthiest commodity, the one staple for which there was always a market and always energy for production. Most residents of Groverton had police band radios in their dens, which they kept turned on around the clock, so that underneath the conversation and TV noise in their homes there was a constant sputter of instructions and reports flowing between dispatchers and patrols. And why? So the good citizens would know what was going on. In addition they kept their eyes peeled for whose truck was parked in whose driveway and for how long; for what new purchases appeared on what backs or in what carports, and whether they were locally bought; what prescriptions were being filled at Moon's Drugs on Main Street; and on and on, down to a level of detail and inference that Sherlock Holmes would have admired.

The day's gossip was juiciest, but most elliptical, with the early morning crowd. Though Traci had lived in Groverton all her life, she usually had to have a couple of cups of coffee before she was alert enough to follow all the allusions and cryptic connections in the talk that slid out of this mouth and that, usually half-muffled by grits or scrambled eggs and a deep country accent. When she did, though, she had the feeling she'd been in on a real insiders' circle—like reading some ultra-early edition of a newspaper, one written only for editors and pundits. "Yeah," she'd tell Eddie O., "if you really wanted to know what's going on in town, you'd get to the Waddle N at six-thirty. If you *really* wanted the scuttlebutt."

"I'm usually there at eight," said Eddie O. "Isn't that good enough?"

"Eight, man. At eight the gossip is so diluted and watered down it's pitiful."

"Like the orange juice."

"Now Eddie O., don't be talking about my other employer. We just stretch that concentrate a *little* bit beyond what the can says—just a little."

"Anyway, why should I get to the Waddle N at six-thirty?" said Eddie O. "I've got an employee doing it for me. My own spy."

"I'm not kidding. When I leave you should always send someone on staff over there to work."

"When *are* you leaving?" Ricky or Kelly would usually pipe in at this point. It was a standing joke at the office.

"Oh, probably never. With the sort of education I'm getting around here, I don't really need my degree."

"Tell me," Eddie O. would say, "what sort of pearls dripped from the lips of the six-thirty crowd today?"

"Oh ..." Traci would shut her eyes and cast back to the early half of her day. "Like, did you know that Claude Nesterson has a real snakeskin toilet seat in his house?"

"Naw!" Ricky, Kelly, and Renée would say. "Hell, Eddie O., that's front-page news if I've ever heard it."

"And it is firmly believed in town that my father has six toes," Traci would go on. "My own father. I've *seen* his feet. But I couldn't shake them from that—um—conviction."

"Oh, Traci, no, they're pulling your leg there. They're just trying to rile you up."

"No-o-o-o!"

But it really wasn't bad; in fact she even liked it, was a little proud of herself for handling it. She was getting to know parts of Groverton that hadn't existed for her before—people, histories, long-standing routines that formed a little world unto themselves. Like raven-haired, blunt-nosed Nelda, who now weighed about two hundred pounds and lived in a trailer a few miles out from town with her daughter and hemophiliac son. In her day she had been a national barrel-racing champion. "I seen her," the men would tell Traci, while Nelda silently refilled their coffee, "I seen her many a time with the crop in her teeth, *flying* around them barrels and the dust just a-scatterin'—"

"Why was she holding the crop in her teeth?" Traci asked once. "Why wasn't she using it?" But they didn't answer. *"Flying* around them barrels," they would muse, instead. "Crop in her teeth."

Nelda always looked unimpressed by their praise, and never broke the rhythm of her stolid pass around their tables, giving just a warm-up to this one, a whole new cup to that one, no refill to the next because she knew it messed up the balance of his milk and sugar. It was really Traci's job to give refills and later in the morning she did it alone, but these earliest customers and Nelda shared deep bonds and long-standing rituals, one of which was for the Barrel Queen herself to tend their coffee.

There were other regulars who appeared during the rest of her shift—Eddie O. and A.M. Bigley and their crowd around eight, a little group of stay-at-home moms who met for coffee at mid-morning—but mostly the later stream of patrons was more

fragmented. Then it was the kitchen where routines were bub-
bling along. Around eight the lunch cooks and dishwashers
started coming in. Traci got to know the men delivering milk,
eggs, meat. The talk she heard as she wove around the big
stainless steel sinks and grill and refrigerators, as she dumped
dirty plates in the vat by the dishwasher, wondering if she'd ever
get the residue of egg yolk out from under her fingernails, was
less collective than what was shared in the public part of the
cafe, and more of a daily update on the staff's immediate
families—this grandchild's colic, that uncle's angina, a planned
reunion, the latest demand of a mother-in-law.

No, the six-thirty customers were definitely her favorites.
Little Gal, they called her. They wore jeans and plaid cowboy
shirts that barely snapped over their bellies, or sport shirts and
Sansabelts, or mechanic's jumpsuits, or overalls. They smelled
of hair oil and aftershave and cigarette smoke, had faces florid
or sallow but almost all lined with sun and age, and spoke in
voices as gravelly and slow as a road-grader. When one of them
made a joke they wheezed their laughter. Much of what they
said was racist, reactionary, sexist, ignorant, appalling to Traci,
and yet she was fond of them, there was something endearing
about them, she got worried if one of them failed to show up.

One topic Traci heard talked about at the Waddle N that fall
was the find on Bryce Torbett's land. Never mind that it
amounted to, at best, one bone—one exposed femur, or femur-
like thing. Never mind that James Donovan and a handful of
zoological paleontologists around the country were shaking
their heads over it, trying to reconcile its apparent antiquity and
its mammalian traits, and that archaeologists who'd gotten
wind of the projectile points on site were now clamoring for
access to it. In Groverton at the Waddle N, there was no doubt
what that bone was. It had grown, multiplied, as if through some
sort of mitosis spurred by talk, or by the replicatory process of
the brooms in *The Sorcerer's Apprentice.* Now it was undoubtedly human; now it was a whole skeleton; any day it would be an
army, a host of human skeletons, American Indian contem-
poraries of Noah himself. The newspaper reports hadn't helped

dispel rumors. Neither had the footage Channel Nine had run from the Waddle N when their correspondent, Nikki Norris, interviewed townspeople about the fossil; those features were short on fact and long on melodrama, as usual. Neither had Bryce's move to block off the bone done much to encourage the community's scientific understanding, beyond further shrouding it in mystery.

Most of the restaurant's patrons believed that this "human in dinosaur-aged rock," as they called it, proved the fallacy of evolution once and for all. They gloated, baiting Groverton's tenth-grade biology teacher, Ken Wainwright, and the other defenders of evolution with their new "evidence." Ken's few allies would finally get so exasperated with the subject that they would stomp off mad and eat breakfast at home for a while. Ken always stayed in there, his blue eyes gleaming, his moustache under the hawk nose bunching and unbunching as he made the same arguments that fall that he had made year after year, every time a court case pertaining to evolution gained attention somewhere, every time some Sunday school class in Groverton studied Genesis. The arguments were by now reflexive, automatic, like much of the banter that went on at the Waddle N. No one's mind was ever changed.

Maybe, deep down, nobody cared; but for form's sake they had to act as if they did.

"Course I believe in God, R.B., that's not the point," Ken would say, sucking on his pipe, unperturbed. "I believe in the Bible in a certain *way.*"

And the round of low comments, bass, baritone, a spectrum of them coming in response, curling up over coffee mugs with the steam, dispatched from neighboring tables—"Methodists just think you can make it up whichever way it pleases you."

"Balanced treatment."

"Balanced treatment, 'sall I'm after. 'Sa democratic society. Present both sides, let the kids make up their own minds."

"Nothing fairer'n that."

"All 'at bill says."

"That's not education," said Ken. "Y'all know that. You don't take every crackpot idea and give it equal time in the classroom. We don't let the flat-earthers into our schools." Ken never really expected to win this argument. He just felt he owed it to his Methodist Sunday school class and his former fellow debaters, and in a way to education and science and religion all three, to state his position. "We're not even really talking about Adam and Eve here. We're talking about two whole ways of looking at the world. There are people who think everything was stuck down here on earth in little compartments, never changing, never changed, and there are people who think it was all more mixed up than that, more related, and more complicated, one thing changing into another and into new things. That's what we're talking about."

"I don't know what you're talking about, Ken, but I'm talking about Adam and Eve."

"Yeah, what I'm talking about is the Bible, the Lord God Almighty."

"And what I'm talking about is equal time. Balanced treatment."

Ken heard them out, shaking his head. "Y'all are like my tenth-graders who walk into my classroom every year telling me they're 'against evolution.' I don't know what makes them so het up about this issue. You can't be 'against' it, I tell them. Are you 'against' *gravity?*"

"Well now, Bryce Torbett's against gravity," drawled R.B. Cowley. "It keeps women's skirts down." At that they broke up.

"And I can think which woman in particular," wheezed Fred Barnett, slapping his leg. "Hee, hee. Whoo."

"Hoo Lord."

Bryce had always supplied the Waddle N crowd with good material, Traci gathered, never more so than lately. He had been noticeable in Groverton since he was little. He was a cute kid. His aunt used to take him to the John Deere outlet, which was next to the Waddle N, and let him sit on all the display model tractors and lawn mowers. Then in high school of course he was in the spotlight, he was the team quarterback and still good-looking, his girl was Deborah Armstrong, and they walked together with that close-knit little sashay of their hips that did not go unremarked. Then he treated her so bad when she went off to college; that must have been good for several hundred cups of coffee at the Waddle N. Then he had that whirlwind romance with pretty Marianne Friel, a north Arkansas girl who came to Groverton to be the hospital dietician, and their baby boys were so handsome, that served up several years of mild notice, and then with Marianne's diagnosis the talk about the Torbett family intensified. Next to sex, the Waddle N crowd relished fatal illness and accidents above everything. Through every phase of Marianne's treatment, the tongues had clucked over the light tan plastic coffee cups, the heads had shaken over plate after plate of scrambled eggs, undercooked bacon, honey buns; then through the death, the funeral. Then there was this matter of the bone Bryce's kid had found. And now Bryce had provided them with the best fodder yet, a whiff of that favorite topic. According to Winston Huett, the closest thing to a good buddy Bryce had, Bryce and Lorene were "just good friends" who had gotten together out of a common interest in the boy's fossil. But Lorene taught the older boy, not the younger; and he'd only just gotten into her class; and anyway it was the younger one who'd found the fossil; so how did that explain anything? Well, he didn't know, said Winston, but it had to be innocent—else why were they being so obvious about it? Her car was at the Torbetts' almost every evening after school. And what did Lorene's father say about it? Jarred had no buddy to relay his messages. It was reported, however, that Irene Hopkins asked brightly after Lorene when she ran into Jarred in the grocery store and he had said firmly that his daughter was just *fine* and was doing a lot of work for the church right now, the Lord bless her. Evangelical, no doubt, the Waddle N crowd agreed. Trying to win Bryce's soul.

20

WHEN TRACI GOT HOME—or to Deborah's house; it was hard to think of anywhere as "home," these days—one night in mid-November, there was a strange vehicle parked in the driveway, a blue Suburban with the state seal on the door. It took her a minute to figure out it must be James Donovan's. The one time she had met him, back in June when she was interviewing him for her initial story on the fossil and he was on good enough terms with Bryce to be in town to get some better photographs, he'd been driving his own truck. But this vehicle had to be his. He and Deborah had been talking a good bit lately, since the day a couple of weeks ago when he'd come to Groverton and taken her to lunch. Traci's mind raced with excitement as she sat in her car brushing her hair before going inside. She hoped Deborah wasn't getting too tired of entertaining him while they waited for Traci.

Poor Deborah. How was she ever going to attract a man? Traci had just about given up on her. She knew her friend was beautiful, smart, and interesting, but what man was going to delve beneath Deborah's brusque manner amd faded jeans to realize that? When it came to men Deborah was scowly and grouchy. She refused to do anything special to win their notice. If she felt like wearing flat shoes and cotton briefs rather than heels and bikini panties, she did. It was going to be hard for a man to take her on her own terms.

So James Donovan must be using Deborah, whom he already knew, as a bridge to get closer to Traci. Well, thank goodness she'd come straight home from the paper today, instead of stopping by her parents' to pick up some more of her winter clothes.

When she came in they were sitting on the couch, Deborah cross-legged on one end, plucking at a throw pillow, and James with one work-booted foot propped on his other knee, scratching Deborah's coon hound, Floyd, behind the ears. The news was on but with the volume turned down. They looked up happily as she came through the door.

"Heyyy!"

"Well, hey, James, how are you!—Hey, Deborah. What're y'all up to?"

"Not much."

"Not a whole lot."

"Where've you been?" said Deborah, as Traci put her purse and jacket on the floor and flopped in the La-Z-Boy. "You're later than usual."

She's been having a hard time making conversation with me gone, thought Traci. "Oh, Lord," she said. "At the planning meeting for the Annual Community-Wide Living Nativity Scene. What a circus."

"What, are you aiming for a role?" said Deborah. "Mary, maybe?"

Traci shot her a look, part pleading, which she hoped said, *Don't make any virginity jokes!* "Eddie O. wanted a story on it."

"Is this a big deal?" said James. "Where's it held?"

"Oh, it's always held at the courthouse. If the ACLU weren't so busy, they could have a field day with this one."

"So how was the meeting? Was there a good turnout?"

"About twenty people were there. This is a favorite event— you always get a good crowd. Let's see: the arguments turned on whether the actors would be allowed to wear their eyeglasses, which aren't authentic, and whether any type of shoes but sandals would be acceptable. Apparently this debate has been running for several years. You can imagine that a shepherd in bifocals with his Nikes sticking out from under his robe is a little less than ancient-looking. But a lot of these guys can't *see* worth anything without their glasses." Traci smiled at James.

"These are the kind of deep topics I'm assigned when I'm not covering paleontology."

"Yeah, I was gonna ask," said James. "How'd that come out, that article on the schools?"

"It turned into a whole series, by the time I interviewed everyone around here who had an opinion in the matter. It came out all right. Thanks for your help. By the way, I think I'll be calling on you again pretty soon." Traci looked at Deborah. "Did you tell him?"

"Tell him what?"

"About my thesis."

"Oh. Oh, no, I forgot."

"Well!" said Traci. "I've decided to do my senior thesis on the whole creation science and evolution debate, using this winter's trial as the case in point. I'm *so excited.*"

"Sounds neat," said James. "That sounds pretty interesting. But what's your major? I thought you were a chemistry major."

"Well, I was," said Traci. "That's why this whole thing has become such a big deal. I'm changing to History of Science. I have some credits in that area anyway and I'll have to petition to have the others counted. I may have to stay an extra semester, but I doubt it. The thing is, for the first time I'm just so fired up about my coursework."

"Do you think you'll still go on to med school, then?"

"Gosh, you have a good memory," said Traci.

"Well, Deborah and I were just talking about you. She was explaining your new living arrangement and what was going on with you."

"I'm just not sure. Who knows?" said Traci airily. "I don't think the change of major will hurt me—and I have all my pre-med requirements. They say that med schools sort of like applicants with more of a humanities slant. But who knows?"

"Do you think you'd come back to Arkansas?"

So he was worried she might not. "Oh, I don't know. I can't see ever living in a really big city, I'll say that."

"You could come back and do for human medicine what Deborah's done for veterinary medicine," said James.

Just then the phone rang. "Which is *what?*" said Deborah sarcastically, frowning, before she picked it up. "Hello.—Sure, just a second.—Traci."

Traci raised her eyebrows inquisitively as she went toward Deborah and, meeting half-rolled eyes, carried the phone around the corner into the kitchen.

"Hey, Traci. This is Stuart."

"Stuart. What's up."

"Not much. I was wondering if you wanted to come over. We could watch TV—make hot chocolate—whatever."

"Um—well, no. I don't think so. Deborah and I have company." She shouldn't have stepped so far into the kitchen; it wouldn't hurt James to know that she was sought after. But in the meantime she had Stuart on the line, like some big fish she wished she hadn't hooked. And as she'd been learning, he wasn't easy to brush off. He was not going to take any arch, veiled, Southern-woman-schooled hints.

"Just 'no,' hunh?"

"Not tonight, Stuart."

She heard his little exasperated blast of air. "You know, you were the one telling me, back in September, that you weren't cavalier about your relationships. I'm not very inclined to believe you."

She was stubbornly silent. In the living room she heard the rise of James's voice, and Deborah's laugh, joining him.

"I wish you'd just tell me what you're thinking."

Finally Traci backed around to the other side of the refrigerator, stretching the cord to the utmost, and hissed into the receiver: "Stuart, maybe I made a mistake, *okay?* You and I would get along fine if we'd never had to leave that lake. Or that picnic site, last month. Maybe it's just the atmosphere some-times, *okay?* There's sort of a spell. But it doesn't last. It's forming a pattern now. As soon as we get back into the real world it's just never the same—I just can't deal with you—*okay?*"

She glared into the silence of the phone, hearing only her harsh breathing, her heart pounding. Her fingers were wrapped in the cord.

"No," said Stuart. "It's not okay."

"Look, I have to go," said Traci.

"Sleep well," he said sarcastically. They hung up at the same time.

She stood by the fridge trying to compose herself. But she didn't want to miss any more of James's visit. In a minute she sauntered back out to the living room. Deborah, in the middle of an anecdote about a client who left a dead horse on her parking lot, glanced at her face and Traci knew she gathered something had happened. Floyd came over and bumbled his big bony head against her hands. A short while later James stood up and said he had to go. He, too, must have sensed her abstraction. He would suspect she was involved with another man, he would be put off ... But Traci tried to be a good hostess, standing by the door with Deborah and cheerfully bidding him goodnight.

21

TRACI HAD TO RECONSTRUCT it all later, from gossip she heard at her jobs—a little at the paper, but mostly at the Waddle N; which was good practice for her new historical bent, for what is history anyway but reconstruction from one form of gossip or another?

The world, as he had witnessed it on CNN the past few nights, seemed to be at a particularly evil pass, and Jarred Strait was wound up. It was a beautiful, chilly November Sunday, with the smell of wood smoke in the air, and of mothballs from winter coats just gotten out of storage. Football scores were on the front of the Sunday papers again, above the banner headlines; cars with deer trussed on their trunks and pickups with muddy three-wheelers in the back were slowly cruising the highways near Groverton. It was a time of year for minds to repent, hearts to mend. And this was what the Reverend Strait was entreating his congregation to let happen in their own lives.

He had been preaching for twenty-five minutes on Nicodemus when he finally started to float downward, imperceptibly to anyone but a seasoned churchgoer, toward his resolution. It was like a cruising airliner's first hitch toward descent, when the tray tables are still littered with plastic glasses and peanut wrappers, but the most sensitive passengers know that they're over the hump—their destination may still be two hundred miles away but at least its existence has been certified by that barely discernible downward tug of the steel tube that encloses them. With the Reverend Strait, it was a certain modulation of voice that started children stretching and looking gratefully up at their parents' faces, nudged women's hands restlessly over their purses, and made the dual mirages of the Waddle N luncheon buffet (fried chicken, sweet potatoes with marshmallows on top, pecan pie) and an afternoon of televised pro football that much more achingly, shimmeringly real for the men.

"And if there are any today who would unite with the living Lord by laying down their burdens before Him—by opening their hearts, here in this fellowship of Christian mortals and of God Almighty, by a public confession of sin cleansing themselves for a rededication of life, let him now rise, and say his piece, and come forward. For when the disciples said, 'What shall I say?' He said, 'I will tell you what to say,' and 'It is good that ye admit your wrong before men, that I can tell ye, Go and sin no more.' For brothers and sisters, I tell you today, if you continue to try to live with the baggage of sin, it will weigh you down, it will burden you like a millstone around your neck even unto death, the fruits of your unworthiness will poison you! But if you cast the burden of your sin upon the Lord, ye who are heavy-laden, He will give you rest, for He is slow to anger, my brothers and sisters in Christ—"

People said later that when they saw her getting up, at her place there by the aisle halfway back, they thought she was going to present a new member, though she wasn't sitting with anyone new. They said that even when she started, they thought it would be just a general testimony, a sort of statement of thanksgiving and recommitment. The last thing anybody expected her to say, including the people who had been saying it themselves for months, was pronounced in a clear voice that trembled at its edges: "I have a sin to confess, brothers and sisters, and I want to do it here in the community of my church and my loved ones ..." They said her voice was sweet and her little posture as straight and poised as a Miss America contestant, and stayed straight somehow even though she started trembling and the tremors rippled through it. She went on, "I have committed the sin of fornication—all kinds of—sexual acts, without benefit of marriage—with Bryce Torbett, and I'm as sorry as sorry can be, as God is my witness." They said the weird thing was she didn't cry or anything. Her face had gotten very pink, and her chest was heaving. But she moved her little shiny chin up a little higher in the air and her eyes looked determined, more than teary—though she was holding on to the pew in front of her with one hand.

The church was motionless and silent for about a minute. ("That don't sound like long, now," said Harold Grubber at the Waddle N the next day, "but you set and watch it go by and think about what was going on in that church yesterday, you'll know how long it was." People were too shocked even to look at each other. They just kept staring at Lorene's figure. "Look like I won't ever forget that dress she's wearing; black, with swirly green things in it, army green, and it wrapped around her so." Harold made gestures around his own blue-jeaned, tooled-belted self. "Tied here.") Finally stout, gray Mae Ruth Earden, who was sitting next to Lorene, reached up and took her hand and started patting it, and Lorene hardly seemed to notice and said, "I—ask you-all to forgive me!"

The Reverend Jarred Strait's face had turned ashy white, though there was some dispute about that on Tuesday at the cafe. "Kindly green, it was," said Phil Nesterson; but "Naw, he went fire-red and then grayish, way he was the rest of the day," according to Phil's wife Tommye. Then he did the thing that marked him as either the biggest Christian or the biggest wimp in Groverton history, depending on your source; he walked forward to the stricken woman and said in a strong voice—

"—shaky—"

"—strong—"

"—shaky—"

Well, at any rate, said, "In the words of our Lord, then, 'Go thou, and sin no more.' " And Lorene lifted her now streaming face to his—"When she started crying, she really let loose; Lord, that makeup was a-runnin' "—and he opened his arms wide to clasp her in them and she fell down on her knees, right there where the sun came in through the window and splashed down in the aisle. After another stricken minute the congregation began to edge out of there, uneasily and quietly but formally—

back row first, like at a wedding or a funeral. A few of them stole glances behind and saw the father and daughter still huddled there like kids playing Freeze Tag.

On Wednesday, Rooster McKay pointed out that "*Go thou,* and sin no more" must mean that Jarred wanted to disown Lorene, even though he forgave her. Rooster was a Methodist, but he had heard the story so many times and in such detail in the past three days that he felt qualified to comment.

"Aw, Rooster," said Harold Grubber disgustedly. "Don't you know those are just the words of Jesus?"

"Words of Jesus or not, I know what 'Go thou' means. Get thee the hell out of here."

"Well, Jesus wasn't *related* to the woman he told that to."

"Sure. So Jarred'd have even more reason than Jesus to tell her to go thou."

"He was telling Lorene to go on about her business," interjected Mavis Wright, the cashier. " 'Go thou on about your business of being my daughter, hon, I love you anyway despite all the pain of it.' "

"Naw, Mavis, y'all're interpreting it the way you want it. If that was what he meant why didn't he say '*Come here,* and sin no more'?"

"What'd she do, anyway, that everybody in Groverton hasn't done? You show me one person who's saved hisself for marriage in this peyton place and I'll show you—"

If Clint Torbett hadn't come in just then for his daily jalapeño burger to go, the discussion might have gone on forever. Clint flushed crimson when the silence fell over the restaurant. The more thin-skinned of the Waddle N patrons tried to make conversation—which sort of fluttered up again, but it just made things worse because it didn't make it far off the ground—like a stunned bird that has hit your picture window and can't fly naturally again no matter how hard it tries.

After Clint left, his head ducked, his face still scarlet, the tongues started clucking again. "Umh, umh. It's those boys I feel sorry for in all of this."

"Don't you know? That Clint, bless his heart, he's old enough

to understand it all."
"Umh, umh, umh."

22

AGAIN JONAS TORBETT was making a discovery, not the kind you stumble upon in a runoff ditch and get written up in the paper for or make by spying on grownups, but the kind that takes much longer to make and that is made in your own head; and not a happy one but a sad one. *Not everyone recognized his new greatness.* In fact, despite all he'd become over the summer—explorer, finder, newspaper hero—school still made him feel the same way, as though right around the corner the possibility always lurked that he might throw up out of sheer nerves; and then everyone would look at him and point, and Mr. Peel the janitor would stonily mop it up, and all the rest of the day people would step around the spot anyway and say, "Jonas Torbett did that ..." So far he'd avoided throwing up, but a certain queasy disappointment dogged him. No one acted like he was anything special. It was all the same monotony and ignominy as before. If not worse. Fifth-graders always used to look so big, muscled and sophisticated, and Jonas had thought that once he was in the fifth grade and had the lime-green science book and the pink speller with 5's on them instead of the old blue science book and yellow speller marked 4, he would be different; he would have reached the Olympian heights of fifth-gradeness himself. Only when he got there he found that he and everyone else in his class seemed just the same as they always had, and suddenly it was the sixth-graders who looked giant and omniscient.

The day Nikki Norris came to interview him from Channel Nine, Clint had informed Jonas that he was not giving back Jonas's football that had been a Christmas present from Uncle

Terry.

"But you just wanted to borrow it," said Jonas helplessly. "I thought you were giving it right back."

"We made a trade." Clint's voice was cold. "If I remember right, you gave me the football and I gave you the act of carrying out the trash last week."

"I *loaned* you the football," corrected Jonas.

"That's right. Loan. And what does 'loan' mean? To give with the intention of getting it back. Now, I could, if I chose, give you the football back. Right?"

"Right."

"Well then, you would have to give me back my act of carrying out the trash."

"I'll carry out the trash for you this week."

"No, no. That's different trash. You have to give me back the same act of carrying out that trash that I traded you for. You have to swap me back the same thing."

"But I can't," said Jonas logically, but with a note of frustration rising in his throat, as he saw where this was going. "Daddy already took that trash to the dump. You know that."

"Well then. You can't give me that act back, I keep the football. It's simple."

"Clint! That isn't fair." Jonas's face was pink, his eyes were starting to glisten, he stuck his chin out toward his brother, who continued to fake a handoff, fade back, and pretend to pass the softly gleaming leather ball.

"Show me how it isn't fair. Prove it."

"We traded—what we traded was—how I would loan you the football and you would borrow it and give it back to me later and in return for that you would carry out the trash for me!"

"Right. And to get back where we started, I could give you the football back, if you could perform the same act for me, of carrying out—what day was that?"

"I don't know." Jonas tried to shrug his miserably hunched shoulders.

"I do. It was Thursday, because it was the day we played Crowdersville. Anyway, so you would need to carry out last

Thursday's trash for me: Thursday, October 8, 1981." Clint had held back his gloating all this time, but finally he could not suppress a big, silver-braced grin.

So after that episode, when Bryce talked cheerily about Nikki Norris at the supper table, Jonas was too despondent to enter in.

The day the feature actually appeared on TV, Clint wasn't around to see it. He was at the state fair with the Baptist youth. He had some Baptist friends he played flag football with that fall—using Jonas's rightful ball. Jonas had begged Bryce, pleaded, to let him go to the state fair with the Methodist youth, when Mikey Rhodes invited him, but Bryce had said no, he didn't think the Methodists were well-supervised and Jonas was too young. So there was no justice, no one respected him, they all just used his bone to make themselves look good and ignored him as usual.

Clint had Miss Strait for general science this year and around Halloween he had gotten to go on a field trip—to the Torbetts' own farm, to see the bone. Daddy opened the gate right up. Clint told Jonas all about it, of course. From what he said Jonas could tell Clint had showed off, leading the way, pointing out landmarks and finally the old bone itself to his classmates, who were slapping their notebooks against their thighs and scaring the girls by pretending to see snakes, while Miss Strait said things like, "Toby, can you see how the Flood waters deposited this human bone here?" and "What do you think of the Mind that could design flowers like that?"

Jonas lay in bed that night and almost cried. In fact tears did trickle down his face, but he did not sob, so that did not count as crying. Ace wriggled over and tried to lick the tears. "Oh, Acey, Acey." Jonas held him. Ace was the best thing in his life. Every day after school he waited at Jonas's bus stop, non-chalantly pretending to be tracking rabbits or just sniffing manure piles. "Yonder's your buddy," the bus driver would say. "He's waiting on you." Jonas would flush, and smile, stepping off the bus, and Ace's head would snap up and, abandoning his cool, he would dash toward Jonas and jump up and get his jeans muddy and bite his jacket. Now Ace stretched against Jonas's chest and belly and then twisted, exposing his own underside, raking his paws in the air and stretching his head back, gums bared, trying to get Jonas to play.

Bryce and Celie were starting to make noise about Ace's getting too big to sleep in Jonas's bed. "And fleas," Celie would add firmly. "I find fleas in that boy's bed, Mr. Torbett." "I put him to sleep every night by my dresser!" Jonas would answer hotly, not mentioning that after five minutes on the floor Ace invariably leaped in one smooth, joyous, Evel Knievel leap up to Jonas's bed, where he padded around grinning and turning until he had decided which part of the mattress he wanted to dominate that night. In fact Jonas was starting to get flea bites, or that's what he guessed they were, since the itching lasted a lot longer than mosquito bites and he wasn't hearing any mosquitoes in his room; but it was worth it to have that warm, responsive, adoring, bossy body so near. Jonas Torbett, mighty explorer, famous discoverer, gripped the dog's body in a hug and then started scratching it in long, sad scratches. How could things be so good and yet so bad?

A postcard came in the mail, saying it was time for Ace's checkup at Dr. Armstrong's. During the Thanksgiving holidays Jonas finally got around to going. He had some questions he might ask Dr. Armstrong, with nobody else around. He hesitated because, after all, it was mainly Ace's health she was supposed to look after, and his questions were about that terrible word he could not think without picturing it printed on his white, stiff, folded report cards: BEHAVIOR. But when Ace created a scene right there in front of the vet's, not coming to Jonas when called because he had found a Tip Top burger wrapper on the curb in front of the Fashion Parade, looking at Jonas defiantly with his speckled, velvety, normally drooping ears cocked out wide, Jonas got just mad enough that he decided to broach the topic.

When he finally caught Ace and entered Dr. Armstrong's clinic, something about the smell—of medicine, flea dip, and clean dog—or the slick floors subdued the dog right away. He dropped his proud head meekly and sat right when Jonas told him to. Mr. Obedient. Jonas patted him and felt his muscles trembling underneath his coat. But Jonas was resolved.

"Can I help you?" said the lady behind the desk. She hadn't been here before. She had a snub nose and short blond hair, and glasses that dwarfed her face.

"Yes, ma'am," said Jonas. "I got this here in the mail." He fished the postcard out of his rear pocket and unfolded it. His jeans had gotten a little wet the day before and the ink had run. He placed it up on the counter.

"Okay," said the lady. "Ace?" Ace politely thumped his tail on the floor. "Let me tell Dr. Armstrong you're here."

That lady disappeared through a swinging door behind the counter, and on its second swing Dr. Armstrong came out. Jonas almost blushed. She was just the way he remembered.

"Hi, Jonas," she said. "Ace!—hey, boy. Let's go in here." They went into the room where she had examined Ace that first night.

"Let me see if I can lift him up here," said Dr. Armstrong.

"I don't think he'll let—" Jonas started, but Ace complied like a lamb, regarding Jonas somberly and with a wrinkled brow from his new heights.

"Ugh," said Dr. Armstrong, rearranging her lab coat. "He's getting big. So how's he doing?" she went on. "Ace—you big sweet thing. Great name." She was feeling him all under, patting him and stroking him as she looked into his mouth and ears and poked his belly. She used her stethoscope to listen to his chest. When she took it out of her ears she said, "So is he turning into a pretty good dog for you?"

"Well," said Jonas. He felt traitorous, and even as he took a deep breath to confess his dog's sins, his heart nearly burst with love for him, that gorgeous tan and black and gray and white spotted bundle of smooth, earth-smelling energy: but he went on. "Sometimes he's bad," he said. "I have trouble getting him to do what he's supposed to. I mean, he's only good when he wants to be. I don't mean he's *real* bad. He's smart. Most of the time he does what I want him to do. Sometimes." He stopped.

Dr. Armstrong was sticking something up Ace's rear. Ace shot a discomfited look at Jonas, and Jonas felt guilty again.

Then Dr. Armstrong turned her back and put the something away and got something else. She turned back around. "Let me draw some blood," she murmured. The dark liquid filled the plastic cylinder while Jonas watched, fascinated. She left the room for a few minutes and came back and gave Ace two shots. Jonas winced each time.

"Okay," she said. "Now go on with what you were starting to tell me. When does he cut up? Give me an example."

"Like when I tell him to sit," said Jonas. "I know he knows what it means. He's been knowing that forever. He learned it in about a day and a half. But he only does it if he feels like it. And if I try to push down on his rear end and *make* him sit, he starts biting on my arms." His voice dropped, with shame for Ace and with fear that she would say, well, then, you better get rid of him, bad dog like that. Jonas knew Ace didn't mean to really hurt him. He didn't bear down with his jaws. But his teeth were still a pup's, needle-sharp. Like a drug addict Jonas had even started to wear long sleeves to cover up the indentations from Ace's teeth and the scratches. He knew about drug addicts from special assemblies at school. They wore long sleeves to cover their needle marks, and their eyes were red, and they put drugs into the sugar dispensers at restaurants so you should only take sugar when it was in the little packets.

"When else?" she said.

"Like when I tell him to come and he doesn't want to. I chase him and chase him and he's still faster than me. And I holler and holler but he still don't come."

Dr. Armstrong was facing him, with one hand on the examining table and one on Ace's neck, gently fingering it. Ace looked deep in dignified thought, like Dan Rather during the credits at the end of the news.

"You need to show him that you're his Alpha Wolf," said Dr. Armstrong.

"Hunh?"

"You are, you know. You're his Alpha Wolf. You've just got to remind him more often."

"Alpha—?" said Jonas.

"When dogs used to live in the wild, the leader of the pack was called Alpha Wolf. All the other dogs would obey that one. They knew who Alpha Wolf was from the time they were small puppies. Now that we've domesticated dogs, the human master—you—takes the place of the Alpha Wolf. Ace will be happier if you show him in no uncertain terms that you are Alpha Wolf. He already *suspects* you are, and he's testing you by disobeying. When he disobeys you've got to punish him—by talking real stern to him if that's all it takes, or whipping him. But you have to punish him while he's in the act of disobeying. Okay?"

"Okay." Jonas's eyes were wide.

"For instance, don't try to *make* him sit. That'll humiliate him. He's got too much pride for that. He needs to decide for himself that he wants to obey his Alpha Wolf. Intimidate him so much that he chooses to sit on his own."

"Okay." Jonas didn't really understand.

"Always, always remember who you are. You are the center of his universe. Once you two have got that established, there's no end to what you can teach him. Does he stay yet?"

"No ma'am."

"Oh, he can learn to stay, and heel, and do hand signals, and all kinds of stuff. Talk to him a lot. He'll understand. Hang on, Jonas—there's a book I'll loan you, that's in my office. Just a minute." She came back in a minute with a white and red paperback called *Dog Training and You.* Then she lifted Ace off the table and gave Jonas a piece of paper to give to the lady at the desk in the next room. "Goodbye," she said. "Let me know how this goes."

"Okay," said Jonas. He told the lady at the desk to send him the bill. He let Ace out into the sunshine and kicked up his kickstand and wheeled off down the road. "Alpha—Wolf?" he whispered into the wind running silkily through his whirring spokes. "The center of the universe: Alpha Wolf!"

He turned into Jim Ray's service station to make the short cut through there, rising off his seat to absorb the bump where the smooth concrete slab didn't join flush with the asphalt road, and noticed Mr. Bledsoe sitting on the curb at the side of the station where Jonas washed cars, his Plymouth parked under the chinaberry tree. He was wearing khaki pants and a maroon sweater. Jonas coasted right up to his former teacher and hopped neatly off his bike before it stopped—a move he had recently perfected, which made him feel a little more like a fifth-grader. He started to say hey but Ace was jumping all over Mr. Bledsoe and he had to drag him off instead.

"It's okay," said Mr. Bledsoe. "Hey, boy, come here. Don't worry about it."

"Were you waiting on me?" said Jonas. "You want me to wash your car? I haven't been doing many since it got cold. Ace, get down."

"It's all right. Yeah, I wanted to talk to you about something."

"He's gonna get your pants dirty," said Jonas mournfully, "and you look so nice. Did I tell you he's a Catahoula?"

"Yeah, I think you did."

"That's a Indian kind of dog."

"That's right."

"You wanted to talk to *me?*"

"Um-hm. Do you have a minute?"

Did he have a minute! No one ever asked whether Jonas had a minute. They always assumed ten-year-old boys had hours, days, to do nothing better than listen to adults.

"Sure," he said.

"Well, why don't you start washing my car, and we'll visit while you do that."

"Okay. Let me get my stuff."

Jim Ray was probably at lunch, and Jonas just hollered into the garage, "Shorty, I'm washing a car" without waiting for an answer as he grabbed his bin of supplies. He turned on the hose, low, just right, the way he'd learned, and started wetting down Mr. Bledsoe's car. Mr. Bledsoe stood in the shade at the edge of the concrete, with his hands in his pockets, looking at his feet, before he started to talk, just the way he used to do in school. Jonas was already sudsing the fender when he finally spoke.

"You know this bone you found."

"Yessir."

"It seems to be a human bone."

"That's what people say."

"Is that what the paleontologist said? The guy from Little Rock?"

Jonas scrubbed at a bug ossified on the right headlamp. "Well, he didn't exactly say that, I don't think. It was something about it might could be a dinosaur too. But since then everybody has said it's a human. The ones from Texarkana did." Mr. Bledsoe was silent. Jonas added, "*I* think it's a human. I think he's lonesome."

"You know, don't you, that all the ancient human remains found around here are Indian? Caddo?"

"Yes sir, sure."

Mr. Bledsoe was quiet some more. Then he said, "Do you remember when we talked about the burial ceremonies in class?"

"Sure. I been to Mi-Ka-Do too. I know about them from there. And from my dad, a little bit." Now Jonas was squatting by a hubcap, on the same side of the car as Mr. Bledsoe. His reflected face looked fat, moon-shaped.

"Do you think your dad would—what do you think your dad's going to do with this bone?"

Jonas's hand, circling the sponge around, started moving more slowly. "I don't know. There are some men who want it. They came and tried to buy it. But he said no. He said he wants to dig them up himself. He wants the pots and stuff he thinks are buried with this person. He can sell them for a lot of money."

"Where are these men from? Are they scientists too, with the Little Rock guy?"

"Naw, Daddy don't, doesn't, let that man come back. He's the one he blocked the road off from. Naw, these men're from I don't know, church or something. Maybe they're preachers. They're

from Texas. They had on suits and they were sort of fat. They want it because—something to do with God or church. Also Mr. Sandifer from Mi-Ka-Do, he would like to have it."

Mr. Bledsoe was squatted down like a baseball player waiting his turn at bat, his forearms resting on his thighs. "It seems to me that this Indian's bones are being treated pretty rudely. They shouldn't really belong to anybody." Now his voice was very, very light and soft. "Maybe he should be buried again with other Indians, under the earth, where no one would disturb him to buy and sell and argue about his remains." Jonas stood up and looked right down at Mr. Bledsoe, and Mr. Bledsoe was looking up at him, looking him straight in the eye.

"He's lonesome, Mr. Bledsoe," said Jonas. "He's all by himself back there. No pots or nothing around him that I can see. I sit back there with him a lot and I can tell how lonesome he is. I didn't mean to find him but I did. Maybe the rain had uncovered him or something. What can I do about it? I don't want my daddy to trash him up. I don't want these preachers to have him either."

"Who do you think he belongs to?"

They were being very still in the shade, with the hose running, running, making little pools around their sneakers.

"His own self," said Jonas, "I reckon. *I* don't know."

"Could you take me to see the bone?" said Mr. Bledsoe. "Let me have a look at it? I never have seen it, and I don't think I can find it on my own."

Jonas winced and looked up at him. "My dad would kill me."

"Why would he have to know? I just want to go look at it, is all."

"Yeah, but if he found out ... He ain't letting—isn't letting anybody back there anymore. Not even Miss Strait." And he felt himself blush.

"Okay." Mr. Bledsoe straightened up. "I'm not going to ask you to do anything that'll get you in trouble with your father. A man should honor his fathers."

Jonas hoped he wasn't mad. "Mr. Bledsoe?"

"Hmm?"

"You know how Indians had secret names that they didn't use all the time because they might wear them out?"

"Yes."

"I've got one, if you need to know it."

"Okay."

"Do you want to know it?"

Mr. Bledsoe thought. So Jonas knew he wasn't just being indulgent, the way grownups always said Yeah sure without really thinking when you said Do you wanna know something. Then he said, "It might wear it out for me to know."

"You might need to use it sometime, like if you ever need a code name for me or something."

"I think you shouldn't tell me," said Mr. Bledsoe. "I think you should keep it to yourself. You'll be glad later. How much do I owe you?"

"Three dollars."

"Thanks," said Mr. Bledsoe. "You take care of yourself, now, Jonas."

"Yes sir!" answered Jonas. "You're welcome. I will."

23

ONE WEDNESDAY AFTER school Jonas was riding his bike toward the drainage canal. It didn't seem as far back there as it used to, maybe because he was getting stronger and had more endurance now, or maybe because he went so often. Almost every day after school, while Clint was at basketball practice, he stuck *Dog Training and You* in the little space between the small of his back and his jeans with the tooled belt that said JONAS and pedaled, then hiked, to the bone-site. There he worked with Ace on all the basic commands and, lately, some of the simpler fetches, which were done with hand signals. He was planning to have his Uncle Terry get him one of those high-pitched dog whistles as he and Ace moved into the back of the book, the more advanced part of the training.

Ace loped alongside Jonas's bike, taking detours through ditches and after rabbits, seemingly not thinking about the lesson ahead, and unbothered by the stomachaches that often plagued Jonas when he was on *his* way to school.

Parking his bike, then jumping over the drainage canal— which was like a narrow creek this early winter—and striding through no-man's-land toward the now familiar gully, Jonas was at peace. The serenity of the plain landscape was already coming over him. After he and Ace had a lesson, he would just sit there on the limestone ledge and be peaceful. He liked the warm sun that washed him day after day, the woodpeckers hammering, and the cardinals flashing in and out of the under-brush. Sometimes he would pull chunks of the crumbling marl off in his hands. He would look for the shark's teeth the scientist had told him about and think about when this part of Arkansas had been an ocean. He had never seen an ocean except on TV, but he could imagine.

As he approached the gully Ace, who had rushed ahead and beat him there, started barking. It was not the single, half-strangulated bark of puzzlement that he gave if he found a turtle or snake; it was his Somebody's-Here bark from home. Jonas moved more quickly, jogging through the little cottonwoods that grew up in the first cracks of the gully, and finally reached its main depression, sliding down the last few feet to the limestone ledge.

There stood Vaughan Sandifer, red-faced, with a chisel in his hand and a knapsack on his back, cussing at Ace but holding out a hand toward him as if to try to make friends. Ace stopped barking long enough to sidle toward Mr. Sandifer with his hackles raised, sneaking up to sniff Mr. Sandifer's pants and, grudgingly, the offered hand. Then he jumped back and started barking again. When he saw Jonas, he bounded toward him, continuing to bark spasmodically.

"Hey, Mr. Sandifer," said Jonas.

Mr. Sandifer didn't look overly glad to see him. "Well—hey," he said. Jonas had the feeling he was trying to decide whether it was Jonas or Clint.

"You remember me? I'm Jonas Torbett."

"Sure, Jonas, I know who you are."

"You come to look at our bone?"

"Yeah." Mr. Sandifer was sweating up a storm. "Your daddy invited me to stop by and look at it when I got the chance."

"Yeah," said Jonas. He looked down at the long, protruding, knobbed, yellow-brown bone, and Mr. Sandifer gazed across at it from where he was standing. "It's real nice, isn't it?" said Jonas finally.

"Yeah," said Mr. Sandifer. "It's fine."

"What's that tool you got there?" said Jonas.

Between his squinched, sun-reddened eyelids Mr. Sandifer shot him a look of pure hate. "This here's to throw at rattlesnakes in case I see any. I'm surprised you come back here without something similar."

"There aren't any snakes this time of year," said Jonas.

"Oh, I don't think you can ever be too sure."

Jonas answered, "Well anyway, I got my knife. A knife I got last year for Christmas. I practice throwing it a lot. Like Indians used to play these games where they would throw knives. Plus, I've got Ace. He barks at snakes."

"Yeah, but even if he barks they could get him," said Mr. Sandifer. "Especially if he finds one already coiled up. Or if he surprises it. I've had many a dog been killed by snakebite."

Jonas felt a clutch in his stomach, a cold lump. "Really?"

"I always carry this snakebite kit," Mr. Sandifer went on. He rummaged around in the knapsack on his back for almost a minute, pulled something out, rubbed it on his pants, and handed it to Jonas. "See here?"

It was a clear plastic box with a snap lid that looked scuffed up, as if it was pretty old. "Can I open it?"

"Sure."

Inside there was a booklet with a red cross on it and some pictures of boys with short hair like in old Scout manuals, ministering to each other, and of snake heads and patterns and tails, and of how you should make cuts and tie tourniquets. There was a tiny knife that looked all rusty and a vial of something, maybe whiskey, and a beige net tourniquet that looked practically rotten with age.

"Wow," said Jonas.

"You want it?" said Mr. Sandifer.

Jonas glanced at the man's face. "Well, sure."

"I'll give it to you on one condition." Jonas looked inquiringly at him. "That you don't tell your dad I was back here." Jonas looked down at the snakebite kit, and a guilty expression must have crossed his face. "He asked me to make a report on this bone for him," Mr. Sandifer said, "and I want to surprise him."

"Oh!" said Jonas, in high, innocent tones. "Sure! I won't tell, Mr. Sandifer."

"All right, then."

"Thank you for the snakebite kit."

"Sure, sure. You take care, now. You and your puppy-dog."

"Are you leaving now? Did you find out what you needed for your report?"

"Believe so, believe so," said Mr. Sandifer, stalking off into the brush toward the Old Murdoch Highway. He had to grab saplings for support. "Bye, then," said Jonas.

"Bye."

Jonas watched the bright blue dot of his knapsack till it was completely blotted out by brownish-green leaves. Then he studied the snakebite kit once more, pocketed it, and sank down on the ledge beside the bone. "Ace!" he hollered. "Come on! You're gonna be tardy." While he waited for his pupil to show up he shook his head. "Wants to surprise him with his report!" he whispered. "He must really think I'm dumb." He felt like Cindy-Lou Who in *How the Grinch Stole Christmas,* when she saw the Grinch making off with the Christmas tree and he told her one of its lights needed fixing. "I ain't as dumb as that," said Jonas fiercely. "I'm Alpha Wolf." He fixed his gaze on Ace, who'd come trotting up to him and now sat at his feet. "I ain't no Cindy-Lou Who."

24

THE GIRL LEFT HIS APARTMENT at eight, just as she had every day that week—right at the time most of James's neighbors were going to work. As he had every day, he winced when he heard her slam the door and clump along the balcony in her sleek leather square-toed boots, and winced at the thought of the picture she made: her figure neat and trim in her navy coat, her just-washed hair (Herbal Essence, she kept leaving the shampoo in his shower) bouncing on her shoulders.

"Hello!" he heard her say cheerfully to the overly curious woman in the apartment on James's right, the woman who always tried to strike up conversation with him when he was stretching out for his run. And just before she reached the steps, to someone else—"Great day, isn't it?" Then there was the quick, fading syncopation of her footsteps going downstairs. James scowled into his half-empty bowl of Wheaties. He'd never mend *this* impression. Not that it was anybody's business. Yesterday as he was getting into his truck his neighbor on the left side, a computer parts salesman, winked broadly as he greeted him, getting into his own Porsche, and shook his head. "And on to the workaday world!" he had said, as if he knew James, Stud Supreme, would prefer to be spending the daylight hours recovering from his night of debauchery.

Yet was it his fault? What else could he have said, when she called up and asked for a place to stay for a week? "I just need to crash on your floor," she had said. What excuse would have worked—"I don't have a floor"? "The thing is, I need to stay for the whole trial," she explained. "If it was just for one night I'd stay in a motel. But for several nights that really adds up. And I considered driving in every day from Groverton ..." It was over a two-hour drive each way, as she knew perfectly well he knew. "Oh, no, no," James heard himself gallantly insisting. (Why had his mother reared him to be so accommodating?) "Um—I have a couch, you know, nothing fancy, um, I may be busy at night catching up on some work ..." (I damn sure will be *now,* he thought grimly.) He couldn't believe she didn't know anyone else in Little Rock to stay with.

Sure enough, she'd arrived Sunday night with her little suitcase, stashing her vanity in his bathroom and her Sweet'n'Low in his kitchen, setting up camp. Monday and Tuesday nights he deliberately ate out and worked late—a refugee from his own apartment. When he got in at nine-thirty or ten she was diligently working at his kitchen table, with notebooks and note cards spread in front of her. "They wouldn't let me bring any of this into the courtroom," she explained. "Not even a notebook. Can you believe it? I have to write down as much as I can remember while it's still fresh in my mind." She wore a chastely cut baby-blue robe in some soft material that nevertheless clung to her figure in all the right places. He would switch on the news and stand there watching it for fifteen minutes without taking off his jacket. She chattered on and on about the trial during the commercials, airily tossing around legal jargon as if she'd known it before that day—"On the cross ...," "On the redirect ...," "But in the voir dire ..."—and got pointedly quiet *(See how considerate I am?)* when the anchormen came back on. Then he would go to the bathroom, come out, gruffly tell her goodnight, and disappear into his bedroom, firmly shutting the door behind him. Sunday night she had come tapping on his door. "I'm having some trouble folding out your couch," she called. Though he was already stripped down to his underwear, he scrabbled in the back of his closet for a robe. "James?" she called. "Just a *minute,"* he said irritably. He found one and put it on, jerking the sash with impatience. He brushed by Traci in the hall, stalked to the couch, and unfolded it without ceremony. "I guess I wasn't pulling at the right angle," said Traci.

"Now," said James, "do you need any help with the sheets?"

"No," she said humbly. "I can get them. Thank you." As he headed back to his bedroom he heard her call, "Goodnight, James."

"Night," he said briefly.

Each night since then she'd managed to fold out the couch herself.

This morning he was going to the trial too, and she'd kept hinting broadly that they should ride together. "No," he said. "If it gets boring I'm going to leave and go straight to work."

"Once you leave they won't let you back in."

"Like I said, if I leave it'll be because it's boring and I won't *want* back in."

"Parking's really terrible."

"I'll keep that in mind."

"Well, I'll look for you inside." Her face brightened again. She was unsquelchable. "I sit in this place where I can see the witnesses' faces really well." Nevertheless he knew it was among the ordinary spectators; with all the national and state reporters there, her *Groverton Weekly* press card hadn't carried enough clout to get her into the jury box or the front row where they were sitting.

He was silent. She'd tried to get him to come hear the testimony Monday and Tuesday, but he'd said firmly he had no interest whatsoever in hearing theologians, he would come when the scientists started testifying, if she could please tell him when that would be. Well, yesterday she had duly begged him to come hear Ruse and Dalrymple, and looked crestfallen when he said he had a meeting at work he couldn't miss; but at least today he would hear Stephen Jay Gould.

Now, as he brushed his teeth, got his jacket, and pulled the apartment door shut behind him, he acknowledged what was really bothering him so much about Traci's visit: *what did Deborah think about it?* No telling what Traci had told her. Not that he really believed Traci would be so devious as to make Deborah think it was James's idea that Traci stay with him ... but could he be sure of that? He couldn't exactly call Deborah and start defending himself out of the blue, lest he seem to protest too much ... And neither could he call Deborah to launch into a diatribe about the pushiness of Deborah's best friend. There would be something a little sleazy about that.

Well, he was supposed to see Deborah this weekend anyway. When he did he would ease around to the subject of Traci and his discomfort with her presence. He'd make sure Deborah knew how he felt about it. By that time Traci would be gone, or at least he hoped she would. Surely this trial wouldn't drag into another week—James couldn't believe there was enough legitimacy to the State's and creationists' claims for it to have gone even past one day—but if it did, Traci would just have to clear out for the weekend. Deborah was coming to Little Rock Friday after work. *That* night it remained to be seen how brusquely James would fold out his couch—if at all ... but, no, whatever they did about that was just a daydream, the fringe of fantasy, that he'd barely admitted into his conscious mind. On Saturday after they got up (from wherever), the two of them were going to drive up to the Ozark National Forest and camp. Since it was mid-December the trails should be deserted, the best campsites barren and empty. It was his favorite time of year to camp—the rock formations showed so clearly without summer's growth, and their subtle colors stood out better—and whether Deborah knew it or not, she was privileged he wanted to show it to her. More than about sleeping arrangements, he was nervous about allotting all that time to spend with just one woman. What if, two hours up the road, they realized they just didn't have that much to say to each other? What if next time he saw her, he didn't respond to her presence the same way—or she to his? Then they'd both be stuck. The solitude of the Highland Trail would seem like a nightmarish trap.

Damn it, now he'd missed his turn. Well, he'd circle around the one-way streets. Downtown the traffic was thicker than usual, and James suddenly pulled over into an empty parking space on Spring Street about five blocks from his destination. It might turn out to be a wise move, but even if it were unnecessary, he wouldn't mind the walk on a crisp winter day. It was eight-thirty-five, and court wouldn't convene until nine.

As he walked up Capitol, he saw a crowd already swarming near the doors of the federal courthouse. A couple of TV cameras jutted above the heads of people like dark periscopes, and on the northwest corner of Capitol and Gaines, where James was just crossing, a man in a London Fog coat spoke rapidly and intently into a big lens two feet away. CBS, read the logo on a van parked illegally at the curb. Lord, thought James, hasn't been this much national press in Little Rock since the Central High crisis. He might not even be able to get into the courtroom.

He jostled around near the entrance, shaking his head at some clown in an ape suit who was cavorting through the crowd, declining fliers being passed out by earnest-looking young men with crosses in their lapels. He hadn't pictured this much of a carnival atmosphere, even with what he'd read in the paper. In the dim main hall of the building people were packed near the elevators. After five minutes James got on one, wedged uncomfortably between a large woman in a brown suit holding a sketch pad and a thin elderly man. It seemed that everybody was going to the fourth floor today. As they lurched upward James didn't check the floor lights; he was still eyeing the weight limit notice when they rocked to a stop.

Just as he stepped forward he was blinded by a flash of white, rainbow-rimmed light. He stood frozen for a split-second before he was pushed on by the crowd behind him.

"What was that?" somebody gasped, and somebody else joked, "A supernova, I think." No creationist there, thought James. Blinking, he saw a phalanx of cameras and reporters settling back against the wall opposite the elevator. He heard them saying, "Nobody—just spectators, artists—" Then a second elevator opened, they sprang forward, and when the first passengers stepped off the blaze of light from two dozen flashbulbs happened all over again. "Move along, son, will you?" said somebody behind James. Son? Obediently he followed the surge down the hall to the courtroom.

There was a bottleneck at the courtroom doors, where men in navy sport coats with badges and walkie-talkies—bailiffs, he guessed—seemed to fall into deep conversation with each person trying to enter. James peered around the man in front of him and saw a bailiff shaking his head, the young man with the fliers waving a fistful of them and talking vehemently. Finally the young man handed the fliers to the bailiff, a disgusted expression on his face. James sneaked a curious peek at them as he shuffled by: *The Word of the Lord will not be sile*— was all he saw.

Stepping into the courtroom he sensed a hush, an enveloping solemnity, like that of a cathedral, and only then did he realize what a furious chatter had filled the halls outside. No ape-man antics here. The room was grave, spacious, filled with an amber light. Its walls were paneled several yards up with a handsome old grained wood, then painted the rest of their imposing height a lemony white. Around the back of the room were stern oil portraits; in front were the flags, hanging solemn, and a clock, and the empty judge's bench. Two people behind James brushed by him, impatient with his hesitation, and he stepped aside to get out of their way. As he scanned the room he saw Traci, already turning, her face also solemn. She gave a little half-wave, moving her coat from the seat beside her. Well, it was a good seat, and he could hardly ignore her gesture. He went and sat beside her, thankful that for once she didn't try to talk.

The press sat in the jury box and in the front rows of the courtroom. The artists had their sketch pads, and one wore what looked like a tiny pair of binoculars attached to her glasses. The two teams of lawyers were at the front of the room—the defense, immaculate in tailored suits and blow-dried hairdos, massed around the Attorney General, and the prosecution a little more varied, with the untidily stylish bagginesses here and there and the weird ties of East Coast liberals. Andy Ropp was nowhere in sight.

The clerk came out and rattled off some statement James could barely understand. Then the black-robed judge entered, and the crowd stood. James wondered if Judge Overton had been up all night reading scientific abstracts and religious tracts. Traci said that he'd been short with the attorneys—particularly the plaintiffs—when any of the examinations went on too long, and that he'd overruled all the state's objections. He started off brusquely enough this morning: "I see you all made it back, and I believe we are about to begin the cross-examination of Dr. Dalrymple."

As Dalrymple took the stand James felt a catch of excitement, almost nervousness, in his stomach—though why that should be he didn't know; it wasn't *his* case. A couple of hours later, when court recessed for a break, his head was spinning. He was trying not only to dust off bits of physical theory he had shelved after exams years before, but also to grasp the quickly stated logic of the experimental manipulation of that theory. Then when a witness had to summarize areas of geophysics James did know well, necessarily oversimplifying them, his mind raced to evaluate the testimony—was anything crucial left out? How would he have put that to the intelligent non-scientist? Meanwhile he was constantly juggling the counterpoint of opposing courtroom tacks that were as much philosophical as legal. And it was clear that, whatever else had caused his jitters, he needn't have felt sympathetic worry on behalf of Dalrymple or the witness who followed him, Morowitz. He raised his eyebrows at Traci and said, "Whew."

"Pretty amazing, isn't it?" she said.

"I feel like I'm back in college."

"I know. It's like, the *adrenalin*—in these *minds*—"

"Well, some of them."

"Your man's up next!" she said.

"Yeah ..."

Gould was short, blocky, with a dark brown beard and infectiously enthusiastic voice. He seemed hardly able to contain himself to the witness stand as the sentences flowed out of him, leis, wreaths, garlands of them, all as intricately and well constructed as the ones James knew from his essays. The testimony started with establishing Gould's credibility—not the toughest of hurdles for the lawyer—and moved on to fallacies Gould noted in the language of the Arkansas bill, and from there to the basic tenets and debates of paleontology; to gradualism, uniformitarianism, catastrophism, punctuated equilibrium, yo-yoing again and again from huge overarching concepts of life to its blessedly concrete, discrete particulars like fish jaws and snail shells—with the lawyer's questions getting fewer and farther between and Gould getting more and more wound up and if possible more eloquent, his eyes snapping more merrily, aeons skipping off his tongue, as the hands on the clock on the wall behind the judge went round.

Then it was lunchtime. "The first day," said Traci, "when we recessed for lunch"—*we,* you'd have thought she was a key player—"the judge said, 'I don't know if this clock behind me is right or not, but it's the one we follow.' "

"So what?" said James.

"Well, I just thought it was funny because it shows like how everything is relative. You know. Look!" She jabbed James with her elbow, and tiptoed to whisper in his ear. "Remember the ones I told you dropped down on their knees and prayed for that witness, that sociologist, when she said she didn't believe in God? That's them."

Though he had no idea what she was talking about, he obediently looked at the three people she was pointing to—two women in longish skirts and hair coiled high on top of their heads, no makeup, Pentecostal probably, and a short man in corduroy trousers and a sport shirt, filing out into the hall with the rest of the spectators.

"So you want to go get a bite?" said James.

"Sure!"

"I don't know where we can go, everything's bound to be so crowded ... Can you walk fast?"

"Of course."

"Let's head for my truck. I'm a little ways down on Spring. We can head west and beat the congestion, and still be back here by one-thirty."

At a cafe on Markham they ordered po-boys and James, after a moment's pause, got a beer. What the hell: he wasn't going to work this afternoon. The cold draft prickled his tongue, and he sipped deeply, appreciatively.

"What are you thinking about?" said Traci.

"What?" He realized that in his brown study his gaze had been resting on her eyes—though he hadn't been thinking of them. Now he noticed that they were a true hazel, neither green nor brown but a blend of the two, with doughnut-shaped paler rings around the pupil. *Radioactive haloes* ... They were wide open, frank and inquisitive, and now they were focused on him.

"You're just staring."

"I'm sorry. I was thinking."

"What about?" She smiled, leaning forward, her breasts nearly grazing the shorn cracker wrappers on the table.

"Well, to be honest, I was thinking about punctuated equilibrium." She leaned back. "Not in a scientific sense, though. I was thinking that it's sort of ironic that not only evolution proceeds that way but science in general ... You know, things go along for a long time with nothing happening and you just have to be patient and wait it out, and then there's a burst of activity with a lot of new ground covered. Or at least that's the way my career goes." He stopped and drank some more beer and noticed with surprise that his mug was almost empty. He shouldn't get beer when he was simply thirsty; ice water would do. He knew, of course, as soon as he'd expressed his thought, that as much as his work he was talking about his personal life: the long desert expanse of plateaus at long last relieved by bluffs, glaciation, canyons—by *incident* ... Deborah. Man, he must be worse off than he thought, to be thinking of her when he drank.

The po-boys arrived. "Another beer, sir?"

"No thanks. Just some water."

Now the girl seemed all subdued. She didn't have anything bright and chatty to say about punctuated equilibrium. He wondered what he'd done.

"What angle are you going to take on this trial, in your thesis? What's your point going to be?"

"Oh, gee," she said. "I don't know." She pushed some cole slaw around on her plate. "I guess I'm a little overwhelmed at the moment."

"Um." Moody, moody. He ate for a while, checked his watch.

"Has he brought the check?"

"Yeah, right there." She had already put her five on top of it. "James ..."

"Yeah?"

"Oh, nothing."

"Come on, let's go," he said. "They probably won't let us in if we're late."

"Yeah, you're right, they won't."

She seemed to recover her equanimity during the afternoon, laughing at several funny exchanges, once even touching James lightly on the leg as she chuckled. When court was adjourned at five-twenty, she told him, "Now I know you don't have to be at your office tonight, so why don't you let me take you out to dinner, to thank you for putting me up this week?"

"Well," said James, "I'd like to run ..."

"Sure, go ahead and run. We can go after your run. That'll give me a chance to shower and pick out where I want to take you."

Maybe she wasn't reading anything into their enforced companionship; maybe she wasn't as aggressive as she seemed; but James had an uneasy feeling about it—a mighty uneasy feeling, he acknowledged as he ran into the winter sunset. He wasn't very good at these interpersonal things but he just had a feeling somebody was reading somebody wrong and he sure didn't know what he'd done to lead anybody astray.

The restaurant she chose was dark and quiet with his least favorite kind of instrumental music, lute or something artsy, playing. His heart sank when they walked in. "Table for two?" the hostess smiled. "It's not like that!" James wanted to shout at her back as she led them to a tiny table by a window, with a rose in a vase by a little candle. "You're not helping matters any!"

While they waited for their ice water, waited for their wine and menus, waited to order, waited for their rolls, waited for their salads, James talked volubly, partly because he was energized from the day's events and from his run, and partly to prevent Traci from injecting anything into the conversation he didn't want her to. She was quieter than usual, but listened to him with eyes that shone in the candlelight and an occasional remotely sad smile.

"So I don't envy those defense attorneys," James said. "Can you imagine having to cross-examine one of those scientists— on the guy's own field? When you're trained as a lawyer, and have only had a few months to be reading up on the subject? 'Have you published in this field?' 'Oh, yes, some five books and a hundred and fifty articles.' 'Okay if he's presented as an expert in this area?' 'No objection here, Your Honor. Any time y'all are ready I'll go ahead and grill him on the salient points of molecular biochemistry and biophysics ...' "

Traci laughed.

"And oh, that was funny, this afternoon, during Morowitz's cross-exam I think it was? When the lawyer was trying to question him about that article on thermodynamics and Morowitz was answering completely by memory—'Oh yes, I've read that, well, I think if you'll read on to the next few sentences following the quotation you've just read, you'll see what point the author's really elaborating on, how he resolves that problem'—and so his lawyer says, 'Maybe it would help if the witness had a copy of the article'—"

"Oh yeah," said Traci, "and the judge is like, 'Doesn't seem like he needs one to me.' "

"Yeah, that was pretty good." James drummed his fingers on the table. "And there was something else funny that happened about that time—"

"I know what you're thinking of," said Traci. "It was the same cross-exam. The defense lawyer, I mean, who is this rinky-dink guy, is lambasting this eminent scientist for not being able to synthesize life in the laboratory, he was like physically throwing his weight around: 'You mean to tell me, Dr. Morowitz, that with all your resources you have not been able to recreate these conditions and produce life from non-life in the laboratory? Can you tell me why that is?' "

"Oh, that was good," said James.

"And Morowitz goes, he waits a beat, like a comedian, and then he goes, 'Young man, it is a *very* difficult problem.' "

"People were getting pretty punchy in there this afternoon."

"To break the tension, I guess."

The silence between them grew for a minute.

"Of course, what really bothers me about the creationists," said James, "is their intellectual dishonesty. That's where the real damage to school kids comes in. If they didn't have to twist and defraud and take things out of context ..."

Traci didn't answer, she just nodded. In a few minutes, just as James cleared his throat and started to say, "Do you remember what our waiter looked like?" he appeared with their plates. They ate quietly for a few minutes and then Traci said, "Well, it really is nice of you to put me up this week—give up your privacy and all."

"Oh." James smiled confusedly. He was determined not to say "My pleasure" so even though she hadn't said thanks, exactly, he said, "You're welcome."

Here came that rueful smile on Traci's face again. "I called Deborah while you were out running?"

"You did?" He almost felt himself blushing.

"Yeah. I charged the call, of course."

"Oh," he said. "I wasn't worried about that. So what'd she have to say?"

The busboy came to clear their plates, and Traci waited to answer. Then she said, her eyes growing shiny again, "She said y'all are going camping this weekend?"

"Yeah!" said James uneasily. "Good! So we're still on! I haven't talked to her in a few days. Why, what's the matter?"

One corner of Traci's mouth had started to crumple and James saw to his horror that she was beginning to cry.

"Oh, no," he said.

She pulled her napkin out of her lap and tried to use that. "I didn't know," she said with her distorted mouth, her eyes shuttering like half-moons to squeeze out the tears. "I just didn't know. Every time I mentioned her you never said anything—and you always seemed so glad to see *me*—"

"Oh, no."

"I'm really sorry. Let's just go, okay? I really need to leave."
She got up, still crying and sniffing, and tried to push her
cumbersome chair under the table.

"We haven't even got the check," said James helplessly.

"Just don't mind me," Traci went on, weeping. James saw the
waiter appearing from behind her, his eyebrows lifted. He
handed the check to James over Traci's shoulder just as she
said, "Never mind. It's just that I'm starting my period, is all.
Never mind." James hastily handed the man some bills and
steered Traci toward the door, past the hostess. "I always take
things hard when I'm starting my period!..."

On their way back to his apartment she subsided, rousing
herself only once to say bitterly, "Now I don't even know how I
can stay with you any longer. I'll have to go back to Groverton
and miss the rest of the trial, I guess."

"Oh, don't be ridiculous," James said. "Don't be silly, Traci."

Across the cab of his truck she faced him. Her face looked
square and wan, her eyes red-rimmed. "You love her, don't you?
I don't know how I could've missed it."

"Who?" he said defensively.

"I could see it in your face when I said I'd called her. You're
taking her camping. I think you really love her."

"I don't know that I've ..."

"Oh, I'm embarrassed to even stay one more night here."

"Don't be silly," said James. "Look. You want me to stay
somewhere else?" In the parking lot of his apartment they glared
at each other, like rival boxers.

"No, that'd be even dumber than me leaving." But he heard a
faint interest in her voice.

"I have a friend I can stay with. Look, I'd just as soon."

"James, that's so *ridiculous.*"

"It won't take me but a minute to give him a call."

Andy Ropp grinned at him, opening the door. "Dame trouble,

eh?"

James rolled his eyes and refused to answer.

"I'm not sure I get the gist of it," said Andy, following him inside. "Or maybe you've missed out on the basic idea. When a single man gets a dame in his apartment, Donovan, the point is to stay there *with* her."

James dropped his duffel bag on the floor by the couch and flopped down. "Oh, you wouldn't believe," he said. "Look, Ropp, just tell me, does this thing fold out or not?"

25

BACK IN GROVERTON, Traci started the weekend of her mortification quietly. As long as she didn't dwell too much on the reason for Deborah's absence, she was glad to have the place to herself, to play hermit—or rather, nun, as was better suited to her current status with men.

Her parents were in San Antonio on some sort of weekend package tour, and Traci's only outing on Saturday was to their house to feed the cat. Groverton was decorated for Christmas, with shiny synthetic Christmas tree garlands strung between its telephone poles, and lights that spelled NOEL (or LEON, if you were heading the other way, as Traci had mused every year since she was six) forming a banner across Main Street. In front of the courthouse stood the rough lean-to where the Living Nativity Scene was now underway each night. With straw scattered on the ground, a few stools here and there for Mary and Joseph and the most tired Wise Men, and staffs leaning against the walls, it looked oddly vacant, stark in the noon light—though in the feed trough that served as manger, Traci did see a flash of pink plastic that must be the doll used for Baby Jesus. (After it was resolved that modern shoes and eyeglasses would be permitted, the next controversy, which Traci had duly reported, was whether to use a real infant or a doll to portray the star of the show. The year before the Nunnally baby, then eight weeks old, was used; he cried unremittingly every night, and turned out to be allergic to hay. This year they were back to a doll.)

Christmas shoppers were out on Main Street in full force.

Some of them waved at Traci merrily, depressingly, and she fled back home.

The rest of the day she spent washing clothes, answering letters to her college friends, and typing out notes from the week past, talking only to Floyd, the dog. She had brought some wine from Little Rock; she drank two glasses with her Lean Cuisine supper and was bored even by the slight buzz that resulted. For a while she looked in vain for something good on TV, finally giving it up and lying in a dejected stupor on the couch. Eddie O. called to find out how the trial was and to be sure she had her instructions to cover the nativity scene Sunday night. It had been running for three nights now, he said, and the *Weekly* had yet to have a story on it because he'd been waiting for her to get back from Little Rock. As a matter of fact he'd expected to see her there tonight—? He ended that statement on a faintly questioning note, but she gave him no reason for her absence, promising instead to cover the event on Sunday. "What time does it start?" "Six-thirty." As soon as she hung up, the phone rang again. It was Stuart, saying he had a fantastic tip for a news story for her. Though she was kinder to him than she'd been the last time they talked, she said wearily that she was under the weather: could they talk about it Monday? When she hung up from talking to him she burst into tears, and fell asleep with her nose leaking into a wet pillow.

She went out for a walk early Sunday morning, came home and went back to bed till noon. Then she straightened up the house and read and finally showered and washed her hair and put on some clean jeans and a sweater, feeling her morale lift slightly with each determined effort. Just as she was picking up her keys she heard Deborah driving up. She went outside to greet her, feeling sheepish: who knew what she and James had been saying about her all weekend?

Act nonchalant, she told herself. Act natural.

"So!" she said. "How was it?"

Deborah climbed stiffly out of her truck, crumpling up a McDonald's sack, her clothes and hair looking limp but her face signaling a tired happiness. "Oh—it was great."

"Really? You had a good time?"

"Oh, yeah." Deborah stooped over to pet Floyd, who had straggled down the front steps to show his master a few swings of the tail in welcome. "Hey, Floyd, baby, sweet thing."

"I think he's actually been awake a couple of hours this weekend. Maybe three. We've been pretty lazy."

"James said the trial was intense. You probably needed to relax."

"Yeah." What else had he said? "Look, can I take something in for you? What else have you got?"

"Oh—my sleeping bag, I guess, some other stuff. But you look like you're headed somewhere."

"How could you forget? The Living Nativity Scene. Eddie O.'s in a big sweat to do a feature page on it."

"In that case, you'd better run on. I think I'll finish unloading later."

"You don't want to come with me, hunh?"

"I'll pass."

The diagonal parking places on Main were already filled, and Traci had to park on a side street. Well, this occasion was certainly a contrast to the last time she'd headed toward a crowded courthouse, two days before. The headlights of cars cruising slowly past threw her shadow in a long, jumpy form stretching out in front of her. Her breath met the night in little plumes of steam. Others hurried along beside her, grandmothers carrying folded lawn chairs, young men with children on their shoulders, hefty middle-agers—most of Groverton, in their cowboy hats and scarves and cheap clothes layered against the cold.

For years she remembered coming to the Living Nativity Scene, first as a small girl, when it held the whole wonder and power of Christmas for her. On the same night they came to the pageant, her parents would drive around to see the lights of Groverton, a multicolored splendor to her childish eyes ... Later, around puberty, she would beg to go with just her friends to the nativity scene—cramming their hands in the pockets of their puffy polyester jackets, talking quickly in a kind of group short-hand to one another as they moved up to the front. But even at that age their giggles subsided when they saw familiar grownups outlandishly clad but still solemn and stiff, like automated mannikins, recreating the old, familiar story: the story that was the reason for the shiny Dillards boxes under the tree, the two weeks off from school ... It was not until the end of high school that Traci had gotten jaded about the Living Nativity Scene and started to view it as ludicrous, embarrassing. It was another of those things she could tell funny stories about at college. Yet what she didn't add, then, was that she could still be touched by the scene, way down: the pathos of these vastly imperfect human beings, out of the homely ennui of their lives, trying to recreate the purity of some original happening.

"Do you think Groverton has changed?" she had asked Deborah Armstrong several weeks ago.

"What do you mean?"

"Well—gone downhill, I guess. Like my mother's always saying."

"No," said Deborah. "I think it's always been this way. I think it's your perspective that's changed."

"Yeah, I guess that would make the most sense."

The strains of "God Rest Ye Merry, Gentlemen," tinny and staticky, reached her ears. She knew it came from a sound system set up behind the stable. At intervals the tapes would be turned off and various choirs standing on the courthouse steps would sing. Eddie O. wanted the names of all the par-ticipating choirs and their directors. Traci had a partial list, but one of her chores for tonight was to find out who the rest of the singers were.

Every year more and more sideshows got tacked on to the basic tableau. They, too, had created controversies. According to some, it all started with the Little Drummer Boy's being thrown in around 1973 or 1974. The next year a contingent wanted to add a North Pole tableau on the other side of the courthouse lawn, complete with Santa's Workshop. The official

organizers' committee refused permission, but a sort of under-
ground North Pole was set up anyway. The next year it became
even more established and co-featured Rudolph and Frosty. The
next year on the traffic island across the street from the courthouse there appeared a City Christmas scene, which caused an
uproar mainly because that site was where, December after
December, a certain church staged its protest against any sort
of theatrical presentation having to do with the birth of the
Savior. For years the main nativity scene and the protesters had
coexisted in good will, and the protesters were of no mind to
give up their prime picketing spot (which was, coincidentally, a
prime vantage point, and afforded the best view of such
catastrophes as A.M. Bigley's crown falling off or Harold Grubber digging under his shepherd's robe to find the Rolaids in his
pocket). Letters to the editor flew to the paper every year like
clockwork, lamenting the commercialization of Christmas, with
the decline of the Living Nativity Scene as a prime example. LNS
organizers wrote stiff letters of self-defense just as routinely,
calling their effort "a community worship experience" and
declining responsibility for the sideshows. But the more of a
circus atmosphere surrounded it, the bigger the crowds were—
the more people flocked into Groverton from all over southwest
Arkansas to see the spectacle.

Traci didn't remember the audience's being this excited.
People were elbowing each other and talking and moving quickly, some toward their parked cars and others pressing forward
toward the lean-to. It took her a few minutes to realize that
something out of the ordinary must have happened. "Come on!"
"—so late getting started?" "Did you hear that?" "—something
about it was Indians done it—" "What?" "It's almost six-forty-
five." "Come on!" "—a shame—" "Come on, they're asking
people to join hands and pray—" "—up to the front." "Who said
that?" "I can't see." "—things are coming to." Now there was a
general surge forward. Traci stumbled and fell into the woman
next to her. She straightened up, excusing herself, but the
woman had already hurried up ahead. Now everybody was
trotting. "What? What's going on?" Traci was asking, but no one

answered her. Finally it was a young boy who helped her out. Running pell-mell back toward his parents from the front of the crowd, he cried out, "Daddy—*they've kidnapped Jesus!*"

"Kidnapped Jesus? The doll?"

"Yes, but they left a ransom note!"

At this rate she would never get close enough to see. Traci started jogging, angling to the side, where people weren't stacked so deep. She wiggled and elbowed her way up front.

The nativity actors were coming out of a huddle. Sheriff Wingate was over at the side, with a grimness of expression befitting only the innkeeper; but his badge and uniform suggested he wasn't play-acting. Henry Brandon, this year's Joseph, was just stepping forward. He had on a fake cottony beard, but even against the white beard his usually beet-red face looked wan and pale. He kept pushing wisps of cotton away from his lips to speak. "Ladies and gentlemen—ladies and gentlemen. It's not usually our policy to speak during the Living Nativity Scene, as you well know. Somebody turn that music off, please."

Jessie Cowley, a teacher who understood the fine points of the sound system, disappeared behind a plywood palm tree that was nailed to the side of the stable. The Star of the East, painted fluorescent yellow-white, lolled precariously in its fronds. Both had been made in the shop at the high school.

At Traci's side, Butter McCollum shifted and clucked. "I told them not to do this. It just gives 'em a forum, whoever it is! It's just playing into their hands!"

"But who—when'd you find out?" said Traci.

"Land, just about ten minutes ago. If that. Such a shame."

Henry was continuing. "But something has happened that makes it a necessity to say something. When the actors got here this evening, the manger that holds the little doll we use to represent the Baby Jesus was empty. In its place was this note, which I want to read to you. I don't know if you can tell or not but the note's made of letters cut out from a newspaper or a magazine." The spectators were utterly quiet. Whereas they usually stood several feet apart from one another, in family clumps, they were now pressed shoulder to shoulder in one close mass.

"This here's the message." He proceeded to read haltingly, word by word. I would've hated to be in reading circle with him in school, thought Traci. "'You to whom the white baby of Christendom is sacred: he will not be given back until the bones of our ancestors, which are just as sacred to us, are returned. We are talking about the ones most recently desecrated. Signed, the Caddo people of Arkansas.'"

"Uh-oh," said Traci involuntarily, and Butter turned her face sharply toward her.

Henry looked up. "I think you can see what a sad situation this is. Us actors have been up here for the past, oh, little while, since we discovered this, trying to decide what to do. We've had some disagreement about it, but I think the majority of us think we can't hardly have a Living Nativity Scene with no Baby Jesus in the manger. We'd like to join hands and all sing 'Joy to the World' before we go home."

There was a jolt of silence. Finally Jessie Cowley started singing, in a range comfortable for her own soprano voice. Tentative, multipitched, swelling and growling, the carol struggled aloft. At the end of the first verse there was another pause, with most people, Traci suspected, hoping that was it. A few diehards started in on the second verse, but over their voices came a shout: "Get another doll, Henry!"

Henry looked up, perplexed.

"Get another doll to be Jesus!"

"Yeah! Can't anybody shut us down!"

Butter stepped forward into the tableau to talk to Henry, who looked confused, and Sheree Blunt edged next to them, grabbing Henry's elbow persuasively.

Now the audience was spewing suggestions, shouting and calling, pressing forward even farther, till they threatened to surge into the crèche itself and scatter the sheep, and made even the Nestersons' big half-dead Guernsey stir in alarm.

"Don't let 'em make us cancel."

"Run over to Wal-Mart and buy another doll!"

"Wal-Mart's closed on Sunday night."

"You'n always find a doll somewheres."

From several feet behind Traci, she heard a high, sweet voice pipe up: *"I got a doll."* And then louder, over the clamor, the piercing voice of a child who is insistent on being heard: *"I got a doll!"*

Suddenly others were saying it too. "'Is little girl has a doll!"

"Why, here's someone got a doll right here!"

"Pass her forward! Pass her forward!"

Traci was craning to see, but at first all she saw was the broad denim-clad backs of those behind her turning around too, and then a buckling, a dimpling, in the crowd. Suddenly, on the shoulder of a tall silver-haired man in a Groverton Indians windbreaker—oh, it was Coach Odum, Traci now saw—a small black girl popped into sight. She was clad in a bright green velour sweatsuit, embroidered around the collar, and her hair was neatly sectioned and pigtailed and clipped with bright plastic clips. Her eyes were large and bright and self-assured, and her face stayed calm as the white man carried her forward. In her arms she clutched a naked, wild-haired, dark-skinned doll whose expression was much more alarmed than her own. And right behind Coach Odum, in the little wake his slow stride through the crowd had made, was a large black woman with her hair in curlers under a plastic net, with a furrowed brow and compressed mouth and a stabbing anxiety in her eyes. When the coach stepped into the pool of electric light and the straw-covered area that signified the stage, the woman halted, but her whole body was bent trembling toward the small, calm form on his shoulder.

A rumble, a ripple, spread through the crowd and Traci, who had debated the existence of God by rote since she was sixteen, now found an instant prayer on her tongue: *oh God, please don't let them say anything!* And the next outcry she heard was "Use that child's doll."

"Henry, Butter, Sheree," said Coach Odum, "this little girl says you can use her doll."

"Well—" said Henry uncertainly, but the child was already thrusting it toward him. All the pink-skinned people stared for what seemed a long, long moment at the dark doll hanging in the air. Then Butter said in a stern voice, "Take it, Henry," just as Sheree Blunt suddenly grabbed the thing and clutched it to her breast. Butter faced the crowd. In the booming south-Arkansas drawl with which she had directed children and grandchildren and Sunday school pupils and yard men and maids in a thousand chores and rituals, she called out, "Now, people, we'll sing one more carol and then we'll get on with the 1981 Living Nativity Scene. First verse only, people, of 'O Little Town of Bethlehem.' " A slight nod sent Henry scuttling over to his proper place beside the manger, where Sheree was crooning over the doll, and a firmer one sent Coach Odum and the little girl into the front line of the crowd. Butter herself stood by them, and took the little girl's mother's hand firmly in her own. Her voice, staunch, nasal, with a hideous vibrato, rang out loudest into the night:

> *O little town of Bethlehem,*
> *How still we see thee lie—*
> *Above thy deep and dreamless sleep*
> *The silent stars go by.*
> *Yet in thy dark streets shineth*
> *The everlasting light—*
> *The hopes and fears of all the years*
> *Are met in thee tonight.*

Traci stood on Stuart's porch, beating on the flimsy wood panel of his screen door. Finally he answered. "Well, hey," he said when he saw her. His eyes swept down her body, almost involuntarily. "You coulda saved yourself some time, if you'd wanted to hear my tipoff last night."

"Well, I wasn't in the mood," said Traci. "And I don't think it's too late anyway. Can I come in?"

"Of course, madam." He bowed exaggeratedly. "It's a pleasure to have you here for whatever reason, even if not for the one I'd like."

"No, I'm not here for that one." Even as she disclaimed it—so airily—she felt a little fillip of arousal within. *That* stood thick in the air between them. In the living room she faced him. "Stuart, when did you get this cute idea?"

"You like it?"

"No, I think it's the most juvenile thing I've ever heard of. You're twenty-six years *old.*"

"It must be getting some reaction or you wouldn't have rushed over. I had a hard time staying away from the Living Nativity Scene, for once."

"Oh, it's getting quite a reaction, all right. You would think it was a real baby that was kidnapped. You would think we were back at Easter and they'd discovered the empty tomb. You would think—" She couldn't think of any more examples, and stopped.

Stuart was grinning. "It looks like you have to come up with a juvenile idea to get the juvenile attention of juvenile Groverton."

She wasn't going to show any approval of him by laughing. "What are you hoping to *achieve* by this?" She reminded herself of a schoolteacher.

"On the record, miss?"

"Goddamn it, Stuart. Well, yes."

"I—speaking not personally, you understand, but on deep background for the Caddo tribe of Arkansas—I'm hoping to get my ancestral remains back. The ones that aren't yet sold to museums or greedy dealers or covered up with a manmade lake, that is. *My* sacred symbol. The bare bones, as it were, of my mythic reality, in which *I* am spiritually invested. Which correspond to the Christians' spiritual investment, I guess, in this." He picked up from the couch a doll made of pinkish hollow plastic, and tipped it back and forth so that its starry blue eyes opened and shut. It had been wrapped in yards of torn white cheesecloth. At this Traci could not contain herself. She burst into giggles. Stuart started snickering too. "Wonderful, Counselor," he said in mock-reverent accents, holding the doll aloft. "Prince of Peace." "Mama," bleated the doll in a mechanical voice. Traci and Stuart stumbled and staggered around the room, holding on to furniture for support. "Oh, my God, are the blinds drawn?" gasped Traci.

Finally they subsided. Somehow they had both flung themselves down on the couch. They wiped their eyes. Stuart tipped the doll again, and again it honked, "Mama." This time they both stared at it, sighing.

"Well," said Traci, "do you really think you're going to get your ransom price for this—treasure?" She pulled her legs up tailor-fashion so she could face Stuart.

"Oh, I don't know. It was just a crazy idea. I guess it was juvenile. I've been so damn bored, Traci"—he looked swiftly into her eyes—"and once it occurred to me I just thought, 'What have I got to lose?' "

"Well, you have definitely created a stir, from what little I saw tonight. I don't know if you'll get Bryce Torbett to cough up that bone, and personally I don't think it's Caddo anyway, I mean I don't even think it's human. But you've created a stir, I'll grant you that."

Stuart was quiet. "I know it may not be human," he said. "The paleontologists and archaeologists have barely gotten a shot at identifying it. But it might be human; and if it's human it's probably Indian; and what's more to the point, everybody around here is convinced it is, and they still don't give a damn."

They were both quiet a minute. Then Traci said, "Everybody's gonna know it's you."

"Well, of course. But what can they do about it? I didn't kidnap a real child. I didn't even steal a doll from anyone, as far as I can tell. I picked up some litter that I noticed on the courthouse lawn, on public property. If they want to take me to court and get into the matter of what this stuff was doing at the courthouse, I'd be more than happy to oblige them. It might be the end of the Living Nativity Scene as we know it." He stood up. "You want something to drink?"

"Sure."

"Hot chocolate okay?"

"Fine."

"Instant okay?"

"Of course."

"Good. It's all I've got." She followed him into the kitchen, idly dangling the doll by its hair—stiff platinum locks that appeared to have been cropped. "How about him"—Stuart gestured—"would Jesus like some hot chocolate?"

She smiled. "Oh, I think not—he's still on mother's milk, these days. Or Nestle formula, since he was born in a Third World country ..."

Stuart turned back around from the stove in time to catch the end of her smile. As it left her face Traci felt a warmth, probably a blush, replacing it, but she kept her eyes steadily on Stuart's. Still looking at her he reached for her fingers entangled in the doll's hair and tugged at them, holding her hand behind her back, until she dropped the doll and clasped his fingers. He was so close to her she smelled his scent, ineffable, something she could never quite reconstruct in her mind but which immediately brought back their lovemaking.

"I wish I didn't miss you so much," he said slowly. "I've tried not to." He backed up to a kitchen stool and sat down, pulled her loosely along by the hands locked behind her hips, stood her between his long blue-jeaned thighs. "No, don't get so alarmed. You think I mean something I don't when I say that. I just mean that I enjoy you. Your company. Isn't it hard enough to—isn't that rare enough between people that you can relax and just leave it alone?"

She stirred uneasily. "I hate it when people get plaintive."

He didn't flinch, just kept looking at her speculatively. "That's not good enough," he said. The kettle started to whistle. "Turn that off, please."

Traci twisted around and turned off the jet, then faced him again. He was waiting.

"How do you know it's not just sex?" she said finally.

" 'Just' sex?"

"Doesn't that bother you? Men are always saying, 'Oh, just enjoy the sex for its own sake, if there's anything else there it'll fall into place'—but I can't do that. I know, Stuart, because I've tried. I asked you once, on that picnic, remember?—I asked you, 'How much of this do you think is purely sexual?' and you laughed and said, 'Oh, about ninety percent.' That really hurt my feelings. And you *laughed* when you said it."

"The reason you asked me that," said Stuart, "was that we had just had such a great time making love. In that moment, for once, you could admit that it's a good thing, a precious thing. You were asking me that like it was something to marvel over. It's simple. You mess it up when you overanalyze it. I'm not going to put myself in the position of explaining it to you, or defending it." His voice didn't rise, and his calmness kept her from taking flight in a puff of indignation or wounded feelings. He spoke quietly, shrugging for emphasis because his hands were still locked behind her back.

"And that's enough for you?"

"Sure it's enough. It's not enough for all time, but it's enough for the"—he cocked his head—"I started to say 'moment,' but I'll say 'day.' It's enough for that day. I don't expect any one person to be 'enough' of everything for me forever. That'd be a pretty big demand to make."

She frowned. "For somebody who doesn't like to talk about it, you do all right."

"Talk about what?"

"Sex. Relationships."

He made a face at the word. "And for somebody who does like to talk about it, at least analyze it, you do pretty poorly."

"Thank you, sir," she said sturdily.

He drew his thighs in, catching her between them, released her hands, and lightly slapped her behind. "Oh, God," he said. "Why do our bodies cause us so much trouble?"

Traci was running her hands automatically along the glass-smooth fabric of the jeans, playing with the thick inseams. "Stuart?"

"Mm?"

"Can I just take a nap here? I'm really really tired."

"You look tired. You look like you've been through the wringer."

To anybody else she would have said pertly, "Well, thanks a *lot!*" and tossed her head, but she just looked at Stuart.

"Now, I have a bedroom," he said, "and I have a couch."

"I'd rather the bed."

"Can I," he said carefully, "lie down beside you? Tell me now, so I don't misunderstand."

"Stuart," she said, *"please* lie down with me."

They left Jesus beside the cold kettle. They hurried to the bedroom, kicking off their shoes as they went. Their stockinged feet rubbed static off each other as they bumped and mingled under the covers, their belt buckles clicked together as they settled into each other's arms. "I really do just want to sleep first," whispered Traci. Her breath was warm in the hollow of Stuart's unshaven throat.

Torbett to Return Bone to Indians
TRACI MORGAN

In a late-breaking development in the case of the kidnapped "Jesus" doll, Bryce Torbett announced Monday
that he would be returning his fossilized bone to Caddo
Indians. Whoever took the doll from the Living Nativity
Scene on Sunday left a ransom note demanding the bone.
Torbett has been in the middle of controversy about the
artifact since June, when it was found on his property by
his younger son, Jonas, 10.

Living Nativity Scene organizers tried to persuade Torbett that his action was unnecessary and would give undue
importance to the prank kidnapping. "It's just capitulating
to the terrorists," said C.W. "Rooster" McKay, president of
the Chamber of Commerce. "I hate to see [Torbett] play
right into their hands." Another doll has been acquired for
the live tableau and the nativity scene is scheduled to run
as planned through December 20.

Torbett says, however, "I want to insure that this doesn't
happen again. This community has given a lot to me and
it's the least I can do." He said he would be on the courthouse lawn at 5:00 p.m. Wednesday to present the bone to
any members of the Caddo tribe who want to accept it.

Stuart Bledsoe, the local Caddo activist, disclaims
responsibility for the prank kidnapping. "However," said
Bledsoe, "I'll be happy to receive this ancient bone on
behalf of my people, no matter what circumstances en-
couraged Mr. Torbett to change his mind and give it to us."
Bledsoe said he would consult with Caddo leaders in Oklahoma for advice on how to consecrate and re-bury the
bone.

26

"AT THIS RATE WE AIN'T EVER gonna get our tree up," said Jonas.

It lay on its side in the living room, a prickly cloud of dark green that made the whole house smell like cedar. The red-and-green tree stand hung limply off its base, and shreds of bark littered the carpet, testifying to the two falls the tree had already undergone that evening. Cardboard boxes brimming with crumpled newspaper and tissue paper sat around the floor, with cords of electric lights looped crazily around them. The boys perched on the living room furniture, waiting for their father to get off the phone.

"I know," said Clint. "Plus, nobody else is gonna be able to call."

"Why, who might be trying to call?"

Clint's face darkened. "Just people."

"Some girl? I bet it's some girl, hunh. That Leslie girl."

Their phone had been ringing off the wall. All the calls were for Bryce, people advising, commending, needling him in this matter of the bone. To some of the callers Daddy said things like, "Well, thank you, Winston. Man can't be too selfish at Christmastime, can he?" And to others he said, "I know that. I know. I didn't do it 'cause I thought I had to; I did it 'cause I wanted to." Once, last night, soon after they got back from cutting the tree, his voice had changed after he said hello. There was the usual pause, and then he said, with a bitterness that made Clint and Jonas look at each other, "Well, you should know.—Hm? I said, *you should know* about public statements ... Since when do I care what a Texan thinks about what I'm doing?

... Yeah, well, you and the Lord can work that out. I think it's horse manure: you drug a lot of other people into this besides you and the Lord." Long pause, then, "Look, I don't want to talk. Merry Christmas to you."

The way he had glowered after that conversation, the boys thought his good mood was gone, but at this time of year they should have known better. Five minutes later he was humming out-of-tune Christmas songs, and he went outside with Jonas to look at the tree once more—where it stood leaning up against the carport wall to soak in Ace's water pail, massive, so dark green it looked black, with cold water trembling in tiny drops on all its fronds.

Now Bryce was hanging up from this latest call. "Okay," he said, coming back into the living room, "y'all ready to raise it up again?"

"I guess."

"Hold the trunk."

Jonas obediently thrust his arm into the tree. To reach the trunk he had to stick his head in the dense branches too.

"Wait," said Clint. "Your arms are too short. You better get back and look to see if it's straight. I'll hold the trunk."

So Daddy lifted and steadied and lowered from the bottom, and Clint grabbed and balanced from the middle, and Jonas stood by the couch and watched with an expert eye, ready to yell "Timber!" any minute.

The phone rang again.

"Oh hell," said Daddy. "Maybe I just won't get it."

"Then *I'll* get it," said Clint. "You think the tree'll fall if I let go?"

"It might," said Bryce, unperturbed. "If the phone's for me I'm indisposed."

They heard Clint in the kitchen: "Yessir, he is, but he's indisposed."

Bryce broke into a laugh.

"Looks straight to me," Jonas said. "Are you holding it?"

"Nope, that's the stand holding it."

"Yay!"

Daddy backed out from under the tree on his hands and

knees, stood up, reached into the dark green foliage, and started shaking the tree wildly. A few dead hardwood leaves fell out.

"Daddy!"

"Well, we gotta make sure it's secure."

Bryce finally let go. Then he dropped onto the couch and lit a cigarette.

"Wow," said Jonas. "I didn't think it was gonna be big enough."

"They never look big enough in the woods," said Bryce. "Isn't it *beautiful?*" he said. He reached over and tickled Jonas in the ribs.

People who thought of Bryce only as suspicious, hard-nosed, and rough, slovenly in his personal habits and disdainful of niceties, would have been surprised to know him as the boys did in December: leading them through the woods to cut a tree; struggling over Christmas cookies in the kitchen; returning from mysterious trips with a truckful of lumpy shapes under a tied-down tarp. He wrapped presents laboriously, holding his big, nailbitten, barbed-wire-scarred thumb over tiny pieces of ribbon while with the other hand he scrabbled for the tape, folding the paper with a care that never really produced worthy results—the Torbetts' gifts always had a wrinkled, lopsided look. He went to elaborate efforts to keep the boys from guessing what their presents were. Once Clint got some Wrangler boots wrapped in separate packages. And when Bryce gave Jonas a pup tent, he put dried beans in an empty Pringles potato chip can and strapped it to the tent before he wrapped the whole thing up. Jonas was perplexed for days about the weird-shaped, rattly present.

Clint came back into the living room and Daddy said, "Let's do the lights!"

"Okay," said Clint. "I been untangling them. That was Mr. Bigley, wanting to tell you you did a good thing."

"Well, well," said Daddy. "Does he want me to call him back?"

"I couldn't tell."

"I better. Otherwise he'll think 'indisposed' means I had a hangover."

"Daddy," said Clint, "why *did* you do it?"

"Do what?"

"Give the Indians that bone. For nothing. When you wouldn't even sell it to those men from Texas."

"Well ...," said Bryce. "Coupla things." He gave them his most roguish look. "Now look, if I confide this in y'all, I don't want you blabbing it all over town. Okay?"

"Of course not." "No sir." They sounded insulted.

"First thing is," Bryce said thoughtfully, picking an ornament hanger out of his sweater sleeve, "sometimes when you live in a town like Groverton—a community like—this—sometimes you sort of get on the wrong side of people, and they start talking about you. Understand?"

They nodded, blushing faintly.

"So, to even things back up, you have to do something above-and-beyond. Something especially good, to get their minds out of the gutter or wherever they've been, as regards you."

"Mmm," said Clint noncommittally.

"So that was one reason," said Bryce. "Even though people said I didn't have to respond to this ransom note, that it was just a silly prank, that the Living Nativity Scene was going on anyway, I sort of figured it was something I could do to earn a little extra credit in folks' mind."

"Extra credit like at school," said Jonas.

"Sure."

"What's the other reason?" said Clint. "You said there were two."

"Well, the other reason." Here Bryce started to grin. "Y'all's daddy's a businessman, you know that, don't you?"

"Yessir ..."

"The other reason I was willing to do this is, I didn't give the Indians the real bone. I gave 'em a old cow bone. I still have the real bone, to decide what to do with."

A grin began to spread over Clint's face too. "You *did?*"

"Um-hm. Figured, what would it hurt? They'll never know the difference. And then I can still sell the real one, if I decide to—to the Texas folks, if I can't get any money for it from the scientists here." Bryce's tone suddenly changed. "Now look! This is a real secret, a grown-up secret, okay? Y'all don't tell a soul."

"Okay," said Clint.

"Cross my heart and hope to die," said Jonas faintly.

"Now where did you put the real one?"

"I dug it up the other day. There wasn't any other bones around it—if there's a whole skeleton down there anywhere, it's busted up and scattered—so I figured I'd go ahead and case it up in my workshop. But I'm not giving up. I've been finding so many arrowheads back there, and a few pot pieces, too, that I still think this might be a treasure trove of relics."

"Wow," breathed Clint. "Find of the century."

"And *I'm* the one who discovered it," said Jonas. But his voice was too vague to carry much authority.

Five

Ezekiel cried, Them
Dry bones
Ezekiel cried, Them
Dry bones ...

Them bones them bones gonna
Walk around
Them bones them bones gonna
Walk around
Them bones them bones gonna
Walk around
O hear the word of the Lord.

African-American spiritual

27

FOR THREE DAYS AND THREE NIGHTS he thought about it. He slept poorly, tossing and turning till even Ace woke up and looked at him askance. Once more he dreamed of skeletons, and of cows and Indians and his father and Vaughan Sandifer and Mr. Bledsoe looming like giants. Santa Claus, laden with an overstuffed bag, struggled down the Torbetts' chimney and then turned into Jonas's school principal; he opened his bag and poured rocks out all over the living room. The scientist from Little Rock walked in and started chipping them open, but inside they were gray and dull. "There's nothing in here," he said. He began to eat them.

Jonas didn't know what the dreams meant and he wasn't sure what his waking thoughts meant either.

He had believed everything his father did was right. You started with that premise and went from there. Even the thing with Miss Strait had not seemed like anything *wrong* Daddy did; it disturbed Jonas, but he figured that was because he didn't understand it well enough.

But this, no matter how he twisted it around in his mind, looked wrong. Like cheating the Indians out of something that should be theirs. Or at least, lying to them about what you said you were giving them.

Once at school Mr. Bledsoe had heard some boy call another "Indian giver." He had stopped everything and given the whole class a lecture on Indians and whites. He told them about treaties and how they were made—and broken. He told them they should never use terms like "Indian giver" that insulted a whole group of people. It wasn't as bad to use them when you were ignorant of what you were saying—here he had looked kindly at the poor boy who'd said it—but now that the students knew, he never expected to hear the phrase from them again.

Jonas winced now to think of his own father breaking his treaty, in a way, with Mr. Bledsoe. Even if Mr. Bledsoe never found out he'd been given a cow bone, Jonas would know. And he didn't know whether he could live with that.

There was a lesson in Jonas's Sunday school book that bothered him. It was about a boy who broke his mother's vase and then buried the pieces in the back yard and lied and said he didn't do it. The moral of the story was "Two wrongs don't make a right." Well, who would ever think they did? When one wrong didn't make a right, how could two? It seemed so obvious that Jonas thought he must be missing something glaringly simple in the lesson. What were the two wrongs supposed to be—breaking the vase as one, and hiding-and-lying-about-it as the other? Or was breaking the vase considered an accident—as Jonas thought in all fairness it should be—in which case the other two actions, hiding the pieces and lying, must be the wrongs? It never made much sense.

But now he wondered: if he did something to try to make things right with the Indians, but had to deceive his father in the process, wouldn't that be trying to make a right out of two wrongs—his and Daddy's? *If* Daddy was wrong, of course.

He didn't know.

Two-wrongs-don't-make-a-right. He tossed and turned, and Jesus didn't come sit on his bed and help.

But one wrong sure didn't make a right, either.

Wouldn't it be better to make what right you could out of a situation? Besides, all he would be doing would be exactly what Daddy had done before him. Maybe it wasn't wrong. Maybe it was just one of those gray-dolphin-like things he couldn't understand yet.

In the wee hours of one of those nights, Jonas lay, unvisited by any visible Savior, and made up his mind.

And waited his chance.

Saturday offered the first good prospect, but at first it didn't appear to be working out. Daddy, in his holiday cheer, made waffles early that morning, with such an excess of zeal and inexpertise that Celie cried out in horror when she arrived at nine and saw the kitchen. Then after breakfast, Clint invited Jonas to go shooting mistletoe with him. The teenagers' Christmas dance was that night. Not that Clint would be going to the dance—the Church of the Rock forbade it—but he would be taking advantage of a party room set up next to the high school gym, where the youth of Groverton's more fundamentalist churches could drink punch and eat cookies and make out without endangering their souls by actually dancing. And Clint had promised to bring fresh mistletoe.

Jonas hesitated, but he knew Clint and Daddy would think it weird of him to decline. So he said, "Sure."

Bryce struck out in high spirits for the bone-ditch, where all week he'd been continuing to turn up projectile points in mint condition. The boys and Ace went in the opposite direction, across the west pastures, heading for the bottomland near the creek. The sky was gray and lowering, but in the woods the fallen pine straw and leaves made a soft, red-brown carpet, the air smelled cleanly of wet bark, and the cold itself was invigorating. They scanned the tops of the bare hardwood trees, looking for the dark clusters that, when shot down, would be a mass of green vine and waxy white berries. Jonas trudged a yard or so behind Clint, carrying a BB gun that felt childish compared to Clint's real shotgun.

"Would you really kiss somebody?" he said. "If you ended up under the mistletoe with them?"

"Why, sure," said Clint.

They walked on.

"*Have* you ever?" said Jonas.

"That's a personal question." In a tone of reproof. "There's a clump," said Clint, nodding up into a pecan tree on a little rise about thirty yards away. They walked a little closer and he brought the gun to his shoulder and fired. Half of the clump dribbled out of the tree. Ace ran over to it enthusiastically. "Hey, get away!"

"Can I try for the rest of it?" said Jonas.

"It's a free country."

A few more tattered pieces of the plant showered down when Jonas shot, and he picked them up carefully.

As they hiked on he said, "What about that other thing— would you do that?"

"What other thing?" said Clint.

Jonas made sure he stayed a step or so behind his brother. "That other thing besides kissing," he said casually. "That thing Daddy does with Miss Strait."

Clint wheeled on him, eyes blazing. "Don't ever say that! That's over, okay?" Jonas stepped back. "Where'd you even hear that?"

"I didn't just hear it, I saw it." Jonas described the scene in the bedroom that day, as best he could. Try as he might he couldn't stretch out his account to more than a sentence.

"I bet you don't even know what it is they were doing," said Clint. "I bet you got no idea."

"I do so too!" cried Jonas. "I do so too!"

"Well, what, then?"

"They were," said Jonas with wounded dignity, "they were— making a baby."

"Oh hell, they weren't making no baby. Dad can't make any more babies. He got hisself fixed after you were born."

Fixed? Was it like being saved? Too much pride was at stake to inquire.

"Well," said Jonas, "I do know what they were doing, but I don't like to say it out loud. I don't even like to talk about it."

Clint turned on his heel and started to walk on. "Fair enough," he said. "You're the one brought it up. Not me."

Jonas trudged a little bit behind. "Clint," he said, "can Daddy do anything wrong?"

"*Of course.*" Clint's voice was bitter. "He's an A-One asshole when he wants to be."

"I thought so," said Jonas. He felt depressed.

They had their usual late, heavy Saturday midday dinner; since Celie left at two they'd be on their own for supper, so they always took advantage of her presence while they could. After dessert Clint said he was taking his mistletoe by the school and going from there to play touch football at the Nestersons'. Daddy said he'd be on the other side of the drainage canal, digging, if anyone needed him. No one asked Jonas his plans. After everyone else seemed to clear out he went to his room, with Ace padding softly beside him. He dragged his desk chair over to his closet and pulled down a box in his closet Magic-Markered BABY CLOTHES in his mother's handwriting. From beneath a stack of small coveralls, booties, and baby hats he took out the cloth sack that contained his secret things. The hiding place was his own idea and he was proud of it.

He'd been assembling this collection for years in anticipation of the holy task, the mission, he knew would someday come his way. Things he knew he would need from books he'd read: some rope, or rather strong nylon cord; a box of matches; a stub of pencil and paper; a pocketknife; a miniature flashlight; some glow-in-the-dark stickers; an invisible ink marker obtained with Froot Loops box tops; and, for tonight, a miniature trowel belonging to a small gardening tool set that had been Mama's. After putting on the hand-me-down army fatigue pants he'd gotten from Clint, he sorted these things into his many deep pockets. He could feel the objects' outlines against his legs. Then he put on socks. He heard gravel crunching in the driveway and lifted his head attentively to look out. It was only A.R., Celie's husband.

Boots. All he had were his cowboy boots from Christmas before last, which were a little tight and had slick soles, not good for hiking, but boots had the look he wanted. A kitchen knife, stuck in a toy holster that also helped to anchor the baggy waist of the fatigues. A black sweatshirt, worn inside-out to hide its message, "Ask me how Jesus Christ changed my life, Vacation

Bible School, 1980." He emptied his knapsack of schoolbooks, put only a pillowcase inside, and slipped it on his back. Dressed, he stood in front of the rarely used mirror inside his closet door and looked at himself hard through narrowed eyes. He folded his arms across his chest and stood with his feet apart. Then he put his fists on his hips. But still he didn't smile. He kept his face tense, his jaw muscles clamping out like Clint Eastwood's.

He remembered one more thing, camouflage face paint for hunting that Daddy had but never used, and dropped to one knee to scrabble around in his hoard for it. He applied it clumsily, still not smiling but breathing a little hard, close to the mirror, so that a warm fog spread over his image in the glass. The greasy smell of the camouflage paint was strong.

He looked at himself some more. He needed something for his head. Without taking his eyes off his own in the mirror he reached one-handed toward his bathrobe and jerked its sash off. He tied it round his head, jerking the knots tight with short, hard movements. The ends dangled to his right shoulder, toughly, satisfying him. He let his arms fall to his sides again, his eyes still intent on his own reflection. *Alpha Wolf.*

Daddy had locked the workshop but Jonas knew where the key was, hanging on a hook between the deep-freeze and the back door. He found what he needed without trouble, in the case Daddy kept for his prize artifacts, where a specimen frog-effigy pot used to be. The display case was locked too, but Jonas knew the combination: 1225—Christmas Day, his father's favorite holiday. He got what he needed, handled it gingerly and wrapped it well. With this in his knapsack he would have to move smoothly, like a brave.

From the workshop his path took him back by the mechanics' shed. There were no workers to call out to him today; the tractors sat idle, the cotton trailers were empty except for a few bolls of the season's second picking clinging to their sides. He went on, across the pasture newly sprung up in rye grass, where mama cows were beginning to calve and big empty cylindrical frames from round hay bales stood around in puddles of water and cow patties. Ace trotted alongside, making no forays, no side trips today, as if he were aware of the seriousness of the outing.

He came to the woods that fringed the winter pasture, which were fairly clear now from the combination of the season and the cows' foraging. There was an old pond back here where he sometimes saw beaver, where he hoped to build a treehouse. Near the pond was the other mound Daddy had found, the one he hadn't excavated. There was a creek running into the pond with a beech tree beside it where Jonas and Clint once carved their names.

Just this side of the creek was a sort of cow boneyard, where Daddy hauled off the dead cows and calves and on rare occasions a dead horse. Sometimes he burned them and sometimes he left them to decay. Then everyone avoided the place for a while, till the smell died down. To Jonas the place had an eerie air. The eye sockets in the cowskulls seemed to stare at him. Their crazy leaning ribs, half-buried in leaves and ashes, made him nervous. But today he started picking gingerly through the bones, hunting for one that might match the one in his knapsack—or match closely enough, at least, that no one would give it a second glance when Daddy sold it to the Christian Texans. He found a couple that might do, and had just eased the knapsack off his shoulders to get out the real bone and see how close the resemblance was, when he heard a noise. An odd, scraping sound. He thought it might be Ace scuffling around in the brush, but when he looked around he saw that Ace too had frozen, with one paw lifted and his ears cocked in the direction of the sound.

The sound repeated itself, regularly. It had a metallic edge to it: the sound of a shovel, digging? And then Jonas heard voices as well. The way they floated through the clammy winter air, the otherwise quiet afternoon, he couldn't tell how close they were.

He tried to slip behind a tree, but the trees were young cottonwoods, too thin-trunked to offer good protection. *"Heel,"* he said to Ace, barely breathing the word but with all the intensity he could muster. *Dog Training and You* paid off. Ace looked at him, almost physically seeming to vacillate, to wobble, and finally relaxed his ears and drew near to Jonas's left side. Then Jonas stole forward to a thicket of smilax several yards away, in the direction of the voices. "Heel," he breathed again, touching his left palm to his thigh. Ace stayed with him.

Why would anybody else be back in these woods today? To look for mistletoe or a Christmas tree? To hunt? But the voices sounded too mean and low for the one activity, and at the same time too boisterous for the other. And besides, the scratching, metallic noises didn't fit ... No, Jonas already felt certain, as he peered through the smilax, that he had company because he was near the Indian mound.

It had been a while since Jonas had seen this mound. His attention, like his father's, had been distracted from it. But he remembered what it looked like—its sides smoothly, regularly sloping up to a flat platform of earth about as tall as a levee, as broad and long as a basketball court. Even though it was overgrown with brush, the basic shape was impressive; it was the biggest of the mounds Bryce had found on his property, bigger than the two he'd already bulldozed. But now it was hardly recognizable. The brush had been cleared off it and dragged to one side. Its sides were pitted and blasted with holes, its top churned up as if a crazy person had plowed it. It looked like Mama's old azalea beds after Ace had dug them up last summer and made Daddy so mad.

At the top of the mound he could see the upper half of a girl's body—she must be standing in a hole. From her width, and the blond hair lying on her shoulders, he recognized Vaughan Sandifer's assistant, the ticket-taker at Mi-Ka-Do. Over to the right he could see a pickaxe swinging regularly, but the thicket hid its wielder from him. A gray van was parked at the base of the mound with its back doors open. "Stay there, Crystal, I'ma talk to a fella about a horse," Jonas heard, and Vaughan Sandifer came out from behind the other side of the van, unzipped his pants and peed. He was only about ten yards away, and it seemed he was aiming straight at Jonas. A faint growl started in

Ace's throat. "Shhh." Jonas stroked his neck, trying to smooth down his raised hackles.

"We're almost done with this load," called the girl. "There's room for a couple more boxes if you want to stack 'em. Otherwise we're full. And I'm cold, and I'm tired, and it's the weekend and we still haven't been paid."

"I think we're about done anyway," said another voice, also a man's, but younger, higher, and more country-sounding than Vaughan's. "All's I'm finding now is chips and bits of stuff. The last whole piece I found was that double-necked bowl, and that was two hours ago."

"Okay." Vaughan zipped up, patted himself, and climbed quickly up the mound toward the others. "I'm trying to think. Time we get to Crowdersville and unload, it'll be three-thirty or so; say four-fifteen by the time we get back here. I'm not sure it's worth trying for a third load today. Our daylight'll be almost gone."

"I keep telling you," said the young man. He had thrown the shovel down and was stretching. Then he picked up something else and from the way he held it, aimed down it, idly, scanning the horizon, Jonas knew it was a gun—shotgun or rifle. "If you do want to dig some more, wec'n rig up that generator, just keep going through the night. Be on the interstate by dawn."

Vaughan grunted. "That's tempting. I want to take 'em home and get some pictures first, though. I want these in my new catalog."

Jonas looked at the open back doors of the van. He slipped the cord out of his pocket and tied it to Ace's collar. Suddenly the two of them were running toward the van and jumping in. Once he got there he thought, What'd you do that for? What'd you do that for?—as if part of himself had stood back and watched the other part act. His heart was beating wildly. Inside the van was dark and full of packing crates and smelled of old earth, a smell sort of like modeling clay. He picked his way to a far corner, bumping his knee once, squeezing between cartons that were full of relics and packing material, and cleared a little space to sit on the floor, pulling Ace in close to him, then pulling a box in front. He was just easing his knapsack off his shoulders so he could lean back without crushing the fossil bone, when an explosion shook the van.

"What the hell!" somebody cried as the noise faded away.

He heard a man's giggling. "I heard a noise, was all."

"Well, goddammit, Tommy"—that was Vaughan Sandifer—"you like to scared the crap out of me. Don't go shooting off like that. Haven't you got the idea we're trying not to attract attention?"

"Why, you didn't hear nothing?" It was the other man.

"No, not till you 'bout blasted my ears out with that gun."

"I heard something. Had to scare 'em off."

Vaughan Sandifer laughed. "Quit worrying. Bryce is two miles away, picking up all the arrowheads I dropped there last week."

"Pretty smart, Vaughan."

"Well, it was the kid gave me the idea. I'm sure it was his kid playing back there who dropped the first ones and got everyone all excited. Indian burial site. That place is no more a Indian burial site than I'm a monkey's uncle."

"Okay!" came the girl's voice. "Look, I got these last three pipes! Where's some more plastic to wrap them in? Did you use all the plastic?"

"There's some shredded newspaper in the top of that last box I put in," said Vaughan. "Just put 'em in there. Make sure they don't touch each other."

Jonas pressed himself back toward the side of the van, where the darkness was thickest. When the girl came to the tailgate he could stare straight at her eyes, the lavender make-up fanning up from her lowered lids as she rummaged around in the tops of some of the crates, nestling them down in the packing material. He kept his hands around Ace's chest so he would feel any growl starting to vibrate there. Finally she stepped back and dusted off her hands. "Okay!" she said. "Now can we *go?*" She shut the van doors with a clang.

28

THE DARKNESS AROUND HIM was disorienting, but he knew he should try hard, through every twist and turn, to pay attention to where he was taken. That was what the heroes in his books would have done. Of course, he had a pretty good idea. He believed they were headed to Sandifer's headquarters at Crowdersville.

First they went slamming and bouncing over the rough terrain in the woods. He couldn't get comfortable on the bare, grooved metal floor of the van; he was thrown around like a kernel of popcorn. How could the stolen artifacts make it through this jolting? The ride got a little smoother, though, and he figured they must have hit the old, old road that came back into these woods, that had once led to a homestead back here. Jonas had always thought it was barely visible when his father talked about it, but he could feel the difference now. If he were right, they would hit the tractor lane at the end of the west pasture, open the cattle gap, come all the way up the tractor lane, and turn into the highway. Simple. He felt a burning anger at how easy it had been for them. It was the rage of humiliation—when your side has been tricked, and easily.

The van made the turns he'd predicted, and Jonas clutched for support against the sliding crates. In about ten minutes there was a slight pause, then a grinding of gears and a turn to the left, and then sure enough he could tell from the regular, smooth buzz of noise and motion that they must be on the highway.

The darkness was complete and he could not see anything—not his hand, not Ace, not his legs and boots. He kept his arm around Ace and burrowed his face into Ace's comforting, homey-smelling fur.

He had jumped on the van out of anger, a desire to avenge his father. It may not have been a smart idea, but it was too late to change that now. He had to keep a plan in place: to stick with these thieves, but out of sight; to see where they took the stolen relics, and to carry a report back to his father and the police.

At last the van slowed—this would be the edge of Crowdersville—and speeded up again, but not so fast; and slowed again, and turned, and started bouncing—over the potholed street that led to Mi-Ka-Do, Jonas would bet. It turned again and he heard gravel sloughing around the tires, and then it backed, and turned, and backed, and turned, and backed, and stopped. Still.

The front doors slammed and Jonas pulled Ace close. Footsteps crunched in the gravel walking outside the van. Then he heard a bang as its back doors were pulled open. He kept his head ducked low, formed himself into a ball as if he were doing a cannonball off the diving board, and prayed that Ace's training would hold true.

He heard the drag of boxes being unloaded off the van. The girl went off into the distance, saying she'd be back. "Turn off the burglar alarm while we're going in and out," Mr. Sandifer ordered. "Okay, okay," said the girl. "Don't you think I got any sense of my own?" So it was just Mr. Sandifer and the young man, Tommy, unloading. Jonas got his first good look at Tommy, who was skinny, and slouched. He had dark brown hair and a giant mustache that seemed like the heaviest, best defined part of him. Like the others, he was wearing old jeans that were dirtied all over with Torbett burial-mound dirt.

After Tommy and Sandifer each took a crate, Jonas raised his head and peeked out. It took him a few seconds to get oriented. Then he realized they must be backed up beside Mr. Sandifer's house, between the house and the museum. The screen door was propped open and so was a door to the house. This was where the two men were taking the crates. Jonas crouched at the edge of the shadows, his knapsack back on his back, awaiting the instant that would be his opportunity. He was going to have to get out of the van in a hurry. The crates were not stacked—the robbers hadn't wanted to hurt the relics—and the first quarter of the van was already empty. And they were taking turns, passing each other on the porch, so that there were only a few split-seconds between when Vaughan grunted and lifted a crate and took it away and when Tommy did.

Now they'd almost reached him. After the next box, he would have to make a dash for it. Jonas wanted to get inside the house, to see where they were taking all these things and just what else was in there, but he couldn't do it through the screen door and porch door they were using. Suddenly he got up and ran, yanking on Ace's collar, before he thought any more. One of his pockets caught on a nail sticking out of one of the crates; he jerked it away wildly and plummeted out of the van, and dashed around the house to the back. He flung himself down underneath a window and lay panting, his heart thudding into the ground.

"—heard something," Tommy was saying suspiciously.

"Jesus, man, you're always hearing something."

"Come on, Vaughan, don't tell me you didn't hear nothing."

"No, I didn't. Come on, we're almost through."

"Why don't I get back up in there and scoot 'em back to you."

"Okay."

Then Tommy's voice came, muffled from being inside the van: "How much did you say we're going to get for these?"

"Oh—man—it's hard to say. Depends on how good a job I do selling 'em, how long I want to take bids on them or how fast I decide to get rid of 'em ..."

"But Crystal and me, we should make a few hundred at least, right? Maybe a thou?"

"Don't be greedy, Tommy." Vaughan sounded cool.

They went inside the house. Jonas stood up and tried to peer inside the window. It was too high for him. He stood on the gas meter a little to the side and by twisting managed to get a view, but was disappointed—it was just the kitchen, empty, with coffee cups and Kentucky Fried Chicken boxes everywhere. He jumped down and edged around the house. Ace was whining the littlest bit back in his throat, but so far he seemed to understand that extraordinary measures were being asked of him.

At the next window, a big double picture window, their voices were clearer. Crystal was talking again. But the blinds were drawn. He could see electric light behind them. This was where he needed to be. He sneaked on around the house, trying to walk toe-heel, toe-heel to make less noise. The porch wrapped around to this side of the house as well. Jonas climbed some big concrete steps and tried the screen door—open. He looked down at Ace. He wanted nothing more than to keep Ace by his side. But he couldn't count on Ace to be quiet inside—and besides, if these people did something to harm Ace, Jonas would just as soon die himself. He slipped Ace's makeshift leash off and whispered, "Hie on!" and crammed the cord back in his pocket. Ace gave him an incredulous look and Jonas told him again. He hied a little ways off, into the yard, but stood looking at Jonas quizzically.

Jonas eased into the porch and tiptoed across the creaking floorboards, his eyes fixed steadfastly on the peeling dark brown paint. He put his hand on the knob of the door—a cheap-looking brass knob. The door had a window on it but it had white ruffly curtains on the inside and he couldn't see what might be on the other side. Carefully, quietly, he turned the knob. No tension: it opened. He peeped around it before he went in. It opened into a little hall. At the end of the hall he could see part of the kitchen again, and on the right was an open door from which the electric light, and conversation, were spilling. There were two other doors in the hall, but they were shut.

He needed a place to spy from. He dropped to his hands and knees and crawled toward the open door. There was nothing in the hall to hide him. If anyone came out of the room he was sunk.

It was hard to crawl with all these things in his pockets, and his knife sheath dragging the floor.

He reached the room and peered around the door jamb.

Now he realized that this room must take up half the house.

It was huge. There were more windows than the one he'd passed and tried to look through, but they were all shuttered. The lights that were on in the room were very bright, tall lamps aimed at a huge table in the middle of the room. Like Daddy's display cases, the table was covered with black velvet. Arranged on the velvet were more Indian relics than Jonas had ever seen in his life. He knew enough to know that they were fine specimens, in great condition: none was broken, and many were unusual, bottles with double necks, pots shaped like various animals, carefully etched and pigmented pipes, mortar and pestles, water vessels. Around the edges of the room were shelves crowded with similar objects. Vaughan was behind a camera, taking pictures of the relics, and Crystal and Tommy were seated on a little bench against one wall, playing with each other's hands.

"—don't understand," Crystal was saying. "If you're not supposed to have these, why are you taking pictures of them?"

Vaughan laughed. "The people I'm selling them to don't care how I got them," he said. "In our market, we need to circulate pictures, catalogs, of the stuff because we can't circulate the pots themselves. The problem is not so much to keep things a secret, as to move 'em fast when we do move 'em."

"And move 'em away from where folks might be lookin' for 'em," added Tommy.

"Right," said Vaughan. "Though, as I said, I think Bryce'll be distracted with his dinosaur, or whatever it is, for some time."

Jonas took his little spiral notepad and invisible ink pen out of one of his pants pockets and, lying on his stomach, started to list the objects in the room. Laboriously he described them as best he could by their color and shape and what he knew of pots and artifacts. He drew a little sketch of the room on the next page. It was hard to draw with invisible ink—you couldn't tell where you'd already made a line—but he did the best he could. Then he wrote down every physical detail he could about Sandifer and his helpers—what they were wearing, how tall he guessed they were. He hadn't read all the Hardy Boys books for nothing.

The room was quiet; Jonas heard Ace's toenails clicking on the porch and heard him whining softly in the back of his throat, but the others must not have heard. Sandifer took pictures for ten or fifteen minutes before he noticed his idle workers. "Look, what're y'all doing? Sitting there playing knick-knack-paddy-whack? I thought you were unpacking these crates and cleaning the stuff up so I can get these pictures done and we can get the hell out of Dodge."

"But after I broke that one you told me you didn't want me cleaning off no more pots," whined Crystal.

"I told you not to wash 'em. I didn't say you couldn't be brushing 'em off, real real soft, with that soft brush I've got over there. Show her, Tommy."

Tommy stifled a yawn and got up. Jonas was watching him, worried that this brush would be outside the room somewhere, and was startled to suddenly see instead, Vaughan heading toward the door, straight toward him, just as Tommy asked, "Where you go—" and Vaughan answered, "To get a—*God-damn!*"

Involuntarily Jonas screamed, and got to his feet and ran. Vaughan's hand scrabbled over his sweatshirt, but Jonas twisted away. He picked another door, opened it, and threw himself inside. It had a lock, a flimsy kind, the kind you lock by pushing the doorknob in and twisting, but it was better than nothing.

He heard the others yelling—*"What'sa matter!"*—*"It's some kind of midget freak, goddamn it! Come help me!"*—as he glanced around the room. He was in a small bedroom. There was a phone on the nightstand. He picked up the receiver and dialed—what did you dial—0. A smooth, pleasant voice said, "—erator will be on the line shortly to assist you."

"Oh please, oh please," murmured Jonas, nearly crying. He heard Vaughan banging on the door and saw the flimsy door shaking in its jamb. "A hammer," Vaughan said fiercely. Then in a booming voice, "Come out, kid, if you want to save your little ass!"

Then there was a muttering on the line. "May I help you?" said someone who sounded grumpy, as if they weren't interested in helping at all.

"Call the police, I'm at Mi-Ka-Do, this is Jonas Torbe—"

The pleasant, smooth voice broke through again and said, "If you wish to place a call, please dial one and the area code first. This is a recording." There was a long buzz. He clicked the button furiously and dialed some more 0's. The live grumpy voice spoke again: "Look, if you need emergency assistance, you've got to—" "Call the police! I'm at Mi-Ka-Do in Crowdersville! Help!" And then another taped message: "Do you wish to place a call?" "Lemme make a c'leck call," he said frantically. He and Clint called home that way from Uncle Terry's. He dialed 0 and his home number, and started to chant. "This is Jonas Torbett. C'leck from Jonas at Mi-Ka-Do in Crowdersville—" The blows of hammer on wood, the splintering of wood, was now drowning him out, and he saw the door beginning to buckle. He would have to go out the window. He unlatched it and pushed hard, hard, with all the muscles he had. He finally raised it about five inches—not enough—and then about five more. He shoved the screen out and stuck one leg through, then the other, and wriggled out just as he heard the door smash open behind him.

He hit the ground hard, all the air jolting out of him. His slick boot soles didn't absorb the shock at all and for the umpteenth time he wished he had on his sneakers. He picked himself up and started running—where, he didn't know. He looked over his shoulder and saw Tommy coming from around the other side of the house, the shotgun in his hands, a mean expression on his face. Tommy had on running shoes.

He heard a faint, demanding bark. Bossy, but with an edge of panic. Here I am! You better do something about it, right away! It was coming from across the compound—away from the entrance and parking lot, toward the burial holes. Jonas started running that way, holding his side where it was hurting.

He dashed up the wooden steps leading to Look-Ma-No-Cavities' and Madam Grunt's exposed graves. Behind him he heard running footsteps.

He didn't think he could outrun this man. He'd have to hide.

Then he could look for Ace. If Ace found him before Tommy did he might give his hiding place away, but Jonas couldn't do anything about that. There was a little ledge inside the circular fence Sandifer had put up around the burial chamber. Jonas might lie on that and press himself very close to the wall, in the shadow, and not be seen. Especially if his pursuers didn't have a flashlight. Under the tin roof, with the lights all out, it was hard to see.

Jonas eased under the fence just as he heard footsteps pounding up the plank steps. He scooted onto the ledge, choosing a point closest to the steps so that if Tommy did pan a light around he might not think to do it there, and lay down. It was harder than he had thought to stay put. The ledge was not flat but sloped down toward the hole. Jonas pressed himself with all his might to the wall and willed himself not to slip.

Tommy arrived. He stood there breathing hard. A cone of light shot out into the darkness and a palm-sized spot of light started moving down the walls of the burial chamber, on the ledge opposite Jonas and then downward.

Ace barked.

"Got-damn!" said Tommy, and the light jerked. "What the hell—! Like to scared the shit out of me, you little son of a bitch." For the second time that day Jonas heard the crash of his gun.

Jonas jerked when he heard the noise and tears started to pour down his face. He felt himself sliding, sliding. Frantically he grabbed the wall, but the smooth, cool clay had no indentation he could clutch. Ace is dead, Ace is dead, he thought, hearing Tommy laugh as he walked back down the steps. The horror and despair that engulfed him were like his falling itself. Already he had lost that crucial moment of balance, his fingernails raked the wall, and like a million cartoon characters he had watched, the force of gravity turned him loose, and he fell, yelling.

He landed on the side of his hip, on top of his knapsack, which had twisted under him, and with his hands, trying to catch himself, crushing something brittle into a soft powder. He lay there for a minute, all the breath gone out of him. I'm desecrating them, he thought, mournfully. Oh, Mr. Bledsoe will hate me. I'm desecrating Madam Grunt and Look-Ma-No-Cavities. And the Old One in my knapsack.

He heard the scratching of a match overhead and smelled sulphur before the small flame appeared. In the margin of its light there appeared a face looking orange and fiendish like a Halloween mask—Vaughan Sandifer.

"You little motherfucker," said Sandifer, very softly, staring at Jonas as if he despised him—as no one had ever looked at Jonas before. "You little motherfucker. See how you make out down there. Enjoy yourself." He shook out the match and the darkness blotted out his face and after a long moment Jonas thought he felt the brush of the little charred match hit his wrist.

Then he felt his ankle. The pain shot up into his calf like an electric shock. Like when he broke his arm. It didn't matter. He was already crying as hard as he could. Sandifer might as well come back and kill him now, since Ace's body, blasted by gunshot, would be the first thing to greet him if he ever got out of this pit.

29

THAT SATURDAY AFTERNOON Traci was pulling a different shift at the Waddle N, to pay back a co-worker who had put in extra hours for her when she went to the trial. Business was slow. The only customers were a threesome of hunters at one of the tables, still wearing their camouflage coveralls and orange caps and muddy boots and downing ham and eggs, and two policemen, Petey Nunnally and Bill Blunt, swigging coffee at a booth in the back. Traci yawned and debated whether to have some coffee herself. Her feet hurt and dusk was closing in drearily outside; she needed a lift. But business would probably pick up in the next hour or so, since people in Groverton tended to eat supper early.

In came Fred Barnett. What was he doing here? He was part of the early-morning crowd. Traci smiled and said hello to him but saw his glasses were fogging up just as she tried to meet his eyes.

"Hoo, y'all got it hot in here," he said. "How you doing?"

"Maybe that's why I'm so sleepy," said Traci. "Table for one?"

"Naw, naw," said Fred. "Just looking for—there they are." He nodded at her pleasantly and went back toward the policemen. Traci watched idly. They looked up at him, with Bill taking long drags on a cigarette, as they listened. Fred talked with his hands in the pockets of his khaki pants, rocking back and forth a little on his feet. Finally he quit talking, and shrugged, but kept looking at the policemen expectantly.

Bill crushed his cigarette out while Petey, his senior, answered.

Traci yawned widely and then saw that the hunters were motioning to her for refills on coffee. As she came out of the kitchen with the pot, she saw the front door to the restaurant opening again. Must be later than I realized, she thought.

It was Butter McCollum and her husband—whose name was Ed, but whom Groverton mostly thought of as "Butter's husband." They too glanced around the restaurant, smiled at Traci, and made a beeline for the policemen. The door opened again and in hurried Jessie Cowley, who did the same thing.

"Got quite a little confab going on back there!" said Winston Huett, one of the hunters, to Traci.

She shrugged in wonderment as she poured his coffee. "Yeah—I don't know what's going on."

"Y'all got any pies ready?" said Winston's son, Jeff.

"Sure do. Just took a new batch out of the oven for tonight. We have apple and pecan."

"Bring me some pecan, with ice cream."

"Me too," said the third hunter, Bud Earden.

Winston scooted his chair back and hollered in a booming bass voice across the restaurant, "Hey, Petey, y'all entertaining guests back there? Looks like the Santa Claus line at the mall in Texarkana."

"Yeah," shot back the older policemen. "What d'you want for Christmas, your two front teeth?"

"How about you?" Traci asked Winston. "Pie?"

"No thanks." He was squinting back into the corner, where four people were now talking persuasively to the policemen. The McCollums had pulled up chairs. "Why don't you go see if they need anything else?" he said to Traci. He laughed. "Then you'n come tell us what they're talking about."

Traci laughed.

"Go on," he said. "Your tip rests on it."

"Oh well," she said. She carried the coffeepot back to that corner and paused as if waiting for entrée into the conversation.

"—but then it might," Butter was saying. " 'Joe Talbot' could easily be 'Jonas Torbett,' and that child's father has a lot to do with Mi-Ka-Do. There might have been an accident. You should at least go check it out."

"—police band radio—"

"Um-hm, mine too."

"Check it out, that's all we're saying."

"—had m'radio on—"

"They tried to call his house too. Didn't get through before the operator lost the connection."

The front door to the restaurant opened again and Coach Odum walked in and headed toward the back corner. "Well," he said as he approached, "looks like y'all beat me to it."

"More coffee?" Traci took the opportunity to say. "Coffee anybody?"

"No thanks." The patrolmen were disgustedly getting their billfolds out of their hip pockets. "Looks like we're gonna have to drive to Crowdersville on a wild goose chase to satisfy all these folks."

"About this kid who called the operator from Mi-Ka-Do, right?" said Coach Odum. "Yeah," he went on as he received some nods. "I just thought I'd come over and urge you to check it out. It didn't sound like the dispatcher thought much about it."

"Well, apparently," said Blunt, "the operator called the dispatcher, the dispatcher called Vaughan Sandifer and he said, no, everything was quiet over there. So we really think this is some sort of prank. The kid hung up before he finished. And it's none of my business anyway. We don't have any proof it's Jonas Torbett or anybody else from Groverton. Gave his name as Joe Talbot, the operator said."

"But—"

"—you at *least*—"

"Worth a trip," chorused the Groverton folks.

"Jonas Torbett could be garbled into Joe Talbot."

"Call Bryce. Ask him where his boy's at."

"Go on, call him."

"—much a coincidence."

Nunnally finally heaved himself out of the booth, and strode over to use the phone behind the cashier's stand. "This is what

I get for working in a small town," he grumbled to the air as he waited for his party to answer. "You think this happens to cops in Little Rock?"

30

GOD HAD TO BE PUNISHING HIM. There could be no other explanation. He had done evil, he had spied on his father and planned to deceive him, and now he had been cast down into the Pit, and his best friend in all the world was dead.

Now that Jonas saw so clearly what was going on, he hated God—hated Him with a raw, fresh hatred strong as the taste of vomit. What had he ever done to deserve this much punishment? Nothing he had ever done seemed as wrong and bad as Ace was good. That booming shot, followed by silence, echoed again in his mind, and propped up against the cold clay wall he started to shake. His grief was coiled inside him like a mass of snakes, weeds, red-hot wires, wrapped like fishing line around his heart, his lungs, his stomach, and tightening, tightening. He clinched his sides, trying to cry to relieve the terrible feeling, but the sobs would not come, and that was worse than really bawling.

For hating God he would be doubly damned—damned before he'd ever been saved. It didn't matter. He couldn't ache any more than he did now, in body and soul. But probably that was because he had never experienced the flames of Hell. He had to just wait here, till he died one way or another and went to Hell, and he'd find out. Maybe he would perish of thirst and starvation. Maybe Vaughan Sandifer and Tommy would come back and shoot him. Maybe his hurt ankle would putrefy and give him an infection all over and he would get delirious like the men in Celie's stories and die that way. Ace's bones would be found near his, with the ancient bones crushed beneath them both like so many corn flakes. They would be buried all together. Mr. Bledsoe would say words over them. But Jonas would never know—he would have gone on to Hell, to the fires licking over him the way they consumed the swollen dead cows he had seen dragged off to the woods. And Ace would be in Heaven, maybe was there already; if dogs couldn't go there, it wasn't worth going to in the first place.

Meantime the night was taking forever to pass. Daylight would surely be breaking soon. Shortly after Sandifer went away, the yellow bulb far above Jonas's head had come on for a few seconds and then flickered off. He had heard someone driving away, and since then it had been silent and pitch dark around him. He couldn't remember whether the moon was full now, but even if it was he wouldn't be able to see it because of the tin roof shutting off the skies overhead.

His ankle was hurting, pressing against the stiff leather of his boot. He took the boot off and touched his swollen flesh gingerly, wondering when the putrefaction would start.

He had never been so alone or afraid. Once when he had gone with his father to tend a dying cow, his father had left him way back in the fescue pasture with the animal while he went to get some medicine from the barn. She was lying in a corner of two fencelines and Jonas was supposed to keep her there, where they could treat her—to wave her back from the open part of the pasture, if she tried to get up. But he didn't believe she ever would again. She took deep, rattling, gasping breaths so far apart that after each one of them he thought she had died. The night was absolutely black, and he knew he was the only person around for acres and acres. He hoped the cow didn't die. He was afraid of being alone with the presence of death. It took his father about twenty minutes to fetch the medicine. Until tonight that was the most alone Jonas had ever felt.

When Mr. Bledsoe had told them about the Indian boys diving naked into cold water, and going through other rites of manhood, he had asked the class whether they thought the young braves were afraid. "No," said the class. He had corrected them. Sure, they were afraid, he said, but that wasn't the point; the point was that they didn't let their fear conquer them. They controlled it.

Jonas thought about that now. Well, he didn't have any choice about conquering his fear. Conquer it or not, he was still huddled at the bottom of a hole shaped like a giant oatmeal carton, freezing, hungry, and needing to go to the bathroom, with skeletons for company.

He thought over what had brought him to this point. He had wanted adventure. He had set out from home to undo something his father had done—to fool his father as his father had fooled other people. But along the way he had seen the thieves taking his father's things. Then he'd jumped in the van to vindicate his father. Did either act add up to anything, to a reason why God should punish or save him? Or whether he was brave, brave as an Indian, or weak?

He lapsed into a dull, blank misery and either slept or passed out. Every once in a while he stirred, dizzy and groggy, but nothing around him had changed, and he would spin back into faintness. Once he heard quick, trotting footsteps approach, and a familiar panting. "Ace?" he said. "Ace?" Then he knew he must have been dreaming, and perhaps his end was closer.

Many hours later he heard a vehicle in the driveway. Two—or maybe three—car doors slammed, and there was a shout he couldn't identify, then nothing else for a while. His stomach clutched with fear. He felt again how he had to go to the bathroom. Vaughan Sandifer would come back, there would be the scratching of a match again and the cocking of a gun, and it would be all over. He wondered if it would hurt to be shot? If Ace had suffered pain? He had to wait, helpless as a cow. He heard sharp barking. He must be dreaming, delirious again, or cruel God was fooling him, but it sounded like Ace. The barking came closer. It was right overhead. Suddenly light came on over Jonas, a ring, a circle of soft yellow light, enveloping him like angel-light-glow, and he looked up into a circle of faces he knew—Daddy, Mr. Blunt, Mr. Nunnally, Mr. and Mrs. McCollum, Mrs. Cowley, Coach Odum—all staring down at him open-mouthed. Ace stuck his head out from between Mr. Nunnally and Mrs. McCollum, his blotchy black-and-gray ears cocked, his black-and-tan-spotted forehead wrinkled in deep concern: Ace alive, unscathed. "We got to get this boy outa here," said Mr. Blunt in a tight voice.

"Oh, *son,*" said Daddy.

All that trying, all those dark hours, and he hadn't been able to cry when he had reason to, and now the tears slid down his face unbidden.

31

ON SUNDAY MORNING WHEN Jonas opened his eyes, sunlight poured in through the window, lighting up dust motes in the air and spilling over his Kawasaki and Ozzie Smith posters, his dresser and messy desk, the pile of clothes he had worn the day before but did not remember taking off, and the white rumpled sheets and thermal blankets of the bed. The room was pleasantly cool, but he felt warm and light, and at his side Ace was a hot, heavy, palpable weight, now bowing his neck and stretching so hard that his paw pads separated. Then he relaxed, gazed at Jonas, and started to pant slightly, completely satisfied.

The phone was ringing and Jonas realized it might have been ringing a while. Now that he thought of it, earlier in the morning he seemed to have waked and fallen asleep again, hearing the phone, hearing Ace get up and walk around and scratch and resettle, maybe even hearing people come in and out of his room. He sat up, and winced at the pain that shot through his ankle. He looked under the covers. It was thickly bandaged, and kept throbbing. Now that he moved, the rest of his body felt flattened and sore—as if Grandmother had rolled him out on her counter with a rolling pin. He glanced at his pillow and saw where the rest of the camouflage face paint had smudged it all over. Celie would be mad.

Just as he was starting to get up, his father came into his room. "Ah-ah," he said. "Better stay put. Good morning. Afternoon, I should say, almost."

"Is it?" said Jonas. "Do I have to go to church?"

"No, you don't."

"What happened to my ankle?"

"You don't remember being in the emergency room last night?"

"No sir."

"Well, it's broken. I guess you broke it when you fell into the burial hole."

Jonas was silent a minute. "How come there ain't a cast on it?"

"They said they'd just put a splint on it for now—you go back Monday for the cast. You know, son, I have a lot of questions to ask you, but so does Sheriff Wingate. That was him on the phone and he's on his way over. So I may as well wait."

"Can I walk on my ankle? How long will I have to leave it in this cast?"

"Um—six weeks, I think he said? I forget. You're not supposed to put any weight on it. We got you some crutches—aren't they up here?"

"I don't see 'em."

"Musta left 'em in the truck when I carried you in. Lemme go get 'em."

"I've got to go to the bathroom."

"I'll be back in just a sec."

By the time the sheriff came, Jonas was back in bed with his plaid robe on and a plate of scrambled eggs and grits in his lap. Sheriff Wingate was a soft-spoken man with a pink face and silver hair. He had a persistent dry cough that went *hoop, hoop* behind his hand in the middle of anything he said. Still, he questioned Jonas almost sternly, fixing his eyes steadily on the boy's, and in his silver-trimmed uniform, sitting in Jonas's short desk chair, he looked big and forbidding. Bryce brought in a kitchen chair for himself, but before he sat down his eye was caught by Jonas's dirty clothes on the floor, which he started to scoop up in embarrassment.

"Wait, Daddy," said Jonas. "There's stuff in my pockets."

"Oh?" Bryce raised his eyebrows.

"Yessir. Um—"

"Here." Daddy handed them over and Jonas felt around till he pulled out the notebook and marker—the most important things.

So the questions started: How did he get to Mi-Ka-Do in the first place? What was he doing there? How did he fall in the burial hole? Where was Mr. Sandifer?

Jonas answered as best he could. He left out what he'd been doing in the woods near the Torbetts' mound in the first place—just said he'd been "playing" back there when he heard the voices. When he told about Mr. Sandifer and his stealing, Daddy didn't turn rigid and red as Jonas expected, but just kept shooting glances at the sheriff. So he must have already known—*how?* Jonas wondered, as he continued to talk. When he got to the part about the room filled with Indian relics, the ones just unloaded from the truck and others, he gave his notebook to the sheriff. "I took notes," he said. "In invisible ink. You wanta read it, you get you some lemon juice in a mister, like you mist plants with, and put it under a hot lamp. I took a lot of notes, all these pages, of everything I saw."

"Invisible ink?" said the sheriff. He was staring at Jonas. In his interest he forgot to *hoop, hoop.*

"Yessir. I got it offa Froot Loops, that's how you get it if you want one. I think it took three proofa purchases. No, maybe four. I'm not sure."

"So anyway—" said the sheriff, laying the notebook carefully on Jonas's desk.

"You can ask Celie. She'll remember."

"So anyway, you were in the hall looking in?"

"Yessir. And then Mr. Sandifer all of a sudden barged out in the hall and saw me and cussed, and I ran. I ran in this other room that looked like it mighta been his bedroom. There was a phone in there and I started to make some calls. But I couldn't get through to nobody and he was trying to bam the door down. Finally it did start to bam down, so I went out the window. Maybe that was when I hurt my ankle." He looked at his father, puzzled. His father was just staring at him, his eyes a little wet. Ace was snuffling fleas. Jonas stroked the dog's neck and went on. "But maybe not, cause I could still run then. That guy Tommy was chasing me. I tried to hide on this ledge up near the top of the burial pit. But he shot his gun and I thought he shot Ace, and I fell. And that's where y'all found me."

"Did you see Vaughan Sandifer, Tommy, or Crystal again once you'd fallen in the burial pit?"

"Yessir, Mr. Sandifer came back and cussed at me some more."

"What'd he say?"

Jonas felt his face heat up. "Um, something like"—he glanced at his father, ducking his chin down and raising his shoulders slightly in apology—" 'Enjoy yourself down there, you little motherfucker.' " He looked down at the bedspread, aware he was probably red.

The men were silent.

Then Sheriff Wingate said, "So! Did you hear or see anything else from them?"

"I think I heard them drive away. The lights went on, then off."

"What lights?"

"There's lights over each burial hole. So, like, on cloudy days, like if your class goes for a field trip, you can still see the— bones—okay. Those lights came on and went right back off."

The sheriff was quiet for a while. Then he said, "Well, Jonas, you've certainly been a brave young man. I'm anxious to see what you're written down in this notebook, because it might help us"—*hoop, hoop*—"excuse me, solve a case. I've already told your father, and now I'll tell you: Mr. Sandifer and Crystal were killed last night in a wreck up near the Oklahoma line. It was a head-on collision and a few of the relics in the van were broken, but not very many, considering—well, I'll spare you that. But we'll have your notes to help us identify the objects. Did you write down which ones you had seen loaded into the van from your father's mound, and which ones were already in the room?"

"Yessir, I think so."

"And will you"—*hoop, hoop*—"tell me again how to make this ink, ah, visible?"

"Yessir, you get you some lemon juice or I think they said vinegar would do too. And you put it in a plant mister and spray it real light over each page and put it under a hot lamp, and it'll turn brown."

"Well," said the sheriff. "I thank you. You're an unusual young man, Jonas." But he still didn't get up, and neither did Bryce. Again there was a pause.

"Mr. Sandifer died?" said Jonas.

"Yes."

"Gee." He rubbed Ace between the shoulder blades. "And Crystal."

"Yeah. Tommy's in intensive care in Broken Bow."

"Gee." He wouldn't have thought he'd feel sad, exactly, but he did: or at least still, and weird. "And you think all those things in his van were stolen."

"We're going to check it out," said the sheriff. "There have been a few museums in the state where things like this have turned up missing, and we've never traced them ... a break-in at Southwest College a year or so ago where all that was taken was Indian pots ... plus some vandalism." He looked at Jonas's dad. "What I was telling you earlier, Bryce, is you can't prosecute very well when they just plunder a grave or a mound. The relics have to be already dug up and cleaned up, you know, in some real—somebody's legal possession. *Then* you've got theft of property charges. Till then it's just petty vandalism."

"Now, there's a black market in these goods as well," said Bryce. "I'm well aware of that. You know this has been a big hobby of mine. But my trading has always been on the up-and-up. I'm in an organization, I get magazines, I go to meetings, and all that. That's all I thought Vaughan was doing all this time ..." His voice trailed off, and he shook his head.

"Well!" said the sheriff briskly. "I think I got all I needed to know for now. Thank you, Jonas, Bryce. I'll let you know what develops, and I'll probably be back to get some more statements from Jonas."

"Sure, lemme show you out, Sheriff."

Jonas sank back into his pillows and watched the sheriff and his father stand in the driveway talking for a minute before the sheriff drove away.

His father appeared in the doorway of his room again and said, "By the way, what's in your knapsack?"

"Well," said Jonas, "I was gonna get around to that."

32

"LOOK," JAMES'S SECRETARY said pointedly, "should I be forwarding your mail somewhere?"

He felt himself blush beet-red. "Why, no."

It was true that during the holidays he had begun to spend a lot of time in Groverton. The geologists often spent their days on fieldwork anyway, and sleeping in Groverton just meant he had a different base for his forays than if he'd started his mornings in Little Rock. But how embarrassing—"Should I be forwarding your mail"!

It was in the heap of correspondence he picked up that day that the letter came from Dan Phillips, a breezy young scholar from U.Penn. who was a little too sure of his own genius for James's liking, but someone he respected nonetheless.

"Donovan: Just opened your letter of some months ago, since I just got back from Borneo, where a colleague (Michael Wu, you might know him) and I have been looking at tortoise subspeciation. But that's another story, which I'm pretty sure you'll be able to read in a forthcoming issue of *ProcSocEvBio* ..." He had to throw that in pseudo-casually, thought James. "At any rate, your question about femur-like fossils from Cretaceous marl brings to mind some work I was doing last year with a family of higher reptiles I came to call Skelesaurs. I can't believe you haven't heard about it, actually; I found a couple of fragments along with one complete, fully articulated skeleton—with the skull, no less. They were hot stuff for a while because of some weird mammal-like things about their limbs—a ball-and-socket arrangement at the top of the femur, some metatarsal fusion, etc. Turns out it was just a case of convergent evolution. They were apparently coast-dwelling. I don't know what's been done on them lately but I enclose a list of references FYI."

That night, back in Groverton, he told Deborah about the letter. The point was moot now anyway, in a sense; Bryce Torbett had given the specimen away in a local publicity stunt, traded it like so much wampum; but as James told Deborah, there was something in you that wanted to know, wanted it settled.

"Anyway," he went on, "I wish I could just check the site deposit again, to make sure I didn't make any mistakes the first time. I'd like to see the outcrop in light of this letter from Phillips."

"Well, I could lead you back there on foot," Deborah said. "If you wanted to do it without Bryce knowing. I've bird-hunted all back up in there."

"Really?" He was intrigued.

"Sure. It'd be sort of fun."

"Well—" James thought. "Could you go tomorrow? After work?"

"In the dark?"

"Sure. The moon's full. Why not?"

"No, I'm helping Traci take some boxes to her folks' house. She's leaving the day after tomorrow."

"She did decide to go back!" said James. How strange it was that people could act so quickly.

"Yeah. She says she's ready, and if she gets there Friday there won't even be a late-registration fee."

"Well, look—are you going to be helping her pack all night long?"

"No, but I'm treating her to dinner after that. Let's go tonight to look at the outcrop."

"Right now?"

"Sure."

So midnight found them sitting side-by-side, hugging their

knees, on a certain embankment between the drainage canal and the Old Murdoch Highway that bounded Bryce Torbett's farm on one side. The moon had come up, and though their bodies weren't touching it threw their shadows into a raffish embrace behind them. It tilted a beam or two into a rough oblong hole, as for a pygmy's grave, beside them.

"Well," James was musing, "what difference does it make, I guess, in the long run?"

He knew Deborah was trying to think as he thought. The long run seemed very long indeed. Looking up at the night sky, even she could sense it. "I guess you could always say that," she said.

"I had the feeling this was going to happen," James went on. "You can see it sometimes when you tell people like Torbett that something has value. Of course you mean it scientifically, from an intellectual standpoint: you're excited and something like this has tremendous 'value' ..."

Deborah lay back, folding her arms in the soft sweat jacket which lay behind her to cushion her head on the flint gravels.

"But I guess it did lead me to you," James added. "That's something." He leaned back on his palms, squinted with discomfort, and moved one hand. In a minute he said, "Hey, what's this?"

Deborah sat up and peered at the object cupped in his palm. "It's a plastic army man," she said.

"Well, I know that. How'd it get here? Seems like an anachronism."

"Jonas probably left it."

"Oh, the boy?"

"Yeah," said Deborah. "I mean, how else would it have gotten here? He's the one that found the bone in the first place."

"Yeah, I met him that first time I came here."

"What're you thinking, it's plastic and it won't decompose for nineteen million years?"

"No," said James slowly. "No, that's true, but that wasn't what I was thinking. If he played here and left these toys maybe those arrowheads were also ..." His voice trailed off.

Deborah yawned. "I'm so sleepy here. Isn't that funny? I could curl up right here on all these rocks and fall asleep. Two hours from now I'll be in a soft bed with a pillow under my head, wide awake."

James looked at her, smiling. Her pupils were wide in the moonlight, friendly and dark, the centered absolutes around which her face, the planes of her cheek, her eyebrows and hair, somehow fell, in lighter, bluer tones. In confusion he felt her studying his eyes, his lips, and almost kissing him. Her glance alone on his mouth was like a slight pressure.

"Are you ready to go?" he said, reaching his hand out.

"Yep." She gave him hers, and together they stood up, unkinking themselves. "If you're going back to Little Rock tonight, you've got a long drive back."

"Yep," he said. "What are we gonna do about that?"

"I guess one of us'll be moving," said Deborah.

"That's what I've been thinking," said James. "One of these days." He noticed as the words stood in the air between them that "one of these days" might happen sooner than it used to for him.

They dusted themselves off, and his hands reached around her waist and locked her firmly to him for a minute, and they kissed, briefly at first, and then longer.

"Come on," said James. They scrambled down the slope with their hands locking, loosed by their sliding progress then rejoining, and found they kept their balance a lot better than they had on the way.

33

EPIPHANY, JANUARY 6, dawned cold and clear. A gusty wind sent the last dried, crumpled, brown leaves of fall whirling around the parking lot of the Little Rock airport. In the pale surrounding sky, the planes taking off and landing looked shiny and hard-edged as toys. The usual good nature prevailed around the automatic doors to the terminal, where two or three lanes of cars were double-parked: skycaps and travelers alike seemed to shimmy around piles of luggage like microorganisms in a drop of water, looking neither particularly hurried nor unhurried, and making no visible progress. More travelers arrived every minute—old black country people getting out of sedate Chevrolets, wearing hats that looked thirty years old; a young couple holding out an impatient hand to a child so bundled up her arms could not hang straight down by her sides; middle-aged red-faced whites, sporting new Christmas clothes. Occasionally people coming from long-range parking, hauling a suitcase, did move with some speed—the women running with short little unnatural steps in their heels and too-thin hose; the men following more slowly, hunched over with carryalls hoisted over their shoulders.

Traci pointed out the last place in short-term parking to Stuart, who was driving his old Plymouth. She jumped out and waited for him to open the trunk. They each took one of her scuffed suitcases and shapeless, bulging nylon travel bags. Traci crossed the traffic lanes and reached the opposite curb first and looked back at Stuart while she waited, impatient to check in, yet still trying fondly to imprint him in her mind. With bare head and hands, but wearing a bulky navy ski jacket that made his legs seem even longer and thinner, he joined her, stepping back briefly to let an elderly white woman clutching her purse precede him. Without speaking they went together to the end of the Delta line. Traci already had her ticket in her hand.

When she'd checked in they drifted down the concourse. "You sure you want to do this," said Stuart. It wasn't really a question.

"Yep," said Traci cheerfully. "You have time to go to the gate with me?"

"Sure."

She stopped in front of a newspaper stand and started scrabbling around in her purse. Stuart handed her a quarter out of his own pocket but said, "I can't believe you're going to read the paper our last few minutes together." She gave him a reproving look as she pulled the newspaper out of the machine and he added, "I'm not being plaintive."

"Oh yes you are." She laughed, reached up and gave him a quick kiss. She knew her good spirits were irritating him, but she couldn't help them. "I just want to read about the ruling."

"You already know what it is," he said. They had heard the news on the car radio: Judge Overton had struck down the Creation Science Act.

"My, aren't we *sulky.*" Again she laughed at him.

She couldn't share his mood. In line at the X-rays and metal detectors, and stepping toward their various gates, people had a sort of cheerful, dieting, black-coffee look. The very ones who'd landed here so exultantly before Christmas, laden with packages and good will, diving gratefully into the collective family lap, now looked like they couldn't flee soon enough. Goodbye to the holiday excesses, the bulging family rooms, the indulgences! Back to business, to solitary routines and disciplines, to severe outlines unsoftened by garlands and lights! Traci felt it herself. Buoyed by new resolutions and plans, she was heading into the neat blank spaces of her new 1982 weekly-organizer calendar. In a little while her plane would rise and from her heights the earth would reveal itself as uncluttered and spare, with every minute detail between here and Boston in its assigned place, like a tiny stitch on a quilt far below.

"I hate January," said Stuart.

They sat down side by side in the waiting area for her flight to Atlanta. Traci opened the paper and shook her wrists crisply to straighten out the front page, and Stuart tilted his head toward hers to read along.

"This is great stuff," breathed Traci. " 'The evidence is over-whelming that both the purpose and effect of Act Five-ninety is the advancement of religion in the public schools ...' Oh, wow." She felt Stuart's breath on her hair.

"Mmm," he said.

" 'Evolution does not presuppose the absence of a creator or God—' " She sensed an impatient movement in Stuart, stopped abruptly, and said, "I'll read the jump page on the plane."

"Good," he said.

She looked hard at him now, trying to remember him already. She knew how it could be to try to reconstruct a face that was not with you. She studied the dark, deep-set eyes, the purplish shadows above and beneath them, the skin a little sallow from winter, the smooth lips whose curves and thin places she knew so well.

"Now, don't mope when I'm gone," she said playfully.

He growled, "I don't intend to mope."

"I'll be back this summer."

"Yeah, sure."

"Anyway, you'll be busy in the meantime," she said with satisfaction. For days she'd been trying to get him as recharged and motivated as she was. It was healthy to plan constructively for one's future, to maintain enthusiasm about one's plans; she hoped he would do both. She went on, brightly, "You'll have your new classes, and this weekend you take the relics to Oklahoma ..."

"Yeah. If Torbett hasn't snookered me again."

"Snookered? That's a Groverton word."

"Yeah, well, that's all I am, a hick Groverton schoolteacher, I guess. Forget law school. Maybe I'll just stay in Groverton and teach."

Every time he'd mumbled this lately, trying to get a rise out of her, she responded brightly, "We *need* good teachers in Groverton." But now she sheered firmly back to the other subject. "I think this time he's sincere."

"Who, Torbett?"

"Yeah."

Stuart just grunted. Two weeks before, he'd gotten a strange confessional phone call from Bryce Torbett, admitting that the bone he'd turned over during the Living Nativity Scene had been a fake. The real bone of dispute was shattered now, crumbled back to dust ... But in reparation, he wanted to donate his Indian artifacts to the Caddo tribe. Stuart could inspect them personally. It was at his little boy's urging, the boy Jonas whom Stuart had had in class ... Now Stuart would go to the tribal council and make arrangements for the relics to be resanctified, preserved.

"You'll have to let me know how that goes, especially," Traci pressed. "I'll be wanting to hear."

"Ladies and gentlemen, we are now ready to pre-board Flight Six-ninety-one to Atlanta. Those passengers traveling with small children or otherwise in need of special assistance may now join the flight attendants at the gate. In a few minutes we will begin boarding passengers with boarding passes numbered for rows Sixty and higher ..."

"Seeing the tribal council, taking the artifacts—" she continued. "That'll be really exciting."

Stuart's eyes were shining as he cut them down toward her. "Not really," he said. "Compared to you."

"Oh, Stuart."

But even as she disclaimed it there came that pang, those unsteady tears in her eyes too. And later, as the plane rose over the rolling city blocks of Little Rock, the river brown as a bared arm, the woods and rice fields and orange-and-white quarry pits beyond, all that scenery quit looking so distinct: the colors blurred into one another. *Not really exciting—compared to you.* What should you pay attention to in the long run, the swoops of your heart someone could start in you, or the great broader

arcs of your journeys? Which were the real turns of your fate?
Could you, evolving, blessed, ever know?

34

JONAS AND HIS FATHER were spending the evening at home. Clint was out on a date, his first real date, at a party at a classmate's house. The transportation plans had been complicated. Since Clint, at fourteen, had to be accompanied by an adult to drive legally, but refused to crowd Daddy, the girl, and himself into the cab of Bryce's truck, they had borrowed Grandmother's car for the evening. Going to the party Clint had driven, his date sat in the right front seat, and Bryce sat stiffly in the back. Then Bryce had taken the wheel and brought the car home. He would go pick up Clint and the girl in a couple of hours.

Clint had been horribly nervous beforehand, even more nervous than he got before football games. He changed clothes twice and double-applied his deodorant. To Jonas it all seemed sort of pointless, and not much fun.

Now Jonas and Bryce were watching TV, and Ace dozed on the floor near Jonas's crutches. Jonas had his foot propped up on the coffee table and Bryce slouched into the cushions at the far end, tapping ash from his cigarette into the ash tray he kept on the arm of the couch. They were watching Miss Strait on cable. All of Groverton was abuzz about her move to Dallas, where she'd taken a job with a Christian television channel. She had announced it right before Christmas and the church had made a big deal about it, sending her off with pride and fanfare. Even people who didn't like her had to admit it was pretty impressive. "Quite an honor for someone from little old Groverton," everyone kept saying, some grudgingly, some not. Tonight the Torbetts had sat through an hour and fifteen minutes of worship interspersed with fundraising, waiting for her to come on the screen—though Daddy kept the volume down, and kept switching over to a basketball game on ESPN, until they actually saw Lorene.

She was sitting on a flowered sofa next to a matching armchair occupied by a man with an auburn pompadour. Behind the two of them, fake birch logs glowed in a little glassed-in fireplace. The suite of furniture where Lorene and the man sat visiting was not in an enclosed room but was on a sort of dais, and beyond it part of a vast choir was visible, wearing teal-green robes, and pieces of some podiums and stage lights and mikes could be seen too and beyond that a huge audience, which the camera scanned occasionally. The audience was of all ages—golden-tanned white people in shorts and baseball caps or leisure wear, who beamed and raised their hands and said "Praise the Lord" at peppy moments and looked appropriately sweet and sad if things got serious. When the camera panned back to Lorene, she was talking fast. Her lips looked covered in wet red goo. Every now and then she half-closed her shadowed eyes, but then she would open them very very wide, raising her eyebrows and smiling.

"—hear it for our Lord! who made heaven and earth. Because, Billy, does a flower, or a simple root, have a mind of its own?"

"No," said Billy, with the pompadour, obediently.

"Or a butterfly, or a sailfish?"

"No, Lorene, it doesn't."

"That's right! And therefore, the planning of these beautiful living things must have been done by the Creator. And really, Billy, the people who think they are smarter than the Lord their Maker and try to say that all this beautiful world of God's came together randomly—really, they are tools of Satan. I hate to say it, because some of them are our neighbors and our politicians and even our schoolteachers. But I feel, Billy, that we must call a spade a spade. They put down special creation for one and only one reason, because they deny the very existence of the Lord." She pressed her lips together and tilted her head back, showing the fine outlines of her chin, her smooth throat. There was a gleam of triumph in her green eyes.

"Wow," Jonas observed. "Her hair has really gotten curly, hasn't it?" Daddy didn't say anything, so Jonas pretended he'd just been speaking to the air. "And blond, too," he answered himself a minute later.

Daddy shook another cigarette out of the pack lying on the table, lit it, and took a drag, still watching the screen. Smoke poofed around the father and son.

"You know, Lorene, I have to agree with you," said Billy. "And I'm glad that you're using forums exactly like this one to talk to the schoolchildren of America, because as you know—"

Ace leaped up and started barking just as the doorbell rang. Jonas cut his eyes toward his father. When Bryce rose too slowly to his feet, still looking at the TV, Jonas started scrabbling for his crutches.

"And now you folks at home are seeing a number flash across your screens. If you want to support this cause, of spreading the word about the Lord's magnificent handiwork—if you want to give Darwin and the evolutionists a run for their money—"

The doorbell rang again, and Ace kept barking hoarsely, but Daddy hardly seemed to notice. Jonas was up, struggling for balance as he worked his crutches under his arm.

"Yes, Billy, I always think of that great hymn: 'Oh Lord my God, when I in awesome won—' "

Lorene's curls and painted face shrank quickly to a mere point of light, and disappeared with a final click of the remote control button as the screen went blank. Bryce ambled toward the door. "Hold your horses, son, I'm getting it. Can't you hush that damn dog? Sit down."

Jonas hollered his sternest *"Come here"* and grabbed Ace by the neck when he reluctantly obeyed. It was probably Mr. Bledsoe waiting out there, and Jonas hadn't seen him in a long time. Mr. Bledsoe had never come to his house before—when Daddy had finally agreed to own up to him, he had done it over the phone—and Jonas didn't want him to think nobody was home and go away.

But that was his voice in the entrance hall responding to

Daddy, sort of dry and flat, a word or two, and then there he stood, in the living room doorway. He seemed to have cold air around him, still gathered in the folds of his coat. He had on jeans and a ski jacket and his face looked a little sharp or set, as if he'd gotten too cold outside, or maybe as if he were mad.

"Hey, Mr. Bledsoe."

"Jonas—hey." Mr. Bledsoe almost smiled. "Ace, boy, hey. You can turn him loose if you want, I don't mind. I heard you messed up your ankle there. You doing any better?"

"Yessir."

Jonas let Ace go and he went over and started sniffing Mr. Bledsoe's legs affably. Mr. Bledsoe didn't notice; his face was tense again as he faced Jonas's father.

"You want to sit down?" Daddy gestured vaguely at the living room. "We were just—ah—watching the tube."

Jonas remembered from class that Mr. Bledsoe didn't think much of the tube.

"No, thanks," said Mr. Bledsoe. "I can't stay."

"Well," said Bryce. "Like I said, I got 'em packed up for you."

Mr. Bledsoe made a snorting, sarcastic noise in his nose or throat, which was probably an accident. But Daddy took it another way.

"Look," he said. He himself was looking at the floor. "I—um. About before. I guess you do have reason to hold it against me. I didn't think it mattered much, I guess. Whether it was a human bone or not. As long as you thought it was." He looked up with one of his most fetching expressions, a wry laugh that crinkled the corners of his eyes and showed his white teeth, but Mr. Bledsoe's face didn't soften. "Jonas here's been telling me different."

Mr. Bledsoe inclined his head gravely and glanced at Jonas. When their eyes met, a flash of gratitude, of love, went through the boy. "Thanks, Jonas."

"So—" Bryce shrugged. "What can I say? I'm sorry."

Jonas had never heard him say that before.

"You want to inspect all the pots? Like I said, I put 'em in crates for you. And each one has an I.D. slip with it, telling where I got it, how old we think it is, what it's worth."

"What it's worth," said Mr. Bledsoe.

"Yeah. Just on a typewritten slip of paper, packed down in the crate with each object. But I could open 'em up and let you look at 'em. I'd understand if that's what you wanted to do."

"No," said Mr. Bledsoe. "I trust you."

"Well." Bryce's face was a little red. He ran his hand through his hair. "Okay then. Lemme help you load 'em up."

Jonas hopped along behind the two men as they strode out the door. Ace dashed into the darkness, glad for diversion. The crates were stacked neatly against the carport wall. Jonas watched as Mr. Bledsoe and Daddy loaded them into the small trailer behind Mr. Bledsoe's car. When they'd finished they shook hands silently. Both of them still looked mad. Jonas could hardly feel too happy when the whole deal was over, and Mr. Bledsoe had driven away, the running lights of the little trailer bouncing erratically in the dark. He didn't even know when he'd see him again.

While Daddy was gone to get Clint and his date and to take the date home, Jonas was restless; but he couldn't prowl around the house too well on his crutches. By the hardest he fixed himself a bowl of ice cream, which he ate slowly, licking every spoonful into a pleasantly smooth shape before he finally swallowed it. He listened to the clock tick but was not afraid. He felt something was different but didn't know what. He gave Ace the melted ice cream in the bottom of his bowl. Ace acted insulted that he couldn't have more.

Then Clint and Daddy got back, and Daddy went straight to bed. Clint breathed a sigh of relief when his father's bedroom door closed and burst into rough giggles. "I'm drunk as a skunk!" he said. "I didn't think I'd make it in front of him!"

"Really?" said Jonas. "You've been *drinking?*"

"Oh, hell yeah," said Clint. He threw his head back and laughed, while Jonas and Ace watched closely.

"What's that like?" said Jonas.

"Oh hell," said Clint. "Maybe you'll find out someday." He swaggered a little as he went into the bathroom, and Jonas heard the sink water running for a long time, and he thought he heard some flushes that the tap didn't quite mask. Maybe Clint was shaving?—something else Jonas had not yet experienced. But he didn't think guys shaved when they got back from dates, only before they went. And there was no need to flush the toilet while you shaved.

When Clint came out, wearing only his underwear, and sauntered a little weakly down the hall, Jonas kept eyeing him. He followed Clint to his room.

"Get out, will you?" said Clint.

"Guess who came by?" said Jonas.

"I don't care." Clint was already crawling into bed.

"Mr. Bledsoe."

"That's just marvelous, Jonas."

"I thought you'd notice the crates were gone from the carport."

"Big deal. He's going to be my teacher, you know." Clint now had the sheet pulled over his face and was speaking through it.

"Who is?"

"Bledsoe. Red Man."

"Your *teacher?*"

"He's going to sub the rest of the year for Miss Strait."

"Oh."

Sadness overcame him at the news. Clint would see Mr. Bledsoe every day. He would become Clint's property to see, to talk about, to quote cavalierly in front of Jonas.

"Now will you please get *out* before I *throw* you out?"

Jonas hopped slowly down the hall, his head dropped as low as the rubber arm pads on top of his crutches. Ace drooped alongside, imitating his mood. Jonas didn't even turn on the light in his room. He shut the door with one of the crutches and lay down, letting the crutches fall beside him, petting the dog who bounded up to his accustomed place.

He lay and thought and could not fall asleep. Then he quit being aware he was thinking but just seemed to feel things, in a stream, and gradually he was less morose. He heard Clint get up and go to the bathroom again. He might have heard a retching sound, but then water started swishing in the pipes beneath the house. Jonas, not knowing why, felt sorry for Clint. It might not be too fun to be his brother either.

He hadn't closed his curtains, and when his head fell to one side on his pillow he could see Orion, fixed in the start of a cartwheel behind the treeline. Those were the first stars he'd seen tonight, but he didn't wish on them. Wishing on stars was for little kids. And things didn't get real easy even if your wishes did come true. It was like being crowned in a game of checkers: you might be king now, and have more elbow room and more directions to go in, but sometimes that just meant you were more confused.

Ace breathed deeply at his side, his feet flittering in a dog-dream, of rabbits, maybe, or thieves or other dogs. The winter starlight came in the window and touched his handsome spots and whiskers and eyebrow-hairs with a steel-blue glaze. Still Jonas lay quietly, awake but not minding it, and after a long while he realized something. For once he wasn't waiting for anything, not to fall asleep or to turn eleven or to get his sixth-grade reader or a ten-speed or to drink or shave or for his ankle to heal or for Clint to come out of the bathroom or for Jesus to come to his bed. Maybe he wasn't yet saved, but he was changed, and the difference was good. Ace, Orion, Indian brave; Daddy at Christmas, Clint in the woods; Jim Ray, Dr. Armstrong, Mr. Bledsoe; skin-diver, Sacajawea-life-saver, angel-glow of flash-lights come seeking him—if Jesus wasn't among all of them, He wasn't worth having around. And if He was, well then your wait was all for nothing, your waiting time was up before it started.